Sofi's Bridge

Christine Lindsay

Sofi's Bridge

Contact Information: titleadmin@pelicanbookgroup.com

Scripture quotations, unless otherwise indicated are taken from the King James translation, public domain.

Cover Art by *Nicola Martinez*

White Rose Publishing, a division of Pelican Ventures, LLC
www.pelicanbookgroup.com PO Box 1738 *Aztec, NM * 87410

White Rose Publishing Circle and Rosebud logo is a trademark of Pelican Ventures, LLC

Publishing History
First White Rose Edition, 2016
Paperback Edition ISBN 978-1-61116-520-3
Electronic Edition ISBN 978-1-61116-519-7
Published in the United States of America

Dedication

This book is dedicated to my son Kyle whose heart of gold always wants to help others. And just as the characters in this novel learn to let their light shine, with pride I watch you doing this too. Continue to let Christ shine through you and in all you do.

1

A blur of white raced along the grounds to the beach.

Sofi froze at the second-story window. Set against the tattered sky of an incoming squall, her sister's nightgown billowed in the dark. For the past six weeks, Trina kept as much distance as she could from the sight and sound of the surf. Sofi raised a shaking hand to her throat, turned, and tore along the upper hall. "Mattie, she's outside."

China shattered as Matilda, their housekeeper, dropped a supper tray.

At the staircase, Sofi hiked up her black silk skirts and pounded downward.

Matilda followed close behind.

Ten minutes ago, Trina had been in the nursery, huddling on the window seat. Though nearly grown, she was always in the nursery since that night when...Trina even slept in the nursery instead of her bedroom, crying for Papa, with Sofi holding her close.

Matilda huffed. "I only left Trina to collect her supper."

A yelping Odin found Sofi at the kitchen hallway. The Springer spaniel bounded, his cold nose nudging her hand. Thank goodness one thing in this house had stayed the same. With Odin barking, she pushed

1

through the green baize door. The dog darted past her.

Inga, their cook, swung around to face her.

Frida, the housemaid, dropped whatever she held in her hand.

A man Sofi could swear she'd never seen before sat at the table, and shot to his feet as she hurtled through the kitchen.

She reached the outer door when the man—the gardener, she remembered now—pushed past her and flung the door wide. He charged across the lawn. The dog yowled and leapt after him. With Inga, Frida, and Matilda running behind, Sofi fled in the wake of the gardener down the trail to the beach.

The man reached the sand.

Odin bolted past, across the beach as Trina rushed along the dock.

Sofi scrambled to keep up, each ragged breath a prayer.

Matilda shrieked, and behind, Frida's and Inga's calls, "Trina!"

Sofi reached the beach in time to see Trina slip into the skiff at the end of the dock. Her sister pulled on the oars and made swift progress out on Puget Sound. At the edge of the dock, the dog pawed the planks, whining.

"Trina!" The wind snatched her cries as Sofi tripped over the shore strewn with rocks and driftwood. *Dear God, please keep her safe.* She had failed in looking after her sister.

The gardener reached the end of the thirty-foot dock and dove. It was hard to see anything other than green phosphorus as he swam toward the small skiff.

Cold brine swirled at Sofi's knees as she waded to the dock. She ran to the end of the wooden planks. It should be her saving Trina. It was her job to look after her family.

Twenty yards out, Trina stood up in the skiff. Her nightgown streamed in the wind, a white sail against the squalling night.

Sit down, Trina. Oh, please sit down.

Swells buffeted the small craft as Trina stood, peering into the depths.

Sofi cried out, but the wind swallowed her words, until a wave nudged the boat, and Trina fell. Sofi screeched.

One moment Trina was there, the next the sea had taken her. Just like Papa.

She wrenched open the buttons of her bodice. She would not remain frozen, but get out of this wretched gown and bring her sister out of the depths.

"No, Sofi!" Matilda gripped her arm. "You're not as strong a swimmer as Trina. She has a better chance than you."

She thrust off Matilda's hand. She couldn't lose her sister. She'd swim in her petticoat if need be. But Inga and Frida had made it to the end of the dock, and now three sets of hands held Sofi, as the rising tempest droned.

Captive, Sofi counted the strokes of the man swimming to Trina. Then he dove, and the night went quiet. Sofi couldn't breathe. All that she'd kept dammed up since Papa's death cascaded over her.

Waves pummeled the pilings and beach.

Odin whimpered at her knee.

A moment later, the gardener came up, gasped for air, and dove again.

Sofi pressed the heel of her hand against her tight chest. *Dear God, don't take her from me.*

At last, the waters broke. The gardener surfaced with Trina coughing in his arms.

Pins and needles flared over Sofi's skin. At last, she could do something. She reached for the life ring, tossing it to the man. It landed on the waves near his head.

Trina batted at him, and he ducked beneath her. Seconds passed. He emerged to take hold of the life ring. He kicked, towing Trina with his arm across her chest. Until he lost his grip on the ring.

The wind and waves flailed at him and Trina.

Hand over hand, Sofi pulled in the rope, and threw the ring out again.

He caught it.

The tide fought to drag him and Trina, but with Frida's help, Sofi hauled them in.

As they neared the dock, Sofi and the women reached down to lift Trina from the waves. Sofi pressed on her sister's back to expel the water she'd taken in.

The man hoisted himself to the dock. Dripping wet, he pushed Sofi away and rolled Trina on her back.

"What are you doing?" She slapped his hands. If anyone would take life-preserving measures, it would be her.

But he shoved her and pried Trina's mouth open. After searching her mouth and throat, he flipped Trina on her front and thumped her back.

A moment later, Trina coughed and spat, and the man stood, leaning down to lift Trina into his arms.

Sofi gave him a shove. "I'll carry her."

"Don't be foolish, miss."

"You can't possibly carry her up to the house after that swim. We'll carry her together."

He swiped his wet hair out of his eyes. "It'll be

quicker if I carry her. She's worn out and she needs—"
He scooped Trina up.

"Please...hurry." Sofi turned and ordered Matilda.
"Water on to boil. Get blankets." Buffeted by the wind,
Sofi walked beside him as he carried Trina up the
incline with the squall whistling.

He kept his gaze on the lights shining across the
lawns from the kitchen.

She kept turning to watch the rise and fall of her
sister's chest, those pale eyelids that remained closed,
that long blonde hair straggling like seaweed over the
bodice of the white nightgown.

When they reached the kitchen stoop, Trina
opened her eyes and looked at the man holding her.

Sofi gasped.

For a moment a spark of the real Trina—sixteen-
year-old Trina—shone in the depths of her blue eyes.

Inside, the kitchen was a warm hive of activity.

The gardener settled a shivering Trina in Inga's
armchair next to the stove.

"A towel," Sofi said to Frida. She dried Trina's
arms and legs and wrapped her in a quilt as Matilda
barged in with dry clothing.

Kneeling before her sister, she'd been prepared to
take charge, have the man fade to the background as a
servant of his standing should, but just as he'd done on
the dock, he pushed her away. Ignoring his dripping
clothes, he leaned close, listening to Trina's breathing.

And Trina latched her blue gaze with his.

In rigid silence, Sofi stood.

Matilda pierced her with a look that asked if she'd
lost her mind.

Sofi put a hand to her head. Was it giddiness at
Trina being alive that sapped her of her usual verve?

No. There was something about this man that calmed her sister like none of them had been able to do for weeks.

"Take your hands off her, ye shameless oaf," Matilda shouted. She'd cared for Trina since she'd been a baby as if she'd been her own.

The gardener fended her off with a pained look. "Matilda, do you honestly think I'd want to hurt her?" He took hold of Trina's wrist, as if he counted her pulse, and hunched down to examine her feet. Rocks on the beach had gashed the inside of one arch. With a tea towel, he wiped away a trace of blood.

Sofi reached out to help, but Trina shrank from her and focused on the fire burning in the grate.

Inga, Frida, and Matilda began to talk at once, while Sofi stood aside, alone in the eye of the storm. It wasn't that Trina rejected her help—she was getting used to being rebuffed by her young sister lately.

But this stranger had taken control.

Frida and Inga submitted to his orders as if they'd known him for years instead of a month. Even the dog sat, his tail thumping as he shifted his gaze between the gardener and Trina.

Only Matilda eyed the man as though he were a hooligan.

The desire to cry crept up on Sofi, but she shoved it deep. She must be exhausted from carrying the weight of what was left of her family to let him take charge. Everything had changed since Papa's death. She spoke to the man in a level tone. "You'll need iodine. Bandages."

"Hot water too." He smiled his thanks when she brought him the basin. "She'll be fine, stop your worrying." His voice flowed in rhythmic Irish cadence.

With a calm Sofi did not feel, she retrieved the tin box, opened the bottle of iodine, while Matilda ripped a clean white cloth into strips. Sofi would let him see to Trina's superficial abrasions. He obviously had first-aid training. But more than simple medicine was needed to heal her sister's mind and heart. To think...only a few months ago, Trina had been at the yacht club, laughing, challenging the young men to a race. Her sister's teeth chattered. But her gaze was clearer than since the day they'd brought her home without Papa. "Leave me...alone. It's my..."

The man's eyes crinkled with a smile. "You're all right. Your few wee cuts and bruises don't worry me at all."

Trina moaned as her shivering eased and pulled the quilt around her. Then that heavy curtain came down behind her eyes. It seemed she grew smaller, shrinking away from them all. At least Trina was safe for now.

Sofi pressed a hand to her stomach.

A frown replaced the gardener's smile as he scrutinized Trina. "Is any tea ready? She needs a cup. With plenty of sugar and milk." He cupped Trina's chin, but she avoided his eyes. "It'll do you good," he murmured, "whether or not you want to talk to me." His brows creased at Trina's lack of response, and he cupped her shoulder. "You'll be fine, so I'm handing you over to Matilda's care before she tears me limb from limb." His smile matched the lilt in his voice.

Matilda needed no further encouragement. She, Frida, and Inga began to cluck over their one chick, Matilda's Scottish r's rolling, the two other women elongating their Swedish vowels.

For now, Sofi would leave Trina in their capable

hands.

Her sister was locked away in one of her moods. Later, tonight, Trina would need her.

Setting her jaw, Sofi studied the gardener in an attempt to remember his name. She and this man had hardly spoken until tonight.

Inga laid out his duties from the time he arrived on their grounds just days before Papa...

Emptiness swelled inside. With Papa's drowning so shortly after this man started to work for them, she'd not had the heart to get to know him. She dammed up the memories of her father again, before grief sluiced through her—a grief she had no time to indulge. Not now when Trina needed her so much. And Mama too.

This gardener's name was...Neil Macpherson. And his manner, his confidence...too controlled to be a mere laborer. His abilities hinted at some training, but he was still the gardener. A man who thought he knew what was best, as Charles thought. But then, Charles, as Papa's business partner, always thought he knew best.

Her voice shook. "You're quite handy at first-aid, Mr. Macpherson."

"Sure anyone could do this. Even me, hired to trim the grass and prune the shrubs." He flinched, so slight, she almost missed it.

Matilda held a cup of tea to Trina's lips.

Trina sipped and leaned her head against the back of the chair, her eyelids drooping.

Sofi felt Neil Macpherson's gaze. "You don't look so well yourself, miss. Take that cuppa that Frida's bringing you."

She rubbed her arms and shook her head. Her

soaking clothes clung. Weariness of heart must be spurring this unfamiliar perversity within her. This need to fight, to protect Trina and Mama.

"Well, if it's not a cup of tea you want," he said, "then perhaps coffee, as long as it has plenty of sugar to counteract the shock." He led her away from Trina, and for a second she wanted to lean against him, like Mama used to lean against Papa.

But this was her family. She must rally herself.

"It's plain your sister's suffering from a prolonged sense of trauma," he said, lowering his voice.

"It's nothing more than a nervous malady."

His brow winged upward. "It's far more than that. She needs help."

She turned away from his all-too-inquisitive eyes. Of course her sister needed help.

Trina just didn't need the kind of help Charles was suggesting.

Inga and Frida whisked away the first-aid materials, and Matilda raced upstairs for an item of Trina's clothing she'd forgotten.

Sofi hunched down in front of Trina. She traced a finger down her sister's cheekbone, along the delicate line of jaw. She turned the young face toward her, only to be met by Trina's vacant stare. Sofi choked back a sob. "Where are you, *älskling*? Where are you?" No response came from Papa's favorite endearment. And really, there was no need for Sofi to ask. She knew exactly where the soul of her sister lay. Six weeks ago, it floated downward with Papa's body to the dark and sandy bottom of the Juan de Fuca Strait.

What the gardener said was true. She didn't need anyone to tell her that her sister suffered from trauma, but there had to be a way to bring her sister back to health other than what Charles was arranging.

Neil Macpherson's officious manner wasn't what angered her. As a simple laborer, he must only mean well.

But as for Charles...she would fight him with everything she had before she'd allow her sister to go to a hospital for the mentally insane.

2

The next morning, from the nursery window high near the corniced peak of the house, Sofi watched Charles's green limousine rumble up the drive.

He'd bought his Cadillac a year after Papa bought his. Everything Papa did, Charles did soon after.

Her insides sank. She no more wanted to talk to Charles today than she did yesterday, or the day before that. He'd been no more help than that doddering imbecile, Dr. Atwood, he'd brought with him.

She turned from the window to the anchor of her and Trina's childhood—this nursery of wooden desks where Trina had created her drawings of boats and Sofi had done her sums and dreamed of designing bridges like Papa.

This was the only haven Trina could bear as she floated through this stupor. At the window seat, Trina rested her head against the warm pane of glass and stared at Neil Macpherson pushing a wheelbarrow through the garden.

Last night's storm had blown itself out, leaving a sham of peace over this house.

But Sofi knew better. A battle waited downstairs.

Matilda flung herself into the nursery. "Mr. Charles Bolton," her Scottish burr rolled with distaste. "The doctor's gone to see your mother. Charles is in your father's study. That blighted man has the admittance slip for your mother to sign."

An iron fist gripped Sofi's chest. She thought she

had a few months to help Trina back to health. "Mama's in no state to make any such decision. Is she in her room?"

"Aye, lass."

"But Charles has the admittance slip, not the doctor?"

"Aye, so he says."

"Right." Sofi clenched her fists. It was time she saw to that wretched man who waited in her father's study. That offense alone made her blood boil. She strode to the door but turned back to look at Trina, her posture and expression unchanged. But Trina's moods changed like quicksilver when a storm roused the water. Or a foghorn blew out on the Sound. "Stay with her, Mattie."

Downstairs in the foyer, the drapes were closed to the water as Sofi had instructed. Until last night, each of the Puget's faces disturbed Trina, whether it hid behind sheets of rain or sparkled like diamonds as it did today. But today a breeze transported the smell of the sea into the house with its invasive reminder of what it had stolen from them. And almost stolen again last night.

With sure steps she strode to her father's study.

Only Charles would have the audacity to invade this sanctum. By the fireplace, Charles lifted one of Papa's antique pipes as if he might smoke from it.

Sofi pulled in a sharp breath and swung her gaze to the walls of her father's study, seeking strength in the framed drawings. All those bridges Papa had built, and those she'd drawn for him, which he'd indulgently framed. But the pain in her chest remained.

Charles returned the pipe to the mantel. A red stain mottled his face at being caught out, and he brushed a speck of dust from the sleeve of his seersucker suit. In his mid-fifties, his hair combed back from a severe part, he was still as dapper as always. He strolled toward her with a smile. "My dear—"

"I told you yesterday, Charles, Trina is not going to that hospital." There was only one way to deal with Charles—head-on.

"Sofi, she's unwell, needs constant supervision." His voice softened. "Trina had another episode last night, didn't she?"

"How do you know what happens in my home? Did you browbeat Frida or Inga for information?"

His mouth thinned. "The sanatorium is the best place for Trina."

The floor seemed to slant. "I know what Trina's suffering from, not that stream of doctors who man-handled her yesterday afternoon. She's only sixteen. She needs quiet, patience." Sofi shuddered. "Not...that hospital."

Charles took her hand, but she tugged it free.

"Sofi, you and your mother and sister are like my own flesh and blood. You used to call me uncle—"

"But we're not your family, Charles." She measured her words. "I don't know what we would have done without you, since Papa...but please don't overstep our friendship." Only the years of her mother's instilled good manners could produce the word *please* at such a time. She slipped behind her father's desk. "Charles, I'm not asking. I'm telling you. Trina is not going to that hospital."

"It's the best institution in the state, as Dr. Atwood and I discussed with your mother—"

"Trina saw Papa drown!" Her voice rang. "She could do nothing to save her father. Of course she's traumatized. But I can help Trina get well. Here at home."

"You, Sofi, are not of an age to be making decisions for your mother and sister."

"I may be only twenty-one, but I know my father would never want his daughter in that place."

He sank to the settee. "Then think of your mother. She needs complete rest. Dr. Atwood is at least pleased with Rosie's progress."

Rosie? The parlor closed in. Only Papa used Mama's pet name. And Mama, what progress had she made, living in a laudanum-induced fog? Sofi attempted to settle her breathing. Clean air. She needed air. Splaying her fingers on the blotter, she articulated through clenched teeth, "Charles, Mama won't be signing that paper today or any other day."

He stared at the carpet until footsteps crossed the foyer and stopped at the parlor entrance.

Sofi couldn't bring herself to look. She recognized the footsteps of Dr. Atwood.

The doctor announced himself with a slight cough.

She held her breath as the two men spoke quietly. A paper rustled between them. Without a word to her, the doctor crossed the foyer. The front door opened and closed.

And Charles met her eyes. "Your mama has signed the admittance slip, Sofi. The sanatorium is expecting Trina the day after tomorrow."

Mama signed the paper. How could her mother be so foolish? Even in her grief, Mama should know better. With her chest held in that familiar vice, Sofi rushed through the open French doors to the patio.

Morning sun flashed, and she gasped for air.

Neil Macpherson, who'd been weeding flower

urns, jumped to his feet.

The pain in her chest almost bent her in two. Between the wrought-iron tables and chairs, the gardener blocked her.

He helped her straighten, his grave look holding hers as he steadied her by the shoulders. "Deep breaths, miss. Nice and slow. In...and out."

Charles's footsteps rang on the patio behind her. "Unhand her, man."

Ignoring Charles, Neil Macpherson kept his gaze on her, his voice pitched low and lilting. "Pay no attention, miss, to anything...or anyone, but your breathing. Again...in....and out."

"I said, take your hands off her," Charles bleated.

Neil shouldn't be touching her. It was not his place. But for the life of her, she couldn't find the strength to tell him so. Her breaths began to slow. Deepen.

"Concentrate only on your breathing, miss. Sure, you're doing grand." His speech, a warm current, eddied over her. His cloth cap shaded his face. A trace of a smile touched his mouth.

She rolled her shoulders back and took a cleansing breath. The pain behind her ribs began to lessen. He shouldn't be touching her, but she was letting him as she'd let him take over last night. Her weakness brought the sting of tears. Tears she refused to let fall. As chatelaine to this house, she must put this gardener in his place. Besides, what was he doing weeding the flower urns on the patio when clearly a private conversation was taking place in the study? "Remove your hands from me, Mr. Macpherson."

His hint of a smile left, he touched the peak of his cap and lowered his hands. "If you're all right, miss, you'll be wanting the patio to yourself." With long strides, he rounded the corner of the house.

Charles rushed to put an arm around her. "My dear, are you unwell?"

As she pulled herself free, his features hardened. "Your vapors, Sofi, only prove you need my help, and Trina will get the best of care at—"

"What you saw was not vapors, but anger, Charles. Pure, undiluted anger...with you."

"Sofi, be reasonable."

She thrust up her hand to ward off the eroding effect of his voice. "No, Charles, I'm being quite reasonable, and I will fight you with everything I have. It is time you left my home."

His eyes narrowed. "You may banish me today, but remember, it is your mother's opinion that matters." He turned his back to her and, thank the Lord, he left the house.

If he'd stayed another minute, she couldn't be held responsible for her actions. But her bravado evaporated, like a puff of steam from a locomotive as it ground to a stop. What could she do? Clobbering Charles on the head with a flowerpot wouldn't help Trina.

Leaving the patio, she took the trail to the rose gardens. Sliding to the ground with her back against the tallest fir on the property, she pulled her knees up to her chest. Odin gamboled toward her, his ears flying. He nudged his leathery black nose into her chin. She buried her face in a handful of his white scruff. There had to be a way to keep Trina out of that hospital.

At first, her mind remained a blank. Then she felt twelve again, when her best friend had died of consumption.

Papa had caught her crying under this very tree. His voice echoed. *Think your way out of your grief. Don't wallow in emotion. Think, älskling.* That was when he'd sat down at these tree roots and taught her to calculate the height of the fir using algebra.

She laid her head against the trunk. With the sun at this angle...the shadow of the tree thirty feet long. Do the equation. Think. Wood and equations sorted themselves out. Her pulse slowed. She had lost Papa. Perhaps Mama, but no one must take Trina from her. Her arms clutching her legs relaxed until the ethereal screech of an eagle sounded overhead. Her hand stroking Odin's head went still. She knew the place to take Trina.

Orchard Valley would surely bring Trina back to health. It could work for her mother too. But since Papa's death, nothing Sofi or Matilda said compelled Mama to leave her bedroom, not even the threat of Trina going to the hospital. Mother stayed hidden away within the refuge of her four walls. In her own private asylum from that little amber bottle of laudanum clutched in her hand, and the hazy fog it induced.

Though it broke her heart, Sofi would have to hide her plans from her mother. Only Matilda could know. And there was no time to lose. She must pack what they would need—food, household stuffs to make the old cabin livable. Gasoline for Papa's Cadillac.

With Odin loping beside her, the making of plans added strength to her stride. But her feet ground to a stop near the house. The gardener.

Neil slept in the room over the carriage house. First thing she must do was remove him from that room. The last thing she needed was him nosing around.

~*~

Sofi found Neil Macpherson sitting at the kitchen table, putting away a substantial lunch of bread, thickly sliced ham, a slab of cake, and a steaming mug of...? She glanced at his cup. Yes, as she thought, tea. With the household somewhat at peace again, Inga beamed at the gardener as if he were a boy who hadn't been fed for a week.

He had saved Trina last night, but Sofi wasn't bewitched by his earnest gaze. His human kindness helped her calm her breathing this morning, but as a gardener, he'd overstepped propriety. She was sure he'd been eavesdropping outside the study earlier. Her lips firmed. This interference from Charles had her nerves strung tight. If she couldn't trust a man she'd known all her life, she certainly couldn't trust one she knew not at all.

The man stood, straight as a rod, in scuffed boots and coarse woolen trousers. Faint stubble darkened his jaw, accentuating its strong line. She caught a whiff of soap. He seemed a decent person, though his dark hair needed cutting, and he pushed it off his forehead to reveal a distinct widow's peak. The memory of his hands supporting her by the shoulders intruded. She glanced away, her face growing hot from the unseemly length of time she'd been gaping at him. Time she could little afford.

He reached for his tweed cap. "Is there anything I can do for you, miss?" His Irish accent thickened.

"Mr. Macpherson, correct?"

"Yes, Neil...Macpherson." That reassuring voice from earlier now stuttered over his name. He didn't seem to be the same man at all who'd saved Trina last night and calmed her this morning. His fingers rolled the brim of his cap.

Too many events were happening over which she had no control, but this was one thing she did have power over. "I'm making some changes, Mr. Macpherson. You will move your belongings out of the carriage house to the top floor of the main house."

"Now, miss?" The Irish brogue came out on a soft lilt.

"As soon as you've finished your meal. You'll be more comfortable there."

"I'm comfortable where I am, miss."

"As I said, Mr. Macpherson, you will move to the top of the house." Did he not hear what she said, or was he being deliberately obtuse?

"May I ask how your sister is this morning, miss?"

"She is well enough. As I was saying—"

"Your family physician has been to visit. I hope his suggested treatment met with your approval, Miss Andersson."

Inga dropped a pot on the floor.

A rim of white outlined Neil's mouth as he clenched his jaw. He knew full well the impertinence of his statement. The world must be spinning out of orbit. Sofi should dismiss him immediately, but she didn't have the heart. "Mr. Macpherson, I am not in the habit of discussing my family's personal lives with the man who—as you say—trims the grass."

Neil's face blanched. "I meant no offense. I only wish to point out, your sister needs help to be released from her overpowering state of trauma."

The gentleness in his voice stripped away the last of her poise. Just like last night, she wanted to lean against him. Unable to speak for fear of unleashing her banked-up tears, she rushed from the kitchen and found her way to the morning room. Bracing her hands on the fireplace mantel, she forced back the desire to cry. Even their gardener could tell that Trina needed special care. What if Charles and Dr. Atwood were right? Since Papa's death, Mama relied more and more on Charles, while every ounce of Sofi's heart said she could not entirely trust Charles to do what was right for Trina. She was right to not trust Mama either. Her breath hitched. But how could she take Trina away from Mama? Keep such a secret from Mama?

The pain in the center of her chest returned. She pressed the heel of her hand against her ribcage. The gardener...Neil...he'd said to breathe slowly. In...out. In...and...out. Gradually the pain dissolved. She rose to touch the photograph of her grandparents and Kiosho standing on the homestead's porch in Orchard Valley. Love would bring Trina back to life, not that hospital.

She must be strong for her sister's sake, for love's sake. The Good Book said, "Be ye therefore wise as serpents, and harmless as doves." Sofi had no concerns about being wily enough to hide their whereabouts from Charles. But as harmless as a dove?

Charles saw her only as a debutante, but if pushed too far, she'd fight and kick and spit like a dockworker to save her sister.

3

Pacific mist swathed the coast.

Neil slipped out of the Andersson home later that afternoon and hiked two miles into Seattle. It was the first time he'd left the private estate since he'd started to work there. All had been well, until Miss Sofi Andersson's order that he move into the main house. But living in close proximity to others didn't suit him. In a way, Sofi's request forced him to a decision. It was time to move on.

Nearing the pier, a gull screeched with the shrill note of a police whistle.

Neil threw a look over his shoulder. No one followed him. His heart settled back into his chest, and he pulled the peak of his cap down over his features. He had to stop jumping at shadows. This wasn't Ireland. Though a few months ago his photograph had been plastered over all the English newspapers at home, the American papers had not carried the story about the murder of Robert Crawford.

But keeping his identity hidden was proving hard. In the past few weeks, Inga and Frida had come to depend on him to treat their occasional cooking burns or sprains. Only Matilda kept her distance. Then, in a little over twelve hours—giving aid to Trina and helping Sofi through her panic—he'd practically unveiled his true profession. If he stayed, it wouldn't be long before they suspected he was hiding his expertise, and wonder why.

A tramcar rattled past. The horn of a Tin Lizzy blared, and he veered away from the paying passengers in front of the Alaska Steamship Company. Hansom cabs and automobiles parked outside the wharves afforded him cover as he slid through the gate.

Shifting his canvas duffle bag to his shoulder, he drew in sea air tainted by the stench of oil and burning coal. Steamers hugged the pier. A ship bound for Anchorage sailed at six, but another vessel for San Francisco was scheduled to leave port at three. He joined a line of stokers hoping for work on the vessel readying to leave. He needed to get away, but the image of Sofi's young sister wouldn't leave him. He hated to see how her treatment was being mishandled. But who would listen to his opinion?

With a sigh he lowered his bag to the wharf. Since debarking in New York two months ago, he thought if he worked at any sort of labor and just lived, he'd find peace, but he couldn't bear to stay in this refuge if it meant he couldn't help people. Like that wee girl shuddering with fear in the kitchen last night.

The line of stokers shortened. Neil stared at the jade smudge of the Olympic Peninsula in the distance. There were places in the Far East where fewer questions might be asked, where he might be able to use his skills. Trina Andersson had her sister to look after her. And what kind of life would there be for him, if discovered and thrown in jail?

A flash of royal blue beside the clapboard building captured his gaze. He'd recognize that limousine anywhere. The blue Cadillac stopped outside the steamship line, and the eldest of the Andersson sisters got out of the driver's seat.

He blew through his teeth. So she could drive. Normally, for what little driving these genteel ladies needed, Charles Bolton sent his limousine and driver. Now, here was Sofi Andersson beating a fast trail into the ticket agency, looking as if she no more wanted to be seen than he did.

Since entering their employ, there'd been no need for him to brush shoulders with Sofi, until last night and this morning. As she'd stood up to that Charles Bolton in the parlor, it hadn't taken Sofi long to cast off the veneer of her affluence, a young woman with hair the color of August wheat, her eyes, the sharp blue of the Irish Sea.

Yet those blue eyes softened when she'd touched her sister with the tenderness of a cat with its kitten. But her sister's pulse had pounded as if the hounds of Hades were after her.

Seeing her father slip beneath the waves could account for Trina's condition. But for six weeks? Family members died every day around the world. He knew that far too well himself. Something more was at the root of Trina's so-called "nervous malady."

He rubbed his eyes with his thumb and forefinger. Ach, he was better off getting away from the whole business entirely.

Gulls squawked overhead. In minutes, he could be making his way up the gangway into the belly of that ship. In a day or two, he could be in San Francisco. In a few weeks, Singapore or Calcutta. Freedom, with no need to constantly look over his shoulder. And people were perfectly capable of looking after themselves.

His stomach turned to a stone weight. If that were the case, then there'd been no need for him to do what he'd done for *his* loved ones.

He could see Sofi through the window handing bills over in exchange for tickets. She spun on her heel and marched back to the limousine. A moment later, the vehicle barreled up the road into town. So that's why she wanted him out of the carriage house. She was planning to whisk her sister away. Sure, it didn't take a genius to sort that out.

A ship's horn blew as it left its mooring. If Sofi was making her own escape, he wished her all the best. He had his own escaping to do. No sense in him staying in the United States, unable to use his real name. Never able to hang out his shingle and open a practice. Sparkling seas and exotic shores beckoned. No sense for him to stay, indeed! With a groan, he formed a fist, slung his bag over his shoulder, and turned away from the lineup of stokers. You'll never learn, will ye, Neil Galloway? He could afford to stay in Seattle another day or two and see that Sofi got her sister safely away.

~*~

Rain chilled Neil through to his marrow. Since he'd returned to the house from the pier late this afternoon, he'd swept the driveway. Now he swept the patio in order to keep an eye on the carriage house. Sofi had arrived back from the wharf before he had and locked herself in with the limousine for the past two hours. He broadened the sweeps of the broom, but his mood curdled when even under the shelter of the trees water splashed down his back. How on earth was his stupid sleuthing going to help Sofi? As usual, he was a fool thinking he had to step in and help. He stopped in mid-sweep, his concentration on the carriage house broken by movement inside the study.

On the other side of the beveled glass, a woman came into the darkened room. It had to be Mrs. Andersson, her chestnut hair piled loosely upon her head, and in elegant mourning finery. The lady had a right to her privacy, and he turned away. Besides, if he had any brains, he'd slip into the dry kitchen. Leave Sofi to her own schemes. But something about Mrs. Andersson's forlorn state pulled at him.

He inched over to the French doors. Aye, he'd heard right. She was weeping. To watch her like this wasn't right, but he kept watching nonetheless as rain ran down his face. She'd lost her husband, poor woman. And what was his mother feeling at home with Da gone, and himself so far away?

Mrs. Andersson paced, touching blotter and ink bottles on the desk, the framed drawings of bridges. Then she pulled what looked like a vial from the pocket of her gown, removed the stopper, and tipped the bottle into her mouth. Not long after, she stumbled toward the settee.

With his Hippocratic oath clanging in his head, he wanted to rush into the room. But it was one thing if she'd come to his clinic back home and bared her soul within the proper confines of doctor and patient. Here and now, with him acting as her blasted gardener, there was nothing he could do.

She fell to one side.

His breath fogged a patch on the French doors.

She didn't move.

Come on, woman, get up. Opening the door, he stepped into the room, listening for any change to her breathing. If he was caught in here alone with her, he'd be in trouble. With the back of his fingers, he touched Mrs. Andersson's forehead. Temperature felt normal, though the room was chilly. He arranged a woolen throw over her, found matches on the mantel, and started a fire. Bracing himself against the back of the settee, he took hold of her wrist and counted. Her pulse beat slow and even. He patted her hands. "Mrs. Andersson. Mrs. Andersson."

"Freddie." She moaned.

Neil lifted the bottle from her lap.

She woke, and reached for his hand. "Oh, my love, Freddie..."

~*~

Sofi secured the ropes, strapping tools on the limousine's roof. Odin sprawled on the carriage house floor, his muzzle resting on top of his crossed paws. She ladled on a thick Swedish accent. "You tink dis vill do the job, *jah*?" She sighed. "I'm not entirely sure why we employ you when you keep your opinions so decidedly to yourself." Her smile died. For one blessed moment, she'd forgotten. What would Papa think if he saw her, covered in dust, a fingernail broken from pulling on ropes? He'd never wanted her to do labor of any kind. He'd only allowed her to work at her so-called hobby if it didn't interfere with her social obligations.

Odin got to his feet and shook himself. His deep-set eyes seemed to question her sudden loss of sense.

She rubbed her grimy fingers, grateful it was Neil Macpherson who'd been living above the carriage house, and not their previous gardener. Old Ruben wouldn't have been as easy to shift.

As it was, Matilda kept Neil busy.

But in midafternoon, Neil had disappeared.

Still, she'd been able to get out and purchase what they needed. There was a great deal to do, and she fought to clear her head. Drawing on an equation to relax, she formed a loop to pull the other end of the rope through. Biting down on her lip, she leveraged against the rope to pull it taut. Like this rope, how much stress was needed per linear foot of twisted steel cable on a suspension bridge? The amount of sway necessary for that structure when winds blew upon it? The secret language of engineering she'd shared with her father brought renewed strength to her fingers, and she tightened the last knot.

Puget Sound mirrored the flat iron gray of the sky when she locked the carriage house doors. She'd have to dash to the kitchen in this rain. When they got to the mountains, they would no longer have to listen to the sea. But her heart clenched. If only Mama didn't rely on Charles's advice. In the kitchen, Sofi shook the dampness from her skirt as Inga's pleasant face greeted her. "What have you been up to, Sofi, getting so dirty?"

She wouldn't lie to Inga. "Taking care of Papa's things."

"*Jah*, that is good, I suppose. And, Sofi, I have good news. Matilda convinced your mama to have coffee in the parlor."

Relief rippled through Sofi like the melted butter Inga stirred into the bowl of flour. If her mother was feeling more like her old self, maybe she could be convinced to forget this nonsense and let Trina remain at home.

Giving Inga a quick hug, Sofi pulled in a deep breath as she rushed into the parlor, to find it empty. A coffee tray sat on a table close to her mother's chair. Sofi stepped into the hallway, about to call for Matilda when she saw light flickering from under the closed door of her father's study. As she pushed into the study, her gaze went to the small blaze burning in the fireplace.

Mama sat on the settee, a woolen throw across her lap.

The back of Sofi's neck tingled.

While outside, showers fell like a deluge, Neil Macpherson leaned over her mother, holding a bottle of Mama's tonic in his hand.

~*~

Light spilled across the floor where Sofi stood at the threshold.

Neil removed his sodden cap. There was no need to feel guilty, but lately guilt, as though from a faulty pump, spouted through him for the slightest of reasons.

Fire crackled behind him, but the gentle waves of heat radiating up his back were nothing compared to the sparks in Sofi's eyes.

"What are you doing?" She rubbed her palm against her hip.

He became ridiculously conscious of the smell of his wet woolen trousers steaming in the warmth.

Her skirts swished as she crossed the room and knelt beside her mother, an avenging angel in black silk. "Mama, are you well?"

"No fussing, Sofi, please," Mrs. Andersson said in a soft Swedish accent. "This gentleman has been kind, but now I am tired."

Sofi took her mother's hand. "Can I get you anything? Please let—"

"No, Sofi. Matilda insisted I come down, but..." Her gaze travelled to her husband's desk. "I find...I cannot. I am sorry." Mrs. Andersson stood on wavering feet.

Neil took hold of her elbow to steady her.

"Mama," Sofi pleaded, "let me comfort you."

Neil's chest contracted at her yearning tone.

"My darling, spend your love on Trina. With your father..." Mrs. Andersson's voice grew faint. "Trina will need your attentions as they take her to the hospital."

"But, Mama, she does not need that kind of hospital. You can stop it, Mama. Please, I beg you—"

"Please, my *älskling*, let me be." Mrs. Andersson's cheeks glistened wet in the firelight. "It is there Trina will get well. *Jah*, you will see. The doctors will help her forget that...awful night." She swept from the room, clutching a handkerchief to her mouth, but turned back, reaching out for the small glass vial. Murmuring her thanks to Neil, she crossed the foyer and slowly took the stairs to her room.

The fire's crackling grew loud in the sudden quiet.

Neil's and Sofi's shadows danced on the wall. Though her clothes were rumpled, he felt far too aware of his damp state, that he needed a shave. Her height struck him too. He wasn't an overly tall man, but Sofi could look him in the eye. She wasn't much older than Jimmy's sweetheart, Alison. He could see she was as worried as Alison and his mother had been the last time he'd seen them at home in Ireland.

Sofi shivered and raised a trembling hand to her throat. But she set her chin at a firm angle.

He waited for the dismissal she was sure to give him. As much as he wanted to help her, though, truth was, it wasn't his place. He was their gardener. Not their doctor. Not even a friend.

"I haven't thanked you yet, Mr. Macpherson, for saving Trina from the water."

He hid his surprise. Perhaps the dismissal was still to come. "You're welcome."

Her gaze went past him. "You lit the fire."

"Aye, but sure your mother was cold. As you are."

"I'm sorry I was rude."

"'Tis all right."

She dipped her head. "Thank you for moving out of the carriage house so promptly."

He injected as much nonchalance as he could muster. "Is there anything in the carriage house that I can help you with?"

"No need." Her voice grew strong as she moved to the door. "I've locked the carriage house. Inga will have your supper ready." Her brow puckered. "Thank you, Mr. Macpherson."

Still, he didn't move. Her mother was taking too much laudanum. But if he told Sofi, she'd only look at him as if he were mad, trying to give medical advice, dressed in these clothes. These waterlogged work boots would squelch on the polished floor when he walked past her. The fraying cuffs of Jimmy's trousers from the shipyard—it wasn't his imagination—the heat from the fire brought out the odor of sulfur and steel dust ensnared in the wool. He raised his chin. If he stood clean and in the suit he'd bought with his hard-earned money, would Miss Sofi Andersson look at him differently? See him as more than a paid laborer? Value his advice as a professional man? Ach, it made no matter. He moved past Sofi, careful to keep his distance. His physician suits and waistcoats hung useless in the wardrobe in his mother's house in Belfast. Maybe Jimmy was making use of them, as he was making use of Jimmy's laborer clothes. Maybe Jimmy had even married Alison in one of his suits.

~*~

The house lay still as a tomb. Fog muffled every creak. Not that long ago, the grandfather clock chimed one. With Inga in a sound sleep in the room off the kitchen, Sofi filled the hamper with flour and baking powder, salt and sugar, as many staples as she could seize.

Odin scratched at the hall door, whining.

She let him into the kitchen, and the tall black-and-white spaniel leapt at her side.

"It's the middle of the night, you idiot." She massaged the muscle behind his ear. "Quiet." She silently left the house and set the few bags she hadn't yet stowed in the car at the carriage house door.

The dog trotted at her side and watched her with solemn eyes as she opened the gates to the main road. He returned with her to the carriage house where she unlocked the doors. A hinge shrieked.

Holding her breath, she waited. No lights flickered on in the house.

Her father's limousine sat exactly as she'd left it. The knots were snug. Something was different, though. This section of rope had given her trouble, and she'd left it somewhat slack. Now it was so taut it snapped when she pulled it. Must have settled with the weight. After stacking the last of the boxes in the passenger compartment, she led Odin by the collar into the house.

They listened at the foot of the staircase. Only the ticking of the grandfather clock could be heard.

She passed her mother's room. She couldn't bear to leave Mama alone in her grief. *Please, Mama, sleep peacefully.*

Inside the nursery, Matilda waited in a chair by the window, a stiff, narrow-boned figure in her buttoned-up Beatrix jacket. A straw-boater hat sat square on her head. "Are ye all right, lass?" she whispered to Sofi.

Sofi nodded. "Did you give Trina the tonic?"

"I gave her the drops when she woke last at one o'clock."

Sofi ran her hand across her middle, queasy at the necessity of giving Trina some of Mama's laudanum. She'd never approved of the medicine Dr. Atwood prescribed so easily to her mother, but she had to be sure they got Trina away from the house without any upset. Sofi moved to the daybed where her sister slept since Papa drowned. If all went as planned, no one would notice they were gone until the morning, leaving Inga and Frida, Mama too, in innocent ignorance.

Odin nuzzled his nose into Sofi's hand. There was no time to waste.

"Come, *älskling*, put this on." Sofi gently pulled Trina into a sitting position to waken her. She guided her sister's arms into a lawn blouse, helped her into a skirt, and knelt to slip Trina's feet into a pair of moccasins. Tonight, Trina cooperated like a rag doll, and Sofi wished for the days when Trina had been anything but compliant.

Matilda buttoned the girl's coat. Together they led her out of the bedroom and down the stairs.

Odin slinked at their side as if he knew they needed stealth.

A breeze stirred the remains of fog as Sofi tucked Trina into the enclosed backseat of the limousine. Her sister fell into a deep sleep on the tufted leather. Matilda sat beside her and placed a blanket over the slender body.

Odin jumped into the driver's seat, and Sofi covered her mouth to hold back the wild desire to laugh. It had been so long since she'd laughed. The spaniel's glance spoke volumes before he turned his head to stare through the windshield. "I'm driving," she whispered, "so in the back with you." She settled Odin on the floor of the passenger compartment. "Watch your tail," she added before closing the door.

Now the hard part. When she released the brake to allow the car to roll down the driveway, the moment of reckoning would come. Out on the road, she'd have to push the starter button and hope the car wouldn't backfire. Grateful for Papa secretly teaching her to drive two summers ago, she pulled up to the driver's seat and began to ease off the brake.

A hard whisper shattered the silence. "Do you know what you're doing?"

Her heart exploded into fragments.

She turned her head to find the stone-like features of Neil Macpherson.

Though the glass separated her from the backseat, Matilda's rapid burr penetrated. Last night, Matilda had assured her that Neil was sleeping in the main house.

Now Neil stood beside the car fully dressed.

Sofi gripped the steering wheel. "I'll pay you two hundred dollars to let us go. I'll pay you another two hundred to leave here and never tell anyone you saw us."

Neil took hold of the steering wheel. "Your sister needs proper care."

For a moment Sofi wanted to laugh. Of course Trina needed proper care. She thrust his hands off the wheel and dug through her handbag. "Here, take the money."

Ignoring the bills in her hand, he put one foot on the running board. "I don't know where you're taking her, but my guess is not the sanatorium. You'll need my help."

"So you do listen at doors." She released the brake and pushed him hard on the chest as he tried to climb into the car. He was just as interfering as Charles.

He fell back and almost lost his balance, but lunged forward to reach in and pull on the brake. The sound screeched. Upstairs, a lamp flickered on—in Frida's room. Light poured down on the carriage house where the car sat halfway out.

"Do something, Sofi." Matilda gestured wildly through the communicating window, as if to swat Neil away.

Neil stood so close his breath moved a strand of hair at Sofi's cheek. "You need my help," he said through gritted teeth. "Truly."

She glared through the windshield at the darkened grounds, listened to the creaking of trees in the wind.

His voice took on an edge. "People might waken."

She clenched her fists, slid over the seat, and pushed the hair from her eyes.

In a blur, Neil placed a duffle bag on the floorboards beside the dog.

Somewhere at the back of her mind, the realization

dawned. The man had been ready to leave. He clicked the passenger door shut, swung into the driver's seat, letting the vehicle roll down the incline and through the open gates. He pulled on the brake and leapt from the car, going to the front. As if to turn a crank.

Her heart thumped.

He'd not driven their car. He didn't know the Cadillac had one of the new electric starters.

At the same time, Matilda shouted through the glass. "Now's your chance, leave the rogue behind."

Before Neil could discover his mistake, she slid behind the steering wheel, pressed the starter button. The engine coughed to life, and she stomped on the gas pedal.

4

Sofi's hands shook on the steering wheel as Neil sprang out of the way just in time. She almost smiled at his open-mouthed shock, the way he punched the air with his fist. Thank the Lord, she hadn't run him over, but now he sprinted beside the car. She concentrated on steering the limousine straight but couldn't get the speed up to outrun him.

Neil leapt on the running board and clung to the roof rack, shouting, "Miss Andersson, for the love of all that's good, stop!" Reaching in, he yanked on the brake, and the limousine squealed to a stop.

She sank her head against the steering wheel.

In the backseat, Matilda prayed loud enough to disturb the dead. "Lord, get rid of this hoodlum."

The house sat a mere hundred yards up the drive. Gas lamps lit the street. It wasn't yet two, but the light in Frida's room still shone. Would Frida alert the house?

Neil grasped Sofi's shoulder.

She'd been so close to getting away.

"I mean you no harm, miss."

She wanted to trust his voice, so deep and reassuring, but there was something polished about it, something practiced.

"Move over, miss. Whether you want to admit it or not, you're shaken."

Everything was quiet in the back. Matilda waited for Sofi to do something. Her sister slept soundly.

Neil's voice grew tight. "They'll soon know you're gone."

Her desire to fight evaporated. This was not the woman in Proverbs she wanted to be, a strong woman, yes, but lighting the lives around her with the peace of Christ. Gathering her skirts, she slid back across the front seat.

Without a word Neil jumped in, took the wheel, and the car trundled down the road while she stared unblinking through the windshield as if locked in one of Trina's dazes.

But while Trina might be trapped within her emotions, Sofi was not going to allow the same thing to happen to her. Her battle for Trina's sake wasn't over. She reached for her purse at the crossroads where south would take them into Seattle, and north to Everett.

"Which way?" he asked. "Quickly, before someone sees how you've loaded this car."

She glanced through the oval rear window. A horse-drawn cart pulled up behind them. Its metal runners on the wheels clattered on the cobblestones, jangling her thoughts. "Why should I trust you?" Her voice rose. "You have been listening to private conversations, probably overheard the plans I made with Matilda."

"That's true, miss, but only on the one occasion, when you were speaking to that Mr. Bolton. I'm not normally so rude. But I have to ask you, in the past few weeks have you ever felt that I would do you any harm?"

"No..." Aside from the notion that he watched and listened, he'd never given her a moment of concern. And no one asked him to jump into the depths to save

Trina. Or light a fire to warm her mother.

"At least let me offer you my protection on the road, miss."

"We don't need help." She firmed her mouth into a thin line. She couldn't trust him when she couldn't even trust her mother right now.

Neil's Irish brogue turned lyrical. "Well, I can understand you bringing Matilda along. She'd make right shrift out of anyone who dared lay a finger on ye. But if you're depending on the dog, he didn't give me a second glance when I came upon you." His attempt at humor fell flat on her ears.

The farmer's cart pulled around the car and was soon swallowed by the fog. There was no mathematical solution to this dilemma. Though she'd prayed and prayed, no clear answers came from heaven. And the roads they needed to travel were rough. "Drive north," she said in a rush, "away from Seattle for a few miles."

Instead, he spun the wheel in the opposite direction, going toward the center of Seattle.

The shock of his flagrant disobedience sucked all air from her lungs, and she gasped. "I knew I couldn't trust you."

At the same time, Matilda rapped on the window, shouting.

"If my guess is right," he rattled out, "you went to the pier yesterday to buy tickets to leave the wrong scent. If you want to go north, lead them astray. Go south a few miles. If anyone sees us tonight and is asked, let them think you're going in another direction."

She slumped back against the seat. What he said made sense, but she was getting tired of that, and his spying.

He shot her a glance. "By the time they notice, you'll be far from their reach."

"They? Who are *they* you are referring to?"

"The two men at the house yesterday."

Charles and Dr. Atwood.

He had heard everything. Her chest tightened, her breathing hitched as the car throttled to a higher speed. "Charles Bolton is no fool. No matter how I may confuse him at the start, he'll eventually figure out where we've gone. He'll come after us in his conviction he's doing right by my sister. And he's not, I tell you. He's wrong."

"Aye, your sister only needs a bit of time. Peace and quiet and time." Neil's voice was steeped in that reassuring tone.

For the first time in weeks, she felt hope, and it came from this man's softly spoken common sense. Her breathing settled. She lowered her tone to match his. "Fine, take us a bit into town. There's a quieter road we can double back on. But if you cross me at any point, Mr. Macpherson, beware. No one is going to hurt my sister."

They saw few drivers on the road as he drove toward Seattle's downtown section. If he went a little farther, they would come to Pioneer Square where her father's engineering firm was situated. That building, filled with its drafting tables, its walls lined with her father's accomplishments, used to be the stimulus of all her dreams. But that had been taken from her with Papa's passing, and Mama burying herself in her room. All Sofi had left was Trina.

Neil slowed the car. "Is that road coming up soon?"

She wrung her hands in her lap.

"Ah." Understanding filled his one word. "Of course, there's no reason for you to trust me."

She didn't trust him. Her gaze rose to the darkened heights of Seattle. Up there in the hills, Charles was building his new home. Like his car, the match to Papa's, Charles's manor would surpass the grandeur of her father's. A few hours from now, Charles would go to her father's office and design the bridges for Andersson and Bolton Engineering.

She looked across at Neil.

He removed his cloth cap, his eyes focused ahead, a vulnerable set to his mouth, as if he searched the curve of the horizon. Who was he running from? Or where was he running to?

"Stop the car, Mr. Macpherson."

He didn't argue. No doubt he heard the note in her voice that said she would no longer brook any argument. The car rolled to a slow stop.

"Were you spying on me yesterday, to know that I'd gone to the pier?"

"No, miss."

"Then why were you there?"

He released a sigh. "Pure circumstance. I was there the same time as you, thinking of taking a ship. That's still my plan." He sent a swift glance back to the passenger compartment. "But before I leave, I'd like to see you get to wherever you're going. Then I'll be on my way."

"Tell me why I should trust you with my sister's welfare, Mr. Macpherson." She held his unwavering gaze.

His dark hair fell like the undercut of a wave across one brow.

In the back, Trina slept on, with Matilda's white

face staring through the window at them.

His voice dropped to a bass note. "I promise you—on my father's grave—I will not harm a hair on your sister's head."

Less than an hour ago, she'd tried to push him from her moving vehicle.

Behind her, Matilda pleaded. "Lass, leave the scoundrel by the road."

She waved to the housekeeper. "It's all right, Mattie dear. I'll deal with this." It was her turn to force a sigh as she faced Neil. "There's a road five minutes ahead. It will take us north."

"Where to?"

"I'd rather not say just yet. You've advised me to leave the wrong scent to cover our tracks. It makes me wonder if that's what you're doing."

He started the car, but his silence gave truth to her words. He was an enigma, kind and gentle, but why did he want to get out of Seattle as much as she did?

~*~

A rising sun melted the morning fog. Where the roads were good, the Cadillac ran smoothly at thirty-five miles per hour. Not so with the out-of-the-way paths Sofi chose, taking them through cultivated farmlands that hugged the water.

Neil kept to a low speed to avoid jarring as the thin tires travelled the rutted byways. They'd come almost forty miles. Now a smattering of small islands floated on the intense blue of Puget Sound. To the northeast, rolling mountains furred with evergreens gradually molded higher and higher. Ireland wasn't the only emerald land, but his halfhearted smile faltered when he glanced at Sofi.

She'd not spoken a word since they'd left Seattle, but sat the whole time with her arms crossed.

Behind them in the enclosed coach, Matilda slept.

Trina had awakened.

He watched her through the mirror.

She seemed more aware of her surroundings this morning, not in that fugue-like condition. Nor did she show any signs of frenzy like she had the other night. Only a slight repetitious rocking, with her arms wrapped around herself, and speaking under a whisper.

Neil ran a hand down his face. He must be mad to be acting as Trina Andersson's chauffeur, and attempting to diagnose her at the same time. He was no psychiatrist. And he was tired, so he was. Last night, he'd waited for Sofi to make her escape in the loaded car. But his train journey almost two months ago from Union City in whatever open boxcar he could find and crossing the northern states had been exhausting. Not since medical school had he been this weary.

"Turn right at that road ahead." Sofi demolished the uneasy silence. Her averted look still didn't invite conversation.

"I need to put gasoline in."

"The cans are in the back." Her terse responses were beginning to weigh on him.

He took one of the cans and filled the tank.

The morning had turned warm, but though Trina sat in the enclosed part of the car, she huddled into herself. Her eyes widened as a sawmill whined within the folds of hills. When a robin trilled, she searched the bird out, a small smile relieving that mask of fear and sadness. Then her eyes took on that forever-haunted look again.

For the next hour, they headed east. As the road began to rise, it meandered around mountains and became increasingly rough. The occasional wisp of cloud snagged on spear-like treetops that stood sentinel on the heights.

Sofi's voice broke. "At long last, the sea is behind us."

Smudges beneath her eyes contrasted against the youthfulness of her skin. A while later, her eyes closed, and her head lolled back against the seat.

He kept himself from uttering a scoff of disapproval. At least one of them could get a few winks.

Yet seeing her asleep somehow lifted his weariness.

The ruts in the road worsened. Just ahead, a small landslide blocked the road. Neil pulled on the brake and turned off the limousine's engine. When the car came to a complete stop, silence rushed in with the mingled scents of cedar and Sofi's clean fragrance. A desire to sit for a moment washed over him.

Her head lay against his shoulder. A strand of her hair splayed like spun gold over his arm, tangling around one of his coat buttons. He untangled the tress and rubbed it between his fingers. He shouldn't. If his mother were to see him now, she'd soon tell him he was taking liberties. But it was only for a moment. Like thick silk, Sofi's hair. And her breath came in soft puffs close to his jaw.

A sharp rap on the communicating window startled him. He dropped the lock of hair.

Matilda sat back with an inaudible huff.

Sofi's eyes opened, her blue-gray eyes mirroring the sky and trees around them so that they melded into aquamarine. Awareness of her situation unfolded as she moved a few inches from him on the seat. A blush pinked her cheeks as her fingers wound her hair into a roll, exposing the nape of her neck.

"I thought you could use a few more minutes' sleep." His voice came out hoarse.

"Apparently Matilda thinks otherwise." She tried to hide a smile.

A warm tide coursed through him. He stepped down to the running board. "There's a rockslide ahead." He hoped his abruptness would cover the shakiness in his voice that her nearness brought on. From the top of the car, he pulled out the rake and shovel. Ten feet down the road, he hauled the larger stones out of the way. It didn't take long to work up a sweat shoveling the loose rock and raking the road smooth. Now, of all times, he didn't need the distraction of a pretty girl, no matter how much she needed help. He should be on a ship to the Far East. Instead, he was on this wild journey, trying to convince himself it was to fulfill his oath. The lunacy of the situation wasn't lost on him. He was not the only doctor in the vicinity. He secured the tools on the roof and joined the women.

Sofi removed her driving coat and pulled the hamper from the car. "We'll stop here for a while. There's a brook down this incline."

As if Trina were an invalid, Matilda assisted her from the car.

He leaned in to help, but Matilda gave him a withering glance.

Trina threw up her hands, cowering in an attempt

to dive back inside the car. "I don't want to go. I have to go back...for...Papa. To find Papa..."

"Trina, Papa is in God's hands." Sofi tried to hold her sister, but Trina slapped at her hands. "Trina, you are safe. Please be brave like you used to be."

"No, I don't want to be brave. I was wrong...wrong..." The girl scrambled back into the car.

Brushing past Sofi, Neil took Trina's hand. "Trina."

At the sound of his voice, she peered over her shoulder.

"Remember me?"

Her eyebrows rose. "You're the gardener."

"Aye, right, so I am." Good, good. Her rigid shoulders were starting to relax. "Will you be coming on out of the car? There's a spot down the hill where we can find out what Matilda's packed for lunch, and if I see rightly, a patch of daisies." He stepped away from the car, and with her hand still in his, she came. He couldn't quite place what emotion tormented her. Fear? Sadness?

With soothing words from Sofi, Trina released his hand and took hers, and then Matilda's.

He followed, carrying the hamper, walking along the roadside adorned by spiky red flowers that reminded him of paintbrushes. The girl's reaction to simply being in a strange environment exceeded any normal apprehension. The spaniel padded at his side as Neil mulled over Trina's behavior. She went from dazed stupors to fits of terror. A person who'd witnessed such a tragedy as losing her father the way she had, might very well react in a similar fashion as soldiers he'd seen return from the Boer War.

Sofi dropped back to walk beside him. "You've

calmed her again when we could not."

"From what I've seen, I'd say she has her moments when she rejects her loved ones for some reason and I distract her from that spiral of emotion that takes her captive."

Sofi remained quiet, taking this in as they made their way down the incline. "From what you have seen? Is this another way of saying that you were snooping?"

Holding the hamper with one hand, he reached out his free hand to keep her from stumbling down the steep hill. He couldn't possibly tell her the truth. What about a partial truth, though? "Miss Andersson, after your father died, I saw how your sister was. I simply wanted to help."

"That's why you were prepared to leave with us last night."

"Aye. It was plain what you were planning."

Her brow wrinkled. "So you'll keep our secret?"

"Miss Andersson, your whereabouts are your business alone."

Her mouth blossomed into a full smile. "I believe you, Mr. Macpherson." They started downward again. "You tightened the ropes on the car."

"So I did." These small confessions eased some of the knot between his shoulder blades.

They reached a grassy meadow near a brook, where Matilda spread a blanket.

Sofi helped Trina to sit, and then pulled pastries and fruit from the hamper.

The stream drew Neil. At its bank, he patted down his clothes to remove most of the caked dust. Splashing water on his face and arms, scrubbing the back of his neck, he relished the cold bite of melted snow. Odin joined him, and Neil caressed the dog's floppy ears as together they stared into the green swirling depths, basking in the warmth of the sun drying his skin.

"You look human again." Sofi's voice startled him.

He hadn't heard her come up.

Trina seemed happy enough sitting on the blanket, mesmerized by a handful of flowers as if she were a girl much younger than sixteen.

A spurt of satisfaction shot through him as he watched the girl lace a daisy chain together.

Sofi noticed his scrutiny. "It's as if going back to her childhood brings Trina peace. But when I try to talk to her, only part of her is there, and she slips away from me."

"She goes back to that day. To lose a father...I'm so sorry."

The image of his own father's laughing eyes drifted away before Neil could savor the joy of those memories. How was his mother faring alone with only Jimmy to look after her in Ireland? He put his hands in his pockets and forced a brighter tone. "Your Scottish terror doesn't have much to say. She never strays far from Trina."

"My Scottish terror...?" Sofi smiled.

The nerves along his spine danced. "Virago, terror, take your pick, miss. Although I've grown fond of the title Scottish Virago. I think I'll keep it as my pet name for her. A name spoken with the highest esteem, of course."

"It takes Matilda a while to like anyone, but once she decides she likes you, you have a friend for life." Her smile grew.

"Something to strive for then."

"Of course, it's harder for some to meet Matilda's

standards. I'm not sure you're up to it, Neil Macpherson."

At her use of the surname *Macpherson*, his surge of joy receded.

Together they strolled back to Trina and Matilda.

He sat on the grass.

Sofi's sister worked on her daisy chain, but thrust it away and bolted to her feet. Wrapping her arms around herself, she stalked a few feet away, her gaze searching the horizon.

Matilda readied herself to follow, but Neil put his arm out to stop her. "You're doing a grand job looking after her, but she's fine where she is for now."

Matilda sniffed and looked away, her gaze following Trina, who strolled through the grass.

"You're taking Trina somewhere she'll feel safe?" He caught Sofi's eye.

At first, she held back. But in one brisk movement, Sofi began packing the food into the hamper. "We're going to a valley in the Cascades." Now that she'd made her decision to break her silence, the dam burst open. "My grandparents came from Sweden and believed in hard work. Fresh air and sunshine. I'm taking Trina there in the hope the valley will bring her back to us."

Matilda stood. "Aye, I'm sure the Lord will fix that poor wee mind of hers there. No scientific blather in a hospital can do what He can do." She stomped off to Trina's side.

Trina glanced at Matilda as if she suddenly awakened, and willingly walked up the incline with her, touching the leaves of low-hanging trees. Some of her haunted look had lessened.

"Don't judge Matilda too harshly." Sofi took her

time folding the blanket. "She's outspoken about everything, including her faith."

He picked up the hamper, shutting out the memory of Da taking him to church when he was a lad. Religion was fine for children and women, or old men, but not for men of science. He held out a hand to help Sofi up. "What was Trina like before?"

Sofi went as still as her sister. "She was always vivacious, annoyingly fearless."

"Did she ever suffer from melancholy? Show an aversion to eye contact? A preference for being on her own?"

"Trina used to thrive on being the center of attention. Why these questions?"

"I've seen this type of illness before, in veterans coming home from war—a prolonged reaction to a traumatic event."

"Did you serve in that capacity, Mr. Macpherson?"

"I've never been a member of the military. And please don't call me Mr. Macpherson."

"Why not? It's your name, isn't it?" Their truce vanished with her clipped statement.

"Call me Neil. If I'm to help you for a while." At least Neil was his real first name. To speak a kernel of truth filled him with the same delight as that brook he'd washed in.

She turned her back to him.

On the next mountain, several hectares of trees were denuded of greenery. The whine of a donkey engine echoed.

"They're logging down there," he said for want of something better to say.

"Are you interested in the timber industry?" Sofi's shoulders relaxed as she took the olive branch.

"I'm interested in many things, Miss Andersson."

Facing him again, she tried unsuccessfully to stop her smile. "I suppose if we're partners in crime—kidnapping my sister—then you'd better call me Sofi."

The June sun at this altitude burned down on his uncovered head, but he shivered. Of course...Sofi wasn't Trina's legal guardian. And him, if he were caught, the authorities would charge him with kidnapping. He gave a brittle laugh. What was the charge of kidnapping when that of murder already hung over his head?

Her eyes narrowed. "I see you're as much of a closed book as before. You clearly have some sort of education, yet you're a gardener. You tell me nothing of your background."

The weight on his shoulders grew heavier as he watched her stumble up the incline. It wasn't physical weariness, but that of humiliation, that stole the strength from him. The memory of the last time he'd seen his medical valise...his scalpels strewn over the pavement...covered in Robert Crawford's blood. So much of what he had been had disappeared with the murder of that man. Neil followed Sofi and reached the road.

Matilda busied herself settling Trina in the car, and the dog jumped in to join them.

Neil drew Sofi behind a pine tree that hid them from Matilda's vigilant guard. "I did work in a hospital. In Ireland. For a while."

"What did you do in this hospital?"

He raised his hand in a helpless gesture. "You need someone to help you with Trina. I need a quiet place to...think for a while. I can't tell you more than that. You're no fool, Sofi. So decide—am I a dangerous man who'll murder you as you sleep?"

She took her time to answer. Then she took his hand.

Every muscle in his body tensed with her touch.

Perhaps they'd left all propriety behind in Seattle, running away with her sister and her housekeeper, for goodness sake? Or was it that they fought together the night before last, in a battle of life and death for Trina, that a lady such as Sofi should cast away her social norms even for a moment?

She lifted his hand to study it, tracing her index finger along the back of it and across his palm. The wind murmured in the cedars. The sun increased its warmth. "You haven't been a laborer for long," she said. "These calluses are new."

He could hear nothing but the flapping of a bird's wings close by, and his own pulse.

"What are you, Neil?" She released his hand. "Who are you? And why do I have the feeling I'd rather not know?"

5

The river churned, its high waters racing through a chasm in foaming green and white caps.

By late afternoon, Sofi's fingertips tingled in anticipation of the next curve in the road. The imagined smell of ink and paper filled her senses. Then, there it was. A honeycombed arc of steel Warren trusses grew out of the cliff, spanning the three-hundred-foot gap and soaring across the gorge—Papa's last bridge. She wanted to shout into the passenger compartment to share this moment with Trina.

But it was the *Cecelia*, Trina's sleek yacht, that had tied the cord of love between Trina and Papa.

Papa's bridges were for Sofi. She blinked back the wetness. Of all the projects for Papa to not see finished. The bridge perched above the gorge, but the joy running through her fizzled out like a damp fuse.

While Papa had been away in Stockholm last year, Charles had finagled until he got what he wanted. He'd arranged for Wetzle Steel to fabricate the bridge structure in his Seattle foundry and transport it here by train. Her father never liked Heinz Wetzle or the steel he produced in his smelting furnaces.

Now the bolt-up crew busily plumbed the bridge. Riveting gangs fastened it together.

Neil studied the bridge as they drove past, frown lines marching across his brow. "I hope your father's company sees to the safety of those ironworkers, laboring so high off the ground."

She tried to see what was behind his hard tone, but he kept his gaze on the road. Back at the brook, Neil had been pleasant to talk to, until he'd all but told Sofi to not ask questions.

A heavy silence ground between them as the road curved away from the structure, heading toward the small wooden bridge that would take them into Orchard Valley.

Sofi looked behind. The new bridge would meet her on the other side of the gorge. No matter who built it, now that she'd seen it, her eyes couldn't get their fill. What had been a series of ink lines actually stood, a thing of grace and strength. If only it wasn't Charles as its consulting engineer. Her chest hurt as she turned away. Some dreams were not meant to be.

~*~

Sunlight slanted from the west as they entered the valley. Farms created a velvet patchwork, and the tang of recently mown hay sweetened the air. The opposite side of the bridge met them at the entrance to town, where the hammers of steelworkers driving rivets into the trusses rang like a welcome home.

Neil stopped at the crossroads.

Sofi savored the outskirts of the town where she'd spent most of her childhood summers. Already her spirits lifted. A high-wheeled freight wagon rolled toward Gronberg's livery stable. Railway lines would make it so much easier to transports goods in and out of Orchard. But there were things she hoped would never change—the red-and-white awning of Helsing's mercantile, the steeple of a white clapboard church that sought the sky. With a quiet nod, she motioned to Neil to take the road following this side of the gorge.

Still within sight of the bridge, Neil drove up to an expansive log home with a wrap-around porch. From the well-cared-for raspberry canes, healthy apple and pear orchards, and large cornfield, it was obvious Kiosho still nurtured her grandparents' homestead. She couldn't wait to see this old family friend who'd emigrated from Japan around the same time as her grandparents from Sweden.

Neil glanced at her.

"We're not stopping here. Take that winding road. There's a plateau—you can't see it from here—hidden behind a bank of trees before the road climbs to the alpine." Her heart grew lighter still as the road switched back and forth up the face of the mountain.

The road took them through a drape of low-hanging cedar, fir, and larch branches. In the center of a clearing, a small cabin of pine logs shone in the late-afternoon sun. A barn listed twenty feet away.

Neil stopped the car.

Sofi jumped down to help Trina out.

Her sister gasped at the cabin with the same euphoria she had earlier when she'd linked the daisy chain.

Sofi pulled her close, inwardly giving thanks that Trina didn't spurn her touch. "Remember, *älskling*? Remember the trees we used to climb. The mud pies we made."

A sad smile lifted the corners of Trina's mouth. Her eyes shone, tracking the mountain peaks, then lowered to the tops of the trees, from the cabin to Sofi. "I remember." But her soft tone brimmed with questions.

Sofi tucked Trina closer to her side. "This is where you're going to get better."

"In the cabin...like when we were kids."

Sofi's insides did a somersault.

Trina showed so few moments of living in the present.

"Remember Kiosho used to bring us lemonade and cookies. Our secret place. Even Papa didn't know, but Mama did."

"Papa..." Trina's gaze withdrew. "Yes, Mama knew, though." She looked a thousand miles into the distance and rubbed her arms as she trailed across the clearing. "Mama always kept our secrets."

Sofi let her go.Mama always used to keep their secrets, but could she trust Mama to do so now? Besides, she had to see to the condition of the cabin.

The sun slid behind a cloud, and the golden translucent wash seeped out of the cabin walls, leaving them a warm shade of gray. The cabin wasn't in as good repair as it appeared when she'd first gotten out of the car, seeing it through the eyes of hope. The walls stood as sturdy as the day Grandpa and Kiosho first hoisted them up. But a lot of years had passed since her grandparents had moved to the bigger homestead at the foot of the mountain. While a great many of the cedar shingles remained on the roof, one corner had blown away, leaving a gaping hole.

Sofi took in the rest of the clearing. The privy would do. The barn hadn't survived as well, but most of the roof remained intact. It would shelter Neil, because though he had his secrets, for Trina's sake she'd bend a few rules. A chuckle erupted from her. Besides, Matilda was here. Scottish Virago, indeed. A trickle of guilt slipped down the nape of her neck. Back at the brook—what kind of woman was she to have taken a man's hand to study it? In order to keep Neil with them a few days, she must cease all familiarity. Passing over the threshold, she stopped in the middle of the main room.

Matilda was already starting up a ladder into the loft.

A raccoon had made a home in the kitchen, and it stood on its hind legs, hissing.

Odin barked and chased it out the door.

Upstairs in the loft, a flurry of wings rushed through a hole in the roof, and Matilda screamed.

Seconds later, a flock of starlings swooped and dove outside, the flutter of their wings matching that of Sofi's heart.

Neil arched a dubious brow, his gaze landing on the broken pieces of an old toy tea set she and Trina used to play with.

But seeing Trina's shining eyes gave Sofi all the confirmation she needed.

Their childhood was soaked into these walls.

Neil led Trina farther into the cabin.

How curious that her sister didn't mind this stranger.

As though Trina were reaching out to touch long-ago memories, she led Neil around the cabin, talking in an undertone for his ears only. When Trina spied the rocking chair, she sat and began to rock. Her knuckles whitened as she gripped the arms of the chair, but something had altered behind her sister's blue eyes. As if she were seeing what was really in front of her, and not something miles away below the waves of the Juan de Fuca Strait.

Sofi caught Neil's slow smile. As though the

earlier coldness between them never happened, a fizzy-lemonade feeling of triumph flowed between them. Breathless, she whirled to inspect the rest of the cabin.

The most important item sat in the corner. If the cast-iron stove worked, they could survive. Small animals used it for a nest for who knew how long. It needed a good scouring, but it would ward off the chill of the nights, cook their food, and heat water. Half the windowpanes were cracked, the frames warped. Then, as she turned, the stenciled words over the door held her fast. Faded by time, the scripture was a verse Grandmama had chosen.

"Let your light so shine before men, that they may see your good works, and glorify your Father which is in heaven." ~ Matthew 5:16

She read the passage again and again. The pricking she felt in her soul did not pertain to her stealing Trina away to this hidden place. *Heavenly Father, what are You disturbing my heart for? Surely You have sent me here for Trina's sake...to hide her, not for the labor that my heart desires. You know I cannot do anything about that.* She must quiet her soul with taking care of Trina, not yearn for impossible dreams.

The remaining glass panes in this cabin needed a good scrubbing. For the time being, they would close the inner shutters. They had enough food for tonight and most of tomorrow until she could make arrangements with Kiosho for provisions.

Water splashing into a galvanized bucket outside reached her ears. Neil had primed the pump already.

Upstairs, Matilda was sweeping the loft.

Trina rocked by the fireplace.

Yes, with help from Kiosho, they would more than

survive here. They'd flourish. Though God pricked her soul a moment ago, she planted her hands on her hips and smiled. Aside from that nudge in her spirit that she didn't understand, she knew He would protect them.

Sofi undid the buttons at the wrists of her shirtwaist to roll up the sleeves and reached for the broom propped behind the door.

~*~

After Neil had a short rest, he cleared the chimney of debris. He teased the first flames from kindling, the logs burned, and the stove began to work like a charm.

Sofi and Matilda swept and scrubbed.

As evening waned, they heated bucket after bucket of water. After several hours of labor passed, they all had a good wash.

Sofi glanced at her hands and giggled, remembering an old Swedish saying her grandmother used. "That our hands show signs of our work is nothing to be ashamed of."

A late dinner of leftover meat pastries went well with the potatoes she'd taken from the larder this morning. Still in their jackets, they'd baked in no time in the fire. At the back of the cabin she'd found the tangled remains of a garden. Some of the vegetables had re-seeded, and she'd gathered enough early peas to finish the meal. Certainly not *haute cuisine*, but filling nonetheless. To her secret satisfaction, Neil cleaned his plate. Her smile played traitor, and she firmed her lips.

He was still, after all was said and done, the gardener.

Trina drifted around the cabin while Sofi climbed

the ladder to lay out their bedding. Though the pain of losing Papa still stung, a sense of freedom sang along her tired arms. She climbed down the ladder.

Neil was sitting at the table, setting out the broken tea set he'd found in the grate. "Do you remember this, Trina?" he asked.

Trina fiddled with the play tea set, trying to connect the broken shards like a puzzle. A frown lined her brow, her mouth clenched tight, as if her mind were throwing out a lifeline to capture floundering memories.

Neil remained equally quiet even as he glanced at Sofi. The look in his eyes resonated with the same triumph they'd shared earlier.

For the first time since Papa died, the tightness in Sofi's shoulders eased. Stars shimmered through the gap in the roof. A glimpse of the Big Dipper drew her outside.

Matilda was washing the dishes.

Neil moved to sit on a wooden settle with his back against the wall and continued to observe Trina.

Sofi strolled to the edge of the plateau and sipped her coffee. An owl hooted. She rolled her aching shoulders, hating the fact she had to leave Mama with only Inga and Frida as a buffer against Charles's meddling. She could only hope Dr. Atwood would stop prescribing laudanum as the answer to all that ailed her mother. But it seemed they'd gotten clean away from Seattle with no one to notice.

Charles would never think that she'd escape to this place right under his nose. Any day, he'd be out to inspect the bridge.

A finicky breeze rippled along her bare arms. A full moon backlit the mountains, and she reveled in the peace the valley gave her. And in today's good old-fashioned labor. Something she'd never been allowed to do at home. A proper young lady had a position to uphold. Here in these mountains, though, she could tap her energy. Of all people, Mama should have understood that and supported her pleas to be allowed a career. Now Papa was gone, she could no more go against his wishes than when he was alive.

Sofi yawned, leaned against the trunk of a cedar, and shoved her loosened hair over one shoulder. There was still so much to do. Tomorrow they must do something about those broken windowpanes. Start chinking the spaces between the logs.

From inside the cabin, Trina's cry broke the stillness, and Sofi's hand flopped to her side. The night terrors had begun already. She ran inside.

"Sofi. Sofi, don't leave me alone."

Neil reached Trina first. "It's all right. You're safe."

"No...I shouldn't be..."

"You shouldn't be what?"

"I shouldn't...be..." Her sister's eyes were dark with terror.

Neil rubbed Trina's back as if she were a child.

Yesterday Sofi would have separated them in a flurry of indignation. But after today, she had no desire to enforce any social correctness. Let this gardener treat Trina as if she was his little sister, for she saw nothing in his face but compassion, and innocent reliance in Trina's.

Gradually, Trina's sobs eased to hiccups.

"Like your big sister has said, it's going to be all right, wee girl, I promise."

Matilda put her arm around Trina's slight

shoulders. "Time you were in your bed," she soothed.

Trina sniffed and looked back at Neil, her eyes as wide and luminous as the moon outside, but she let Matilda lead her up the ladder to the loft.

Neil picked up the quilt laid out for him.

Sofi started up the ladder behind Matilda and Trina.

"Has she spoken of your father's death at all?" Neil asked in a low voice.

"Nothing. All we know is the *Cecelia* sank in the strait off Whidbey Island. Papa's body was never found, and fishermen rescued Trina when they found her floating on a life ring."

"The *Cecelia*?"

"A small racing yacht Papa and Trina built."

Behind her, a log in the fire fell in a hiss of steam and crackled with new flames. He placed his hand on the doorframe. "If I've read the map correctly, that strait is like open sea." That blade-edge in his voice had returned. "A bit irresponsible of your father, wouldn't you say, to allow Trina to take her yacht out that far?"

It took a moment to catch her breath. "My father may have been a lot of things, but he was not irresponsible. A storm took them unawares." She pressed a hand to her middle. "We won't know the full truth until Trina can tell us."

"You can't deny he took a risk, putting a human life on the line like that. Trina could have drowned too." His voice softened. "As he did."

Neil strode from the cabin before she could gather a response, taking with him the camaraderie they'd shared all evening. She listened to his footsteps recede. Neil barely disguised his insult that her father was to blame for the foundering of Trina's craft. With a shaking hand on the mantel, she stared into the fire until the log shrank to embers. Neil's accusations smoldered like hot coals at the front of her mind. Why had Papa and Trina been so far out on open sea that day? Had they not checked the weather before leaving the marina?

Odin sprawled in front of what was left of the fire as Sofi climbed to the loft.

Matilda lay on the other side of Trina and woke when Sofi undressed and pulled on her nightgown. Shivering, Sofi crawled in beside Trina and pulled the bedding up under her chin. Her feet touched something warm, and she reached down to pull out a hot object wrapped in a blanket. It was a stone that had been heated in the fire.

Matilda leaned over the somnolent form of Trina. "'Twasn't me, but him. He heated the stone in the fire while you were out having a dander under the stars. Did the same for me." She rolled over and muttered to the wall something that Sofi only half caught. "For the life of me, I don't know what to make of the man."

Sofi pushed the stone to the foot of the bed again. Neil's insult to the memory of her father raced through her mind, followed by his promise this morning to protect Trina on the grave of *his* father. Like her, his loss had to be recent. Still raw. Grief had torn her family apart. It must have done the same to Neil. To his loved ones.

She curled her cold toes around the wrapped stone. In the barn, Neil had no such comforts, only that one thin quilt. Grabbing two more of the quilts she'd packed, she crept down the ladder, pulled her canvas driving coat around her, and slipped on her boots.

Outside, the barn rose up, a dark shape against the night. If he was inside, it wouldn't be proper to barge in.

She tapped on the side of the frame where a door used to be. No answer. She knocked louder. "Neil?" Inside the barn, she called his name again, and with no answer, climbed to the loft. The quilt lay on top of clean cedar boughs next to his duffle bag. She added two more and hurried back to the cabin.

She climbed up to the loft and turned down the wick on the oil lamp. A small flame cut the darkness in the event Trina woke in the night. Sofi's eyelids grew heavy as she prayed, listening to her sister's breathing.

Neil's Irish brogue teased her memory. As the fronds of cedar trees tapped against the cabin, the questions he wouldn't allow her to ask drummed. He'd worked for them for a little less than two months, coming to them shortly before Papa died. Practically a stranger. It was obvious he was far more than a gardener, yet she trusted him, and not Charles, whom she'd known for years. Her toes curled at the bottom of the quilts. A man intent on hurting them wouldn't heat a stone to warm their feet.

~*~

Night air fragrant with cedar fell damply on Neil's face and arms as he tromped down the mountainside. He pushed away fir boughs as if he could push away the memories that talking with Sofi evoked. Her father had been a wealthy builder of grand steel structures, just like the man responsible for his own father's death in Ireland.

Corn stalks brushed at his knees as he waded

through the field to the gorge. Moonlight etched each steel cable as the bridge arched. At the abutment, he took his first steps toward the bridge deck. At the wooden ties, nothing but space existed between him and the frothing white caps of the river. The girders felt solid to his touch, though. Rivets holding this bridge together were no different than the rivets his father and brother had pounded into the plating of ships at home in the Belfast shipyard.

But what did Neil know? He was no engineer of bridges or builder of ships. He was a doctor. He knew nothing of steel, but of human tissue and organs. If the bodies of his patients weren't too broken from illness or accident, he was able to knit those tissues and bones together again. And sometimes, not. Like the day the ambulance car brought the shattered body of his father from the shipyard to the hospital.

Except for the want of basic safety equipment, Da would never have fallen from the ship's deck to plunge fifty feet to the ground. But to men like Robert Crawford—and perhaps the late Frederick Andersson—five fatalities a year remained within the confines of acceptability. Their balance sheets and ledgers never showed the scores of accidents that took lives or left numerous laborers maimed. Men like Crawford were more interested in finishing the job on time than in caring about the loss of one man...one husband...one father.

With a shudder, Neil slapped his hand against a steel girder. Had any justice been served with Crawford's death? Neil struck the girder again. No! And he needed to contain his anger. Sure, look what anger had torn apart—his mother, himself, and Jimmy. He walked to the center of the bridge.

Lights from the ironworkers' campfires winked on the bank of the river. The low hum of voices travelled in the night. One man strolled across the bridge deck, swinging a lantern in his hand.

Neil's trousers and shirt were dark, but all the same, he stepped closer to the triangle of a steel girder to blend in against the bridge. For Sofi and Trina's sake, and for his own, he needed to remain invisible. Neil slipped below to the ribs supporting the deck.

The lantern ceased swinging with the man's gait. A tiny red glow of a cigarette spiraled into the dark as the man tossed it into the river. A moment later, the man returned the way he'd come.

Neil grasped a steel beam to hoist upward, but stopped as his fingers pushed through a crumbling piece of metal in the center of an eyebeam. Between his fingers, he moved loose fragments of steel. He was no bridge designer, but surely this steel was substandard.

6

An aroma of brewing coffee wafted out to Neil on the bluff overlooking the valley. He'd been sitting on this tree stump since first light, trying to compose a letter. He raised the pen from the page.

Blue smoke spiraled from the cabin's chimney. Inside the cabin, the stove lid clanked as it dropped into place, and a stream of chatter came from Sofi's lips all for Trina's sake. Sofi's willow-like bone structure and Nordic lightness of hair were an illusion. She might have been raised in Seattle's high society, but rolling up her sleeves yesterday, she'd paid no heed to the sweat dampening her shirtwaist. Or her hands growing red and chapped like the frontier women who'd crossed the prairies in covered wagons.

He and Da used to take turns reading stories of the Wild West to entertain a wide-eyed Jimmy when he was only a wee lad. But that was a lifetime ago. Da had been buried almost three months, and Jimmy was a man now. Had he married his girl back home? Wasn't that what Neil's banishment had been for, to let Jimmy do right by Alison?

Neil placed the fountain pen back on the paper. It was a bit of a chance, but if he addressed the letter to Alison, care of her mother who lived several streets away from their house, surely the police wouldn't notice. Alison would pass the message to his mother and Jimmy that he was safe. Alison would be the making of Jimmy. And the Good Lord knew, Jimmy needed to be made a man.

Odin pattered across the grass. Caressing the dog's ears soothed some of Neil's rawness.

The cabin door swung open and Matilda struggled across the porch with a half barrel. He hurried over to help, the dog cantering at his side. Neil set the barrel beneath the pump. "What else do you need?"

Matilda looked at him askance, but her dour mouth softened. "I suppose ye could bring out yon pot of water I have boiling on the stove."

He nodded in deference, wanting to win this paragon's favor. After bringing the steaming pot out to Matilda, he emptied it into the barrel, and she thanked him with a brusque nod of her own.

A great many repairs needed doing to the cabin, but this morning, the orderly place smelled of fresh coffee. A cedar log burned in the fireplace to ward off the morning chill. The stove threw off heat, and biscuits fresh out of the oven sat on the warming shelf.

Sofi had packed the car to create this temporary home. Even a few wild roses in a bottle graced the scoured pine table.

Trina sat in the rocking chair, staring into the fire. She wasn't confined in one of her dazes, but her hands gripped the arms of her chair. Yesterday's progress wasn't showing today. But what she'd said last night repeated like a refrain in his mind. *I shouldn't be...* She shouldn't be what?

He couldn't barge to her side and engage her in conversation. It took time for trust to grow. Time he didn't have. If he had any sense at all, he'd be on a ship leaving Seattle, instead of trying to stitch Trina's memories together again.

Sofi removed a pan of biscuits from the oven.

His stomach rumbled at the whiff of scones.

She poured a steaming cup of the strong black brew she drank so easily and brought it to him.

"I need to apologize," he started, "for what I said last night about your father."

"We were both tired last night."

He returned her smile. "To a new day then." He took a sip and held the cup away from him, crinkling his face. "My, how you Swedes like your coffee strong."

"Too robust for your delicate tastes, Neil Macph—." Her eyes danced.

"Not at all. We Irish like our tea just as strong."

"But is the coffee to your taste?"

He leaned against the wall, his voice going husky. "'Tis grand. Sure I prefer it."

"You prefer tea, don't you?"

"I do miss a pot of tea, one where the leaves have been stewing so long the spoon can stand straight up in the cup. Does that satisfy ye?"

Their combined laughter lifted to the eaves. Their gazes locked.

A faint flush caressed her cheek, and she glanced away.

It felt so long since he'd held a simple conversation with another person. Catching the first ship out of Ireland, lying about his name as he came through Ellis Island, had not allowed for genteel talk of any kind. Even when he'd found work at the Andersson estate, grief imprisoned the whole house. He'd probably stayed there as long as he had because their emotions mirrored his own. Now, sipping coffee with Sofi, he could almost pretend that life held the promise of hope...of freedom. He sought her unguarded eyes.

"Thank you for laying out the quilts for me last night."

"And you, for the warming stone."

He ran his hand across Odin's back as the dog sat at his feet.

Sofi fussed over the coffeepot at the stove.

In proper society they'd never be alone like this, even if Matilda's footsteps did stride from the porch to the pump outside.

He couldn't take his eyes off Sofi's hair that hung loose. His face grew warm at the way her waist tapered to the gentle flair of her hips. It was his turn to glance away.

She didn't notice his embarrassment and poured another cup of coffee. She took this and a biscuit to Trina, but her sister waved the food away. Sofi hunched down in front of her. "In no time at all, Trina, you'll be your old self."

Trina pushed out a harsh sigh. With trembling hands she took the cup, sipped a few times, and passed it back to Sofi. She cuddled the biscuit in her hand, but turned to look into the fire. As Sofi returned to the table, he was sure he heard Trina say on a wisp of breath, "Sorry...Sofi, sorry."

While Sofi sat opposite him and drank the remains of Trina's cup, he kept his gaze on the younger girl.

Trina continued to mouth the word *sorry*.

"Ever since I was a little girl, I've always thought I had to fix everything." Sofi's brow furrowed.

"Are you doubting your decision?"

"No, I am convinced I am doing the right thing for Trina." Sofi propped her elbows on the table. "Trina seems to trust you, and with just one night in this place, she had the first good night's sleep since...since we lost Papa. I got some rest too. Maybe that's why I feel optimistic today. As the Lord promises, His compassions are new every morning." She smiled, but her eyes held questions.

The silence took on a tangible quality, and he felt his slight smile harden to a mask.

"You mentioned you had plans to leave Washington soon, that you needed a place to think." A blush started at the base of her throat and winged upward to encompass her cheeks. She placed a hand on his wrist that rested on the table. "I'm not asking for your life story, but would you consider staying with us for a while? Trina likes you and..."

The feel of her fingers on his wrist did something to his insides. A rose petal dropped from a bloom in the center of the table. Silence beat in his ears as Sofi removed her hand, and he reached for a biscuit, hoping to regain his equilibrium.

"I'm a good judge of people, Neil, and I'm right about you, aren't I? These things you don't want to tell me, they're nothing serious." She lifted her gaze, her blue eyes seeing clear through the fabrication of Neil Macpherson, surely.

The biscuit stuck in his throat. He gulped the hot coffee. What would Sofi say if she knew that Scotland Yard wanted him for the murder of Robert Crawford? And with Crawford being the right-hand man to an English peer, no doubt an English police inspector was already on American soil, searching for him?

~*~

An hour later, the sun shone strong as Neil attempted to fix a hole in the roof with rough branches. A noise he recognized rent the tranquility of the valley—hammers on steel. He jumped to the ground. Work on the bridge was far enough away to sound like a chorus of discordant bells. Memories of burning coal and sulfur from riveting forges rushed upon him. He might have been at home in Belfast close to the shipyard, until the cedar and pine scents of Washington's mountains brought him back. He was far from Ireland, looking down on a valley hardly touched by civilization.

From the porch, Sofi's wistful gaze latched onto the web of steel in the distance. "Seven o'clock," she said.

He leaned a shoulder against the porch post.

The hem of Sofi's fresh skirt brushed the tops of a sturdy pair of boots. She'd attempted to roll her hair into a twist at the back of her head, but the straight strands wouldn't comply.

A rumble of laughter deep in his chest wanted to escape. A feeling he'd not felt for months. For the life of him, he'd never let on. Only a few days in her company, and he already knew her hair would tumble to her shoulders by noon.

She was quick-witted, though, and he transferred his look to Matilda before Sofi read the twitching of his mouth that would give him away.

Matilda tugged on a pair of gloves and fastened a hat on her head as if she were going to high tea.

Neil rested a foot on the porch. "You're sure you can trust this caretaker you're going to see?"

Sofi smoothed the front of her shirtwaist. "Kiosho is no caretaker, but half-owner of the timber business he and my grandfather built. He'll see to the supplies we'll need, and no one will be the wiser that we're up here."

"Trina will be safe with me then."

Sofi's eyes glistened. "I know."

"Will you post this for me?"

She glanced at the name and address as she took the letter. "Of course."

A moment later, she and Matilda crossed the clearing and ducked through the opening in the trees.

He turned to study the clearing. The stack of wood he'd split earlier would provide for the rest of the day. Until they got more tools, there was little he could do to repair the cabin.

Inside, Sofi had left the main room tidy, even propping her thick sketchpad on the fireplace mantel. He thumbed through pages of concise architectural sketches of bridges. Below every drawing she'd listed the structure and location—Eads Bridge, connecting Illinois and St. Louis. Brooklyn Bridge. A long wooden bridge built in the seventeenth century that crossed the Rhine. He stopped flipping pages when he came to a series of detailed drawings with highly developed mathematics. Equations working out the tension of eyebeams, floor beams, the ribcage of a bridge, its cords. These were no sketches, but fully fledged blueprints.

Trina came to stand beside him like a shadow. This was no good, and he returned the sketchpad to the mantel. He wanted a glimpse of the girl he'd seen yesterday. "Come now, Trina, let's get some sun on our faces."

Her mouth hardened.

He didn't give her the chance to argue, and, thank goodness, she didn't revolt as he led her outside to sit on the stoop. Nothing changed in her expression for a long while, still a pale reflection of a sixteen-year-old girl. He understood, though. It hurt too much to remember. Sure, he knew too well how that felt. But as a half hour passed, he sensed she'd reached a point of peacefulness. "Trina, my name is Doctor Neil..." He wished he could give her his real surname. "I want to help you feel well again."

She jerked her head up to look over the clearing.

He took her wrist between his fingers and thumb.

Her pulse beat as though she were running. She swallowed convulsively though she didn't appear to be in any physical pain.

He rubbed a hand along his chin. "Trina, it's proper to feel sadness like you're feeling. But you will get better when you can tell someone what frightens you. You can tell me, if you like."

Her cascading hair obscured her expression until a blue jay cawed and she jumped.

"'Tis only a bird. Your sister and Matilda are only down the hill. You're safe here."

Her eyes took on that haunted look. "My father isn't safe."

Whatever he'd expected her to say, it wasn't this, but her wide blue gaze, so much like her sister's, flew to his.

"Tell me about your father, Trina."

"He's buried at the bottom of the strait. I should..." Her gaze followed an eagle circling over the valley.

Just as he'd sensed that door opening to her, he felt it close.

During his studies, he'd barely touched on psychiatry, concentrating on preparing for general practice. He'd read some of Sigmund Freud's work, the latest papers by Carl Jung, but he knew so little of modern-day treatments for this type of illness. The asylums he'd visited convinced him there must be a better way. Maybe there was wisdom to getting a person to talk their way to emotional wellness. He walked a few feet from Trina, his hands in his pockets.

Clouds scudded past. The pounding of rivets at the construction site reverberated over the ranges. Odin, who slept in a patch of sun, sat up, his ears alert. With her interest captured by the eagle, Trina noticed nothing.

But someone was close by.

Neil couldn't see past the first line of trees. At the edge of the clearing, evergreen branches parted, and a man stepped through.

A tall man, big around the chest and shoulders, walked up the incline to the cabin.

Odin jumped to his feet, but the dog didn't growl.

Neil's muscles tensed as the intruder approached. In order to get the man to leave, he'd have to bluff it out.

~*~

Fog rolled in and smothered Seattle. Horns moaned out on Puget Sound. It was midmorning, yet dark enough to feel like twilight.

Roselle Andersson stood at the door to the parlor where her husband's partner waited. Her thoughts swirled like the dense mist outside, but for the sake of her daughters, she must think clearly.

At the mantel Charles picked up one of Fred's antique pipes, studying the intricate carvings of the bowl. Such fanciful and expensive things that in her opinion only collected dust. Though she loved Freddie with all her heart, she never understood his desire for such items—Chinese porcelain, Japanese paintings, lead crystal from who knew where.

When Charles saw her, he set the pipe back on the mantel and rushed toward her, his hands reaching for hers. "Rosie."

She pulled her hand away. She had never invited him to use Freddie's pet name for her. He must have read the reproach in her face because his cheeks and ears turned red as tomatoes. "You always did admire Fred's scrimshaw collection, Charles."

Charles led her to the settee. "Everything Fred owned was of the highest quality. Like this house. Like you." He gave her a wan smile. "I didn't grow up like you and Fred. My mother and I had not even a slice of bacon from week to week, though we managed somehow."

"What makes you think I know nothing of working hard for plain food?" she snapped, glancing at the richness of carpets, paintings, chandeliers, fripperies that had made up her home for years. "As the child of poor Swedish immigrants, I grew up on the old saying, 'Manure and diligence make the farmer rich.' Freddie's father made money from his timber business, but I came to our marriage with nothing but love."

The look Charles sent her almost made her laugh. He acted as if she had uttered a vulgar oath.

"I have never heard you speak in such a fashion, Roselle."

"You mean like a farmer's daughter, *jah*?" There was another word Freddie had not wanted her to use. It clearly offended Charles too. Always say *yes* instead of *jah*. Always say *Mrs. Jones* instead of *Fru Jones*. These men, when they made money, put on such airs. She had known Charles for more than twenty years as Freddie's partner, and it was as though he had never once seen the real Roselle, the girl she used to be.

In the darkened room, flames from the fireplace threw shadows on the walls. This was not the sun-filled valley she had grown up in. This was mist-drenched Seattle. This graceful mansion echoed with emptiness now, her longing for Freddie, her fear for her daughters.

Charles turned on a lamp.

Light burst from crystal droplets, and blinding beams shot pain through her head. She raised her hand to shade her eyes, her puny spurt of strength melting like butter on a hot griddle. She needed his help to find her girls. "I don't understand what's happened, Charles. Sofi has always been sensible. Why has she done this?"

"She's just a girl, Roselle."

"Sofi is no girl. But though she is a woman, she is still my child." Her chastening of Charles turned to tears. She gripped her handkerchief, angry at herself for crying again. "I should have listened to Sofi. Should have taken them to Chicago. To my aunt. Better still, the valley. Trina needs me. Not a hospital."

"I'm dreadfully worried about them too, but don't be too hard on Sofi. It's been my experience that despair can drive people to do the unthinkable."

She wiped at her face with the handkerchief, but it did no good. Tears flowed. "The unthinkable? Yes, that must be it. Sofi would never have done anything like this...unless she felt her loved ones were in danger. It was me who did this by signing that admission slip for Trina."

He put his arm around her and patted her

shoulder. "I've hired investigators. We're not sure yet if they've gone to Portland by train or taken a ship to San Francisco. I've put notices in all the papers. I'll get them back for you. Now, with Fred gone, all I want to do is what's best for you and his daughters."

She shrank away from his hand on her shoulder, holding back a fresh sob.

"Roselle, dearest, you mustn't let yourself become ill with this weeping. Where is your medicine?"

She shook her head. The movement brought a wave of dizziness. "Sofi said I shouldn't take it. She said it's best to face my grief. Not sleep it away."

"Of course, very sensible. But you're fragile. You've lost your husband, now your daughters, and Dr. Atwood knows far better than Sofi. Tell me where you keep your laudanum, Rosie."

"I don't like how it makes me feel." Traitorous tears filled her eyes.

Sofi would never have taken herself and Trina away if Freddie had been here.

Charles clucked his tongue. "This distress is most unhealthy. Where is your medicine, Roselle?"

She waved to the desk by the window. Perhaps it would be best to take the tincture.

He brought the amber glass bottle to her.

After adding the drops to a glass of water, he supported her as she sipped, as if she were an invalid. Yet she sighed as soon as the bitter taste hit her tongue. As much as she hated the dullness of mind the laudanum brought, it also brought a strange salve.

"That's good, Rosie dearest, drink it all."

She sank against the settee cushions. Yes, it was best this way. A few drops of the laudanum. Charles had begun the search for the girls. Soon they would be home. And now...in only a little while. Only a little while. The dreams would take her...

A foghorn blew out on the water.

It took a long time to realize Charles still held her hand. He should not be doing that. Her mind reeled.

"I'm going to take care of you, Rosie."

It must be a dream. A gray dream set against the felt of her eyelids. She felt Fred's cool lips—it had to be Freddie's lips—against her burning forehead. "I'll take care of you, Rosie."

7

No hesitation slowed the intruder as he strode up to the cabin.

Neil returned the man's steady gaze and waited. To have their small party discovered so soon riled him. Still, if he could bluff out the man's inquiries and send him on his way, all might not be lost.

The stranger stopped three feet from the cabin and held out a hand for the dog to sniff. "Whoa, boy."

The dog didn't growl, nor did he move from his protective guard of Trina.

The man appeared to be in his late forties, early fifties. Of Nordic descent, Neil guessed. He wore dungarees and a plaid shirt. Sunlight glinted off blond hair sprinkled with gray at his temples. He stopped short when he saw Sofi's sister sitting on the stoop. "Trina girl, is that you?" The man frowned when she didn't answer at first.

She almost smiled, though. "Hello, Uncle Henric."

The back of Neil's neck prickled. So the man was a relative.

"What are you doing here, sweetheart?"

The question brought a wrinkle to her brow, and weary of her little amount of speech, she drifted inside the cabin.

The man's eyes, blue ice drifts under blond brows, narrowed on Neil. "Where's the rest of the family?"

Neil's stomach formed a knot. This *uncle* was a good four inches taller than Neil. Still, Trina accepted him. The dog flopped at the man's feet, his tail thumping.

The man looked through the window, saw the results of Sofi's domesticity, and glared at Neil. "Why's Trina alone with you in this shell of a cabin?" His question was more of a growl.

Neil returned his glare.

The chinking sound of a horse's bridle broke over the clearing, followed by the clip-clop of hooves.

"Uncle Henric," Sofi shouted from a large wagon pulled by two Clydesdales as it emerged from the trees.

Matilda sat in the back, and an Asian man drove the wagon up to the clearing.

At the welcome in Sofi's voice for their intruder, tension eased from Neil's neck and shoulders. With a name like Henric, the big man had to be of Scandinavian descent, but only a hint of Swedish flavored his speech, as it did in Sofi's. First generation in the U.S.? Second?

The deep crevices between Henric's brows eased too. His ice-blue eyes warmed at Sofi.

She slipped down from the wagon and embraced Henric. "I'm so glad to see you, but I know that look in your eye." She sent a twitch of a smile to Neil. "No need to beat him senseless, Uncle Henric. At least not yet."

Matilda dropped down from the wagon and ran inside the cabin to Trina.

Neil extended his hand. "Neil...Macpherson," he said, inwardly cursing himself for stuttering over the false surname.

"Henric Petersson," came the gruff response as they shook hands.

Sofi drew the Asian man to her side. "This is Kiosho, my grandfather's dearest friend." Neil reached for Kiosho's hand and concealed his surprise at the man's grip. This Japanese gent had to be in his eighties. Slight in his dungarees and collarless flannel shirt, his hand held great vigor, so too did the strong planes of his face under a fringe of gray hair. His steady brown eyes studied Neil.

Sofi shooed them all inside the cabin.

Henric turned to her. "Kiosho would look after you better than this, or you need to come out to my place. This old cabin's not fit for a grizzly, never mind Fred's daughters. And where's Rosie?"

Matilda set Trina in the rocking chair, where Trina sent a trace of a smile to Kiosho. A moment later, her face pinched as if she were trying to place him.

The elderly man hunched down, took her hand, and murmured, "Granddaughter, you are like your mama, sheltered too long, and are now a feeble tree."

Sofi opened her rucksack on the table. With a raised eyebrow at Neil, she placed a box of black tea leaves close to the stove. A smile played around her lips. "I left your letter at the homestead for Kiosho to mail."

Neil smiled his thanks in spite of this unexpected mob in the small cabin, when he thought they were to be living in seclusion for a few weeks. Their presence overwhelmed him.

Yet Sofi had the look of one settled into her family. A strange mixture of family, but family nonetheless.

The big Scandinavian sat at the table. "Last time Kiosho and I saw you, Sofi, was at your father's memorial service." He cast a look Trina's way and lowered his voice. "What's going on, Sofi? I didn't see

Trina at all that day. That officious partner of your father's told us she was ill." He sputtered and turned red. "Nor did I get within five feet of your mother."

At the stove, Sofi poured coffee for Henric. "I've a lot to explain. Mama's...as well as can be expected."

Neil understood the plea in her tone. Whatever was going on with her mother embarrassed her, and she wanted to be alone with Henric and Kiosho to discuss it. He picked up the axe and left the cabin. With such stalwart advocates as these two men seemed to be, he should be able to leave Sofi and Trina with good conscience, catch a ship to San Francisco or Anchorage. That knowledge should have given him a sense of release, but it didn't.

A fallen log lay in the thicket. He could use it for firewood, maybe use parts of it to fix the roof. But what did he know of repairing log cabins? He was a doctor, for pity's sake.

The tail end of Henric's conversation filtered through the open window. "Are you telling me you don't know anything about this man? What's happened to that sharp mind of yours, Sofi? If you won't find out who he is, then I, sure as shootin', will."

Neil froze. He'd been so consumed thinking about Sofi, he'd forgotten his own predicament. He took a step in the direction of the thicket, but that was foolish. These two men had no way of knowing what he was running from in Ireland, or who he was. He waited as the big Scandinavian's boots thumped across the cabin's stoop.

Sofi followed and looked across the clearing to Neil. "Uncle Henric. I trust him."

Neil's gaze flew to hers. That she trusted him sent a ripple of light through him. For the first time in three months, someone trusted him.

Despite Sofi's faith in him, Henric's mouth remained clamped.

Neil tried to weigh what was going on behind the Swede's heavily lowered brows. That faulty pump inside him began to sluice guilt through his veins. He didn't deserve Sofi's good faith. Somehow Henric knew that.

Henric lifted Sofi's chin with his large hand. "Come out to my place. We'll bring Kiosho too. The Lord knows my place is empty enough without Margie. And you two girls are the children she and I never had."

"Uncle Henric, we love you too." She shook her head. "But your sawmill has people coming and going. This here is an isolated spot on my grandfather's property. Besides, I don't want to ask you to go against Mama's decision about Trina. It's bad enough that I had to."

"To keep a secret like this from Rosie galls me to no end." New energy infused Henric's tone. "What do you say I go to Seattle and bring her here? This is where she belongs. Why, she used to be the light in this valley...the way she used to sing in church..."

Neil held himself back from speaking, but he needn't have feared.

Sofi reached for Henric's arm. "Mama isn't herself these days. I believe with all my heart that she's best left to grieve in peace for Papa, and give me a chance to help Trina." She glanced over at Neil. "There's one more thing. We left Charles in Seattle, but he'll be checking in with the chief engineer at the bridge site now and then. He could show up in town any day, but he has no idea the cabin exists."

"Charles is the reason for all this secrecy. I should have known." Henric's voice took on that growl again.

"He's the one who talked Mama into signing the papers for Trina to be placed in the sanatorium."

Henric's chin went tight. "Never did like that man. But, Sofi, are you sure a hospital and doctors aren't the best thing for Trina?"

Neil stepped forward. "Trina will receive the appropriate care here, from Sofi and Matilda."

Henric sent him a dismissive glance. "But hospitals have medicines. Treatments."

"What kind of treatments?" Neil thrust up a hand and let it drop. "Lock her in a padded cell? Hot and cold baths to shock her out of her fugue-like state? They're developing more compassionate ways of dealing with trauma and melancholy. They're not prescribing opiates like laudanum as much as they used to, but it's anyone's guess how Trina would fare in a sanatorium."

"Is laudanum dangerous?" Sofi asked.

Like so many patients and family members he'd seen in his practice, Sofi's gaze reached out to him for assurance, a remedy for her loved one.

His desire to heal warred against self-preservation. He'd already let out far more medical knowledge than he'd planned. But even if they realized he was a doctor, the people in these mountains would never associate him with Dr. Neil Galloway that Scotland Yard was looking for. The words were out of his mouth before he could stop them. "People can become dependent on opium tincture."

Henric slanted him a look laden with questions.

Sofi rushed to the big Scandinavian. "That settles it. With Mama the way she is, I can't take any chances for Trina's sake."

A moment later, Henric lifted his gaze to the treetops. "Your father was like a brother to me. And he always said you were the smartest in the bunch, Sofi." When he looked back down at her, the lines between his brows eased. "I'll keep your secret, for now. Mostly because I don't like that Charles. He was always pushing Fred to expand the business in ways Fred had no interest in." Henric looked past her when Trina came out of the cabin, escorted by Kiosho and Matilda. Stillness settled over the big man, and he harrumphed. Pulling at his ear, he turned to take in the cabin and clearing. "I guess it could work, Sofi. The trees make a thick blind. As for your smoke, well, it could very well be me or Kiosho burning bush. All right, you win. This evening when it's dark, I'll start hauling up supplies to make the place weatherproof. Cut some cedar shakes to fix that roof. Try to make life a little easier for you."

Neil watched the soft smiles travel between Sofi and Henric.

"And, Sofi girl," the big man added, "you think it an adventure to live the frontier life like your grandparents did, but without help from me and Kiosho, you'd find it mighty hard. Still though, if anyone can make it work, it's you."

Sofi smiled at him, and then went to her sister on the porch.

Henric used the opportunity to step closer to Neil. He narrowed his eyes and spoke under his breath. "That girl may vouch for you, but it's not right just you and these three women up here alone. We're both men. So I don't need to spell it out."

Neil pulled himself to his full height. "You have my word as a gentleman."

"That may be, but know this. Matilda will keep an eagle eye on you from here. Kiosho's just down the hill. And you'll never know when I'll show up. So, you make the smallest indiscretion toward those girls, and I'll tear the skin off you."

8

With the tail end of her apron, Sofi dabbed a few beads of sweat from her brow. July had turned the valley into a blazing kiln.

This afternoon Matilda and Trina were taking a walk to cool off in the forest.

Henric left Neil around the side of the cabin to finish chinking between the steeple-notched logs and joined her in the shade of a cedar. She handed him a cup of water. Being with her father's oldest friend kept up the illusion that Papa was only away on business. That any day he'd motor up in a limousine with Mama beside him. Better that way. She had no time to indulge her grief. Trina needed her too much.

Henric tossed back the water. "That Neil's a hardworking man."

Neil was planing a log in the middle of the clearing. These past few weeks as they'd playacted at living the frontier life, he'd become bronzed. His face...his hands. His arms...as they smoothed out that log...were slick with sweat. Heat rushed up her face. Shame on her for looking at a man in that way, admiring. With an impatient hand, she shoved her hair off her shoulder. He could use a drink of water. She started to rise.

But Neil was already leaning his head under the pump. Water gushed from it, slaking his thirst and soaking his shirt. He returned to the sawhorse without a glance in her direction.

Henric's voice yanked her back to her surroundings. "Trina say anything yet about what happened the night her papa died?"

Sofi shook her head, her gaze tracking to the bridge to stop thinking about what Trina must have experienced that night.

Tree crickets increased their chirping with the searing heat.

For the crews working on the bridge, it had to be dreadfully hot, standing in the open sun on those slender riveting platforms, metal reflecting the blinding rays. Her gaze strayed from the crew, to the bridge's abutments, and below to the foreman's shack.

Even from this distance, she could make out the dark green Cadillac belonging to Charles. Each day, through Henric's field glasses she watched for Charles's car to pass the crossroads into town. Each week, he would stay a few days at the company Pullman car on the new railway branch. After a few days inspecting the bridge, he'd return to Seattle. The first time she'd seen his car, her heart nearly failed. But as each day, then each week passed, that fear dwindled.

"Do you know how the bridge is progressing?" She hadn't meant to verbalize her thoughts, but now they were out in the open, she wanted answers. "I see they've finished a few sections. I can't help but wonder why they're going at it so fast."

Henric's mouth puckered as if he'd tasted something sour. "That's Wetzle Steel for you, always wanting to get on to the next contract. I'm of the opinion that Wetzle's inclination to hurry things caused our accident last year when the foundations were laid. He didn't take enough time to clear the area before blasting."

Sofi didn't bother to cover up her wince, though it had been over a year since the fatality. Deaths occurred during constructions—*but please, Lord, no more deaths on this bridge. Not this bridge.* "It was Johanson who died," she murmured. "How's his wife?"

Henric took a moment to answer. "Grief doesn't go away overnight. Mrs. Johanson knows that. Nor was it easy for me when my Margie died. We can heal if we let God lead us through the pain, though." He touched her hand. "Sofi, there's a difference between being strong in the Lord and ignoring the suffering He allows in our lives."

"Not now, Uncle Henric," she croaked. "I can't crumble until Trina is well."

"All right, Sofi." He rose to his feet. "Time I got back to the sawmill anyway. I've given Neil as many lessons on frontier cabin repair as I can."

They strolled to the porch railing where he'd tied up his mare.

Sofi ran her hand down the mare's shoulder. "As soon as Trina shows signs of improvement, I'll drop by the Johanson home. In the meantime, will you find out for me if there's anything I can do for the widow?"

He nodded as he swung up into the saddle and then rode through the drape of trees.

If only she weren't hiding up here. She'd go down to the site and insist that the chief engineer do things the way her father always insisted on. But as usual, there was nothing she could do when it came to Papa's business. He'd left that in Charles's hands. And she had Trina to take care of. She'd left a pan of dirty dishwater on the table. She needed to throw it on the garden she'd been coaxing to life.

On her way to the garden, she pinned up a strand of hair. It was always tumbling down, and water from the basin slopped the front of her dress. She didn't look the Seattle socialite these days. She'd slipped into the role her grandmother filled fifty-odd years ago, and that brought a spring to her step.

Neil put the tools away and was raking the yard of wood shavings when Trina and Matilda came through the trees. Trina carried an armful of wildflowers. They must have been out by the narrow bluff on the other side of the forest, Sofi's favorite place, that afforded the best view of the bridge.

Matilda went inside the cabin to start supper, leaving Trina to sit on the stoop with Neil.

Sofi couldn't make out what they said, but her sister wore such a placid expression answering his gently put questions that Sofi didn't want to break the spell. She hurried around the side of the cabin to empty the dishwater on the rampant, growing beans. Letting Neil stay had been a good plan. These past few weeks, he'd soothed Trina's terrors away. So why did the sight of him smiling down at Trina fill her with this emptiness?

Was it because she was letting her concern for Trina take over her life? The sensible, the urgent, the necessary, must be done. True. But before Papa died, she'd wanted to do more with her life. Wanted to be like Trina and plunge forward to pursue her heart's aspirations.

Taking her time, Sofi returned to the front of the cabin.

Trina had gone inside.

Matilda was talking to her while she peeled potatoes.

Neil cupped his hands under the outside pump and scrubbed his face, his hair dangling in his eyes. He wore the new dungarees Henric had given him. Unable to get to town to a proper barber, his hair gleamed like a raven's wing down the back of his neck. With one last slosh of water, he raked the dark strands off his face, and his widow's peak stood out like an arrow against his forehead.

She hurried along the porch and inside the cabin before he noticed her. Once inside, she smoothed down her wet shirtwaist and put damp hands up to cool her flaming face. With all she had on her mind, she didn't need wayward thoughts about a man to pull on her already-strained nerves. That was like setting light to an already-short fuse.

~*~

Firelight flickered against the log walls.

Sofi shifted her position so that light from the oil lamp fell on her sketch of the lower ribs of a bridge. She tried to concentrate on the algorithm, but her thoughts were too scattered.

At the table, Neil pieced together the broken tea set. With a smooth stick, he applied the glue, tied the shards together with twine, and got up to set the mended pieces on top of the mantel, only a foot away.

When their eyes met, a frisson of electricity shot through her.

His gaze fell, and he returned to the table and tapped the lid on the tin of glue he'd been using.

Light flashed at the window. A thunderstorm? Oh, please, no.

Mattie sat by the fire, mending a tear in one of

Trina's dresses.

Sofi couldn't bear a repeat of that last stormy night in Seattle.

Trina sat in the rocking chair, staring into the fireplace, her eyelids drooping.

Sofi set her sketchpad on the mantel beside the repaired tea set. A storm coming would explain why she felt so keyed up. Her restlessness had nothing to do with the way Neil looked at her. She cupped her sister's shoulder. "Come, *älskling*, you look ready for bed."

Trina shrugged off Sofi's hand. She seemed to be in one of her between times, part of her here in the present, part somewhere else.

Matilda picked up her sewing and, with Trina, climbed to the loft.

At the base of the ladder, Sofi waited with her hand on a rung.

Neil sat in a chair by the fire and cracked open one of the books Henric had loaned him, Dostoevsky's *Crime and Punishment*. Odin stretched out on the floor beside him, and the image of Neil by the pump this afternoon came over her. The way that dark hair fell into his eyes as he washed. His strong, tanned throat moving as he slaked his thirst. Her face scorched. The sight of him made her insides shimmy like light on a rippling pond.

He looked up. "Do you mind if I read a while longer?"

He couldn't see her flush in the dim room. "Read as long as you like." She climbed the ladder, forcing the image of him from her mind.

A rumble echoed far away, but there no answering flash of lightning.

Downstairs, Neil dragged a chair closer to the fire.

Trina coiled on her side beneath the blankets. Matilda slept close to the slanting roof. They'd gotten used to going to bed early and rising before dawn.

Sofi undressed, pulled her nainsook nightgown over her head, and lowered the wick of the oil lamp so only a tiny flame wavered. She lay down and rested her hand on Trina's slender hip to let her know she wasn't alone. The day's weariness crept up, and pictures of the bridge passed behind her closed eyelids. Only the rising wind disturbed the darkness, but the remembered sound of rivets being hammered into steel trusses resonated in her ears and strangely lulled her. Sleep wasn't far off. And there was Neil reading downstairs...

A high-pitched wail woke her.

Thunder crashed.

Trina!

Sofi bolted upright, her heart lodged in her throat.

Matilda scrambled from her side of the loft.

Trina screamed, flailing her arms.

Lightning split the sky outside and cast the loft in brilliant pink that faded to a green glow. It wasn't lightning. Fireworks. The Fourth of July. Somehow the lamp had blown out. In the town below, a scattering of explosions cracked the night air, scattering Sofi's pulse as they did.

Her sister screamed again and again, far worse than her normal terrors that consisted of whimpers and staring wide-eyed into the dark.

With trembling fingers, Sofi fumbled in the dark to find the oil lamp.

A burst of blue and green flashed.

Trina screeched.

Sofi couldn't find the matches to light the lamp. "Dear Lord in heaven, where are the matches?"

Matilda pulled the flailing Trina into her arms.

The thunder of fireworks almost covered the sound of Neil racing up the ladder. He flew to Trina's side and took her from Matilda, throwing a box of matches to Sofi.

She lit the lamp and turned the wick high.

Matilda tried to take Trina from Neil, but Trina clung to him.

"Come, wee girl," he said in a lilting brogue. "Don't be afraid. Cry it out on my shoulder." In a whisper over Trina's head, he spoke to Matilda. "Get her a drink of water, if you please."

Sofi stroked Trina's back, feeling as if each of Trina's shrieks emanated from inside herself.

Her little sister cried inconsolably, until another explosion clapped and yellow starbursts flecked the sky. She thrashed and kicked.

Neil kept his arms around her, taking the brunt of Trina's driving fists and feet.

Trina cried, "Papa!" and flung away from Neil to the opening in the loft floor and peered into the darkness below. "Papa!"

Neil grabbed hold of Trina as she tried to lunge downward.

She brandished her arms into the dark, empty space as if reaching for something or someone.

He took Trina's hands, forcing her to look at him. "What is it, Trina?"

"I've lost him. I should never have..."

With each blast from the fireworks in town, Trina screeched and looked up as if she saw beyond the eaves of rough-hewn cedar. Between screams, she cried, until at last, the festivities ended.

Trina slumped in Neil's arms, heaving gasps. A moment later, she took a few sips of water from Matilda and closed her eyes with a whimper.

Neil laid Trina down on her pillow. "You're all right now, wee girl." He took Trina's wrist, counted her pulse, smoothed the damp hair from her brow.

Trina's nightgown clung to her with sweat.

Matilda pulled a dry gown from the trunk.

"Let her be, Mattie," Sofi whispered.

Matilda sniffed back tears and tucked the blanket around Trina. "She's quiet now, poor thing."

Sofi sank to her knees and gradually became aware that she trembled. Her teeth chattered.

With such a reaction to simple fireworks, what had her sister lived through that night? Images of Trina floating on a tiny lifebuoy on a raging, open sea with lightning flashing around her jabbed at Sofi's imagination. The memory of the telephone ringing in the house the next day to tell her and Mama the awful news jangled in her ears.

A rasping sound of someone struggling for breath blocked out the memory. All she could hear was her own pulse thumping in her temples. Feel the vise in her chest. Cutting off her breath.

"Sofi?" Neil took her by the shoulders. "Breathe, Sofi. Slowly. Breathe."

Through a haze, Sofi recognized it was she making that rasping noise. She wasn't at home in the foyer with the telephone receiver in her hand, listening to Mama screaming. She was in the cabin in the valley.

Neil lifted her chin. "Take a breath. In through your nose, out through your lips. Nice and slow."

She did as he said. Her heart beat double-time. She

glanced down. Trina was safe and sound in the makeshift bed not two feet from her. Sofi's breathing began to slow.

"Matilda, stay with Trina." Neil stroked Sofi's hands and smiled with each successful breath she took. "A hot drink will help."

Matilda looked over the sleeping form of Trina to Neil. "I'll take care of this lamb, if you'll take care of the other."

Neil helped Sofi down the ladder and set her in the rocking chair.

Odin ambled to her side and whimpered until her hand fell to play with his ears.

The night wasn't cold, but Neil retrieved her coat from a peg by the door and directed her arms into the sleeves. His hands lingered on her shoulders. She wanted his hands to stay there, warm and strong. His hands, his voice, helped her breathe. Blotted out the loneliness, the grief.

He left her to throw kindling into the stove. The wood started to burn, and the metallic sound of the kettle meeting cast iron made her heartbeats settle. Sparks flew as he threw a log on the fire. He knelt in front of her, and her breath had become normal.

"Won't be long," he said, "and you'll take the Irish answer to all that ails you, a good strong cup of tea, strong enough to walk on, with plenty of sugar. None of your black Swedish coffee that would make your hair curl."

She managed a wobbly smile.

"That smile tells me there's hope. You're a fighter, Sofi, and that's what you need to be."

"I am a fighter only if need be. Trina's normally the brave one."

"Aye, well, there's more than one type of courage, Miss Sofi Andersson."

"And if...if what you say is true about coffee, then why did it never curl my hair? I've been drinking it since I was a child."

His smile started in his eyes and travelled by slow degrees to his mouth. "Well, curly hair is fine for some." His expression grew serious. "However, if someone were to ask my opinion, I'd say that straight, blonde hair hanging down a girl's back...like corn silk—well, there's nothing more lovely."

Heat invaded her, gradual and slow.

Neil touched her forehead with the back of his hand. "You suffered delayed shock along with Trina tonight." His fingertips pressed the inside of her wrist.

Her heart rate sped up.

His eyes met hers and widened, at the possible knowledge that it was his touch that quickened her pulse. Laying her hand on her lap, he hurried away to check the stove. Seconds later, he grumbled, "The wood's gone out. Sure, I left the matches upstairs when I took them up to you. I'll be back."

The firelight pulled her into a place of no thought. Later—she hardly knew how long—Neil pressed a cup of hot tea with milk and sugar into her hands.

He set a chair beside hers and sipped from his own cup.

"How did you know to bring the matches upstairs earlier?" She needed to talk of something mundane.

"You prayed aloud. Obviously, you wanted God to bring the matches, but I was closer. I didn't think He'd mind."

A giggle escaped her and she touched her head, feeling dizzy.

He looked down at his clasped hands. "Sofi, your sister has buried her feelings deep. I don't know if I can help."

Her eyes brimmed, but she willed the tears back. "She is not going to that sanatorium. Please, Neil, don't give up. The Lord will answer my prayers."

"You sound like my father." His smile softened the skepticism on his face. "I've seen people get better on the sheer strength of belief. Was it God who made them better, or something inside their psyche that healed their body? A lot of good my da's faith did him. As for me, if there's a logical solution to a problem, I'll find it." His voice trailed away.

She smoothed her hand over her knees covered by the canvas coat. "I believe in the common sense God gave us. He expects us to work hard. Do our duty. But I've learned that the real work of life is accomplished through prayer."

"I trust in science, but who am I to tell you not to pray? Believe in God if it gives you peace."

The Lord used to bring her peace, but since Papa died, she'd only been able to pray for Mama and Trina, not for herself. She got up to stand by the fire, clenching her fists to hold back the sorrow.

"Tell me more about Trina, about your childhood." Neil stood beside her, his voice matter-of-fact.

She grabbed hold of the change in their conversation, anything to stop from entering the valley of grief. The warmth of the fire, the clean, soapy scent of Neil gave her strength. "Whatever Trina wanted, she went for it. She swam the farthest, climbed the highest trees. A fearless risk-taker. And she likes—liked—drawing. When she was six, Papa built a dinghy for her. Her first of several crafts. I remember the day we all had to stand at the water's edge and christen her racing yacht, *Cecelia,* with a bottle of sarsaparilla."

"*Cecelia.*" His chuckle reverberated from deep within him.

She echoed his chuckle. "For several years Trina's entered the annual yacht club junior race, *and* won each year. Papa urged her on. Before...before he died, I'd have said there was no one more daring than my little sister."

He looked into the darkened corner as if it held the answers. "All the same, your sister was helpless out on the open water, unable to escape her dilemma. It's as though that powerful force of wanting to escape or do something to help your father got trapped in her nervous system. She has no way to release it, so she shuts the door to her mind."

"Will she ever open it again?"

He wrapped an arm around her shoulders. "From my observation, females tend to worry more internally over their fears. Not like men who battle against their trauma with exploits. Not always the right kind of exploits, mind you. Men try to force things. Make things right." His brows pulled together. "Seek revenge."

A log fell, sending up an array of sparks. A wave of dizziness, perhaps, made her lean closer to him. He settled her cheek against his solid shoulder. She took in one long draught of air while he stared into the fire. His chin rested close to her ear, his mouth brushed against her hair.

At the same moment, they became aware of their closeness.

She pushed away slowly.

Christine Lindsay

Neil unwound his arm from around her and bent to stir the embers in the fireplace. "I think you're feeling better, Sofi. It's time you went up to the loft."

At the bottom of the ladder, she stopped, trembling again. "You admit you trust in science. Why is it I know you're a healer without you telling me plainly that you are? Who are you really, Neil?"

He had no answer.

She climbed the ladder. Still trembling, she huddled under the quilt next to Trina. Tonight she had felt such closeness to him—and he most likely had a girl at home in Ireland, probably that girl, Alison, he'd written to. She remembered his precise script on that envelope he'd wanted mailed. She must watch that this closeness between her and Neil went no further.

9

Silver hooks screeched along the curtain rod as Frida wrenched open the drapes to the sun glittering on Puget Sound.

Roselle shielded her eyes from the sunlight. "It is too early."

"It is three o'clock, madam."

"Three?" Roselle raised herself up. "How could you let me sleep so long? This is shameful." She swung out of bed, but when she sat up, she swayed and clutched at Frida for support.

"I could not wake you, madam. I telephoned the doctor, but he said it is good your medicine makes you sleep."

Roselle put a hand to her brow. This was no good. What would Sofi think of her mama dragging from bed in the middle of the afternoon? "Frida, bring me strong coffee." She held her stomach as her insides listed. "Run me a bath too please, Frida."

Roselle saw herself in the gilded mirrors and pulled away. Perhaps it was best Sofi was not here. How could she help her daughters looking this way? Freddie's face flashed into her mind. The way he smiled before he and Trina had left to go sailing that day. Freddie too would not want her to wallow in grief, but be the lady he insisted she be.

In the marble bathroom, Roselle removed her robe and stepped into the hot, scented bath. She clicked her tongue in disgust—the middle of the afternoon. As a girl, she got up at four in the morning to help her papa milk the cows. There were times she wished she could spend her summers running through cornfields, walking barefoot in raspberry rows, feeling soil between her toes.

But Fred had not wanted this for her. He had come a long way from the only son of a timber baron. As his wife, she must be a fine lady of society.

She sank lower into the bubbles. And fine ladies of society took laudanum for their nerves. *Isn't that right, Freddie? Oh, Freddie, isn't that right?* And if it was, why did she feel so ashamed?

~*~

After Frida's ministrations Roselle swallowed a few bites of Inga's freshly baked *äppelkaka*. They insisted she eat more, but she sent them to the kitchen so they would not see her cling to the banister and inch her way down the staircase to the parlor.

She sat on the settee and laid a heavy wrist over her eyes. Her head felt like a fifty-pound weight. Her eyes stung. The laudanum produced fitful sleep, strange dreams, but she needed it more and more to get through the nights.

Inga found her a while later and brought her coffee and spritz cookies.

After Inga left, Roselle sipped the coffee but pushed the cookies aside. All the while, the amber bottle in the desk sent out a beacon to her brain, like the lamp of a lighthouse, whirling, whirling. Only the laudanum gave her rest. Her fingers itched to open the desk drawer.

The front bell chimed. Frida answered it, her voice

penetrating through to the parlor. A moment later, Frida rapped on the parlor door and swung it wide.

Two men strode in after her.

Frida plumped cushions at her back. "Madam, a policeman from England and a man from Pinkerton's Detective Agency."

Roselle, dazed, struggled to sit up, shaking. Had they found Fred's body? Were they bringing him home at last?

The taller of the two—a blond man—stayed in the shadows, holding a black Stetson.

The other man pulled his chair close to her, his brown bowler hat on his knee. "Mrs. Andersson," he began in a crisp English accent. "I am Inspector Webley of Scotland Yard. This is Joel Harrison of Pinkerton's. He's assisting me on American soil. I've been following the trail of a man, seen in this area." He laid a photograph on the table before her. "Have you seen this man?"

"I do not understand. Are you the detectives Charles hired to look for my daughters?"

The policeman frowned. "Madam, I know nothing of your daughters."

Frida interjected. "Sofi and Trina left home. We have heard nothing of them since the beginning of June. We think they took a steamship to San Francisco...or perhaps the train to Portland."

The inspector's eyes narrowed. "Did your daughter's disappearance occur around the time your *gardener* was here?"

Roselle shrugged her shoulders. "My gardener?"

"Will you look at the picture, Mrs. Andersson. Have you ever seen this man?"

She studied the photograph. A young man. Dark

hair...kind eyes. A dream? Standing in this room...by the fireplace...his hand on her brow.

"You recognize him."

"*Jah*, maybe. No. I do not know this man."

The inspector laid another photograph on the table. "This man?"

Roselle moved the second photograph with one finger. Younger, resembling the other man. A brother? "Who are they?"

"Good-for-nothing troublemakers, but that's the entire Irish race for you." The inspector glared at Frida. "You, have you seen either of these men?"

Frida's voice came out like a squeak. "What has he done?"

He? Roselle arched her neck to look at her maid.

The inspector's eyes pinned Frida. "You have seen this man, haven't you?" He stabbed the first photograph with his finger.

Roselle clutched the inspector's sleeve, her voice hardly able to get the words out. "Why are you asking of this man? Has he abducted my daughters?"

The inspector didn't answer, but Frida did. "No, madam. Remember, Sofi left that note saying she was taking Trina away for a while. There is no need to fear of kidnapping." Frida looked up at Inspector Webley. "Why are you looking for this man?"

The detective from Scotland Yard stuck out his chin. "Interesting that you mention abduction. I wouldn't put anything past these Irish blackguards. I want to question the younger one, Jimmy Galloway. As for the older one, he's under suspicion for brutally murdering a man in Northern Ireland. His name is Neil Galloway. Dr. Neil Galloway."

~*~

Neil scraped cold ash from the stove grate. Through the window, he kept an eye on Sofi outside as she lifted dry clothes from a rope he'd strung between two trees. August sun dazzled white through the sheets. Every once in a while, Sofi would bring a piece of fresh laundry up to her face to breathe in before setting it in the basket. As soon as she entered the cabin, he scraped the ash free with more vigor than necessary.

Trina sat on the stoop, staring off into the forest. The terrors from the Fourth of July's fireworks had not lessened after all these weeks. Shadows still smudged under Trina's eyes, and Sofi's ever-watchful gaze grew less and less hopeful.

For weeks he'd encouraged Trina to talk, but each time, her blue eyes dismissed him with little interest. In other circumstances, he'd think she was looking down her perfect little nose at him. But today that slightly disdainful look gave him hope—hope that maybe Trina, the real firecracker Trina whom Sofi described, was fighting to get out.

Matilda assured Sofi she'd look after Trina, and Sofi slipped out of the cabin.

Odin lifted himself from sleeping under the table and plodded after her.

Neil pulled out his father's watch. Sure enough, in half an hour, the hammers would stop, and the riveting gang would file off the bridge.

Sofi was taking her daily, solitary walk.

He finished the stove in quick time and washed in a hurry under the pump. Late-afternoon sun angled through the tops of firs and cedars. The path, thick with fronds, muffled sound as shade cooled his face and arms, until sunlight burst upon him at the narrow bluff overlooking the river.

With the dog at her side, Sofi leaned a hip against a sun-warmed boulder and looked out at her father's bridge. She appeared relaxed. And why shouldn't she be? Her life was an open book, while his remained nailed shut. He half turned to go back the way he'd come, but stopped as her eyes that mirrored the sky invited him closer. Without speaking, she went back to watching the workmen file off the bridge. Up here, the trees created the perfect blind to hide the two of them.

With one foot planted on the rock face behind him, he leaned back, crossing his arms. "Quite the structure, so it is."

She nodded, her gaze unmoving from the bridge. "When it's finished, it must be strong enough to support its own weight—what's called a dead load—as well as the live load of trains that will pass over it. We get powerful winds racing through these ranges. As the canyons narrow, the airflow funnels and gathers speed, making those winds stronger than a locomotive."

"Takes a great deal of science then, to build a bridge."

She suppressed her laugh, and he found himself saddened that she didn't release it fully. "You're not the only one who enjoys science. My father had me calculate stress computations from the time I was twelve."

"An interesting hobby for a woman." He watched her carefully.

Her expression froze. "As you say...an interesting hobby. For a woman."

"But drawing bridges is more than a hobby to you, isn't it, Sofi? I've seen your sketchbook."

"My father told me that one doesn't build a bridge just so people can cross from one place to another. A bridge conveys some of our deepest human emotions—a step of faith."

He glanced at the last of the riveting gang as they walked along the structure forty feet above the river. "A charming notion for poets and artists, I suppose, but when you come down to it, it's only mortar and steel. Something to convey people in safety."

"Safety should be uppermost, of course." Her voice reached a warmer groove that ignited something within him. Her eyes lit. She was lovely, so she was. Alive, flushed with fervor, her silk hair caught the breeze. "But this particular bridge," she went on, "well, the design of this bridge meant a great deal to my father. And to me. If I'd been a son, he would have had me work with him."

He held back the desire to touch the curve of her cheek. Since leaving Ireland, he knew what it felt like to be barred from the precise labor that made sense of his being. "I don't suppose being the daughter of a wealthy man, you could flaunt convention and take up this career you want."

She looked at him as if he'd suddenly grown a second head. "My father didn't want that for me. But...some women have done things. Built bridges even. Like Emily Roebling when her husband was too unwell to leave his bed. She acted on his behalf as chief engineer. Their Brooklyn Bridge is an example of one of our nation's greatest."

He moved closer. "I've known one or two lady doctors in the hospital I worked in back home." His voice found a deeper level. "Intelligence, when it's marked enough, Sofi, can march outside the boundaries of society."

Her eyes shone with laughter. "Flaunt convention! Step outside the boundaries of society—why, Neil Macpherson, you shock me."

He felt his answering smile. "From up here I don't see much society a'tall."

For a moment, they savored the levity, until that familiar awkwardness wedged between them.

"No," she added. "Not much society up here. But the achievement of goals up here—oh yes—for men and women. The first few years after they arrived from Sweden, my grandfather found work building railroads. My grandmother stayed behind to run their farm. She butchered their meat, repaired the cabin, hunted for food, as well as all the womanly arts of caring for a home."

He couldn't keep the sharpness from his tone. "If you were a poor woman, Sofi, you'd still be doing that, working your fingers to shreds. My parents did. My da did in the shipyard. When a person is concerned over having a few potatoes and a bit of cabbage—if any—to put on the table at night, they don't think of careers and such. They think only of paying work."

She grew quiet. "You're right, of course. I've been indulging myself. I must endeavor to find more womanly avenues for my tal—"

"Sofi, I never suggested you do any such thing!"

A blush stained her neck and cheeks. "That was waspish of me. And not what I really believe. In some cases, God ordains people to go against society. But not all. My father would never have approved. I cannot go against him. I loved him."

"Aye, Sofi, I understand. I loved my father too and would never want him to be ashamed of me now he's gone." And here he was, a fugitive running from the law.

She sent him a sideways grin. "I'm sorry for arguing. Reminds me of how I fought you those days before we left Seattle. In the frame of mind I was then, I'd have punched anyone in the nose who crossed me over Trina."

"And they call us the fighting Irish. Who'd have thought to be scared of the Swedes?"

Her unleashed laughter made it impossible for him to think straight, and he laughed with her for the sheer joy of it.

The hammering on the bridge had long stopped. The bridge was completely empty as the wind whisked their laughter away.

He cleared roughness from his throat. "Speaking of a fighting spirit, there've been other women who threw convention to the wind. You'd not be accepted readily. I'm speaking plainly, Sofi, because I know what bottled-up fervor can do." He yanked a frond off a nearby branch and slapped it against his leg. He'd seen the devastating results of that in Jimmy's life— anguish bottled until it fermented and ruined lives. Ruined his career as a doctor.

"Sometimes I think it would be easier," she said, "if I didn't feel the urge to use these natural abilities—I think God-given abilities—but to do the more expected tasks of a woman in my social position. Strangely, my father considered it more socially acceptable for my sister to enter yacht races than for me to consider a career."

She raised her gaze. "But what about you, Neil?

With all this talk about life's purposes and the toil of one's brow, what are you doing with your life?" The sun nestled between two peaks as she tensed her weight against the sun-warmed granite.

Her natural perfume intoxicated him—not the overpowering colognes of society, but the scent of soap, apples she been paring earlier—stirring the desire to touch her cheek, her hands, her arms. What if he closed the gap between them? How would the softness of her cheek feel against the roughness of his? What would her lips taste like?

His breath quickened.

Sofi's eyes widened.

He couldn't tear his gaze from her softly parting mouth. A muscle tapped at the base of her throat.

Had one of them moved closer?

He pulled in a breath. When a man and a woman cared for each other, they should speak the truth. He wanted to tell her about the thrift clinic he'd partnered in for the poor back home. Tell her of the work he'd done in the hospital. If he shared his pride in those accomplishments, he knew her eyes would shine in understanding.

Aye, right, ye fool. Then tell her you left the clinic and your position in Belfast City Hospital, as well as all your patients, to run to Washington State to be a gardener. How could he possibly tell her about the night that stole his life from him, and all with one slash of a knife? He rubbed the pressure between his brows. "Time we were getting back to the cabin."

"Right. Of course." In a fluster, she smoothed her shirtwaist. Her eyes that moments ago were shining turned a dull slate. She set her profile to him. "Foolish for the two of us to stand here any longer."

~*~

Sofi led the way through the forest. Beneath the canopy of trees, the last vestiges of sunlight couldn't reach them. She picked up speed as it grew darker, not knowing who to hurt for most. Papa, who lay in a watery grave. Mama, who seemed equally lost. Trina, after all this time a helpless ghost or rebuffing those who loved her. And then there was her. Fool. Fool. A fool wanting to be held by a man who shrouded his life.

At the cabin, Matilda stirred a pot of beef tea for Trina.

Sofi began to clear away the supper dishes.

Outside, Neil chopped wood. Good.

He could stay out there the whole night for all she cared. In fact, she should send him packing. He'd stayed too long.

Trina sat in the rocking chair. Her hands gripping the armrest gave the lie to her placid exterior. Energy simmered beneath that false composure.

Sofi steadied herself against the solid table her grandfather had built. This was her duty, taking care of her sister. Neil, and foolish, unreachable dreams designing bridges, mattered not in the least. She knelt beside Trina's chair and held her sister's hand against her cheek. "You're going to be all right, *älskling*. You will be the girl you used to be."

"That girl is gone!" Trina shouted, her eyes dark with intensity. Her face flushed as she shoved Sofi's hand away. "She's gone. Forever. Like Papa. Now leave me alone."

Sofi backed away as if slapped while Trina

returned to her fierce silence.

The coppery glow of twilight followed Neil into the cabin, where he dumped an armload of logs on the hearth. With his hands on his hips, he studied Trina. He took Sofi's sketchbook from the mantel and carefully placed it on Trina's lap along with the box of pencils.

Trina's restless brow smoothed at first and became pensive again. But on her lap, one finger curled and uncurled.

Sofi ignored Neil's attempt to whet Trina's interest. Hadn't she tried all sorts of activities to entice Trina back to life?

With a frown, Trina ran her hand over the book as if it were Braille and she blind. She stuck out her lower lip in that pout Sofi was getting so tired of. "Leave me alone."

"If you can't put it into words," Neil said in his softest voice, "then draw me a picture."

A ripple of confusion crossed Trina's face.

Sofi stomped outside. The spot between the peaks where the sun sank was now a deep mauve. Her chest tightened. Her hands needed something to do to break this endless cycle of hope and disappointment. She wrenched the broom from where it stood and swept the porch with a vengeance, until she came to the end of the pine boards and returned to the doorway. And froze at the soft scratching of a lead pencil on paper.

Inside, Trina bent over the sketchbook and drew with swift, aggressive strokes. Her hand moved in wide sweeps over the page.

Sofi moved as if afraid to wake a sleeping person.

Neil raised his finger to his lips.

From behind the rocking chair, she peered over

Trina's shoulder and clamped her hand to her mouth.

Trina had drawn the *Cecelia*, perhaps in its last moments before it slipped beneath the waves. Using the flat side of her pencil, Trina's hand roughed in the basic lines of keel and ribs, the incisive S-shaped curve to the hull. With bold strokes, she captured the sleek lines of her racing craft. But this view of the *Cecelia* was from its side as it lay on the surface, filling with water.

And in the waves...trying to reach the boat...Papa.

Coldness climbed Sofi's spine. Washington's twilight shut off abruptly. Darkness filled the cabin her grandfather had built. Smooth, pine-scented walls closed in. She couldn't breathe. The room spun.

Matilda reached for her. "Sofi!"

Neil gripped her upper arms.

A lamp was lit. The scent of cedar and pine told Sofi she was here in the valley, but she could feel the strength of the waves her father must have battled. The *Cecelia*'s insidious slide into the depths. The drawing dredged up the grief she'd tried to keep at bay. What Trina must have gone through, watching that? Sofi put her hands up to her ears to smother the sound of Trina's imagined screams.

Oblivious to them, Trina continued to draw. In her sketch, the nightmare remained forever entrenched in time. Yet, though tears wet her cheeks, a peacefulness cloaked Trina.

A peacefulness that floated far from Sofi.

Neil laid a hand on Sofi's shoulder and led her outside.

Her voice broke. "I didn't want to...feel the loss...of Papa. All this time, for Trina's and Mama's sake, I've kept myself..." She stumbled from the porch and ran to the edge of the clearing. Cedar branches lashed at her.

She had to get away. Do something to shut out the pain. An owl screeched. The memory of her mother's crying and Trina's nightly terrors echoed in her ears, while wind hissed in the trees. She ran into the night, down to the stream that bubbled over smooth stones.

Footsteps followed. Out of the darkness, someone caught her and pulled her against a warm, human chest. Neil's arms tightened around her. She laid her head against his shoulder and sobbed, soaking his shirt. The memory of her mother's cries and Trina's screams stopped. Blessed silence strummed. A cooling breeze moved along her bare forearms.

His hand smoothed her hair from her face. "You've bottled this up far too long."

No sound penetrated the night air except their breathing. She felt nothing but his arms around her, his lips at her temple, smelled the heady mixture of his shaving soap, the tang of wood smoke clinging to his clothes.

Consumed by the need to feel life, the steady pulse of a heart to shut out the loss, she pressed her hands against Neil's chest. Lifting her head, she could see nothing in the darkness, but knew where his mouth was. Sensed where his lips were.

His mouth met hers, cool at first...warm as their kiss deepened. He breathed in sharply and crushed her to him. The safety of his arms. For once, someone watching over her. He pulled back and tried to speak, but she placed her hands on either side of his face, feeling the slight roughness to his jawline, and drew him close. His lips took hers. The warmth of his hands caressed her waist, her back. Her hands roamed his shoulders, the strong column of his neck.

Too soon, he set her free. He placed her palms

together and held them between his own. Lifting her fingertips, he planted a brief kiss on them and set her from him. "This isn't right," he whispered, his breath ragged.

Her hands flew to her raging cheeks as she flung back from him.

The moon's silver light etched the stiff lines of Neil's face. "I'm sorry. That was no way for a gentleman to act."

She felt winded as if she'd been hit in the stomach.

He apologized.

But it was she who'd foisted herself on him. Was this any way for a godly woman to act? Arms wrapped around herself, she fled to the house, tripping over tree roots. Her hands broke her fall, but she hardly felt the sting of grazed palms. Behind her, Neil rushed to help, but she got up before he reached her. She couldn't bear for him to touch her.

At the cabin, Neil started to lead her to the slatted chair, but she pushed him away to remain standing by the door.

"Sofi," he chastised in a pained voice. "You're overwrought." He was right.

She knew better than to act like a child.

Her sister sat in the rocking chair, sleeping the exhausted sleep of someone who had tried to tell all.

Matilda stared at the sketchbook, her lined cheeks damp.

Sofi had no desire to look at the drawing, but the fight went out of her, and she let Neil lead her to the chair. As if nothing had happened, he treated her with the same deference he always did. At the stove, he poured her a cup of hot coffee. "Drink this."

He gently removed the sketchpad from Matilda's

hands. "Take Trina up to bed now, dear. You've all had enough shock for today. You can trust me to look after Sofi for a while."

Matilda gave a short nod. "Aye, laddie."

Sofi took a sip of coffee, her teeth clattering on the rim of the cup.

Neil had earned Matilda's respect. If Matilda only knew what she had done outside—throwing herself at Neil—she'd certainly have something to say.

Neil wakened Trina.

Sofi caught a glimpse of her sister's face soft with sleep.

"Papa's gone," she whispered, as if she'd been privy to Sofi's lament outside.

"Yes, Trina, your papa is gone. And that hurts." He led her up the ladder to the loft, with Matilda following.

Sofi gulped the coffee, listening to their footsteps above.

Neil returned and threw a log on the fire.

The wine-like fragrance of sap hissed from the flames.

"What happened outside broke all rules of propriety." He spoke in a low, measured voice. "I'm more sorry than I can say."

She couldn't look at him. With this hard edge of grief over her father, Neil's words swung like a door shutting between them. But still...she hoped. Hoped madly, insanely, that he'd take her in his arms.

He studied his clasped hands in a strange way, as if his calloused hands didn't quite belong to him. "You've been so busy caring for Trina, you haven't given yourself time to grieve. That's what prompted what happened outside. I take full responsibility."

Gone was the man who'd kissed her with what felt like longing. A levelheaded stranger sat in his place as if she spoke with a lawyer, a professor...a doctor.

The small flame of hope that their kiss meant something to him guttered out. Tonight she'd suffered a temporary madness to think she could trust him with her heart. By morning, she'd be over it. She had to be.

Without another word he opened the cabin door and stepped out into the darkness.

She stared into the dying fire.

It was time for Neil to go.

10

Neil tossed, hour after hour in the barn loft under the eaves. Rain pattered on the roof, while images assaulted his mind. The black-and-white sketch of Sofi's father moments before he drowned. His own father the last time he'd seen him, broken and bleeding in the Belfast City Hospital.

Then Jimmy's face when he'd dashed into the clinic a few hours after their father's funeral. "You should have seen him, Neil, that blighted man—walking down Newtownards Road. What right had Robert Crawford to be living when he was the reason our da is dead?" Jimmy's voice echoed from that night.

An hour before dawn, Neil thrust the quilts off to tug on dungarees and a shirt.

Odin, sleeping on the cabin porch, woke and sauntered beside him to the edge of the plateau. The dog's leathery nose quivered with the scent of morning.

The valley lay like a lake of mist where only the tallest cedars and firs poked through, but Washington was a dream he couldn't afford to indulge.

He imagined, far from Ireland, Mother making Jimmy's tea for when he'd come home from the shipyard—bacon and eggs, potato bread. And how was Alison's pregnancy progressing? Was Jimmy making good use of Neil's banishment? A finch sang nearby, and Neil winced at the beauty of it. To think of Jimmy as a married man with a child on the way...but himself...would he ever find a safe place in this world to have the same? A wife to hold? Children of his own? Last night, he'd wanted to pour it all out to Sofi. With her compassion, her intelligence, she, of all people, might understand.

In the east, a slim beam of light parted the clouds. Thankfully, he'd kept his family's secret to himself and not blabbed it all to Sofi as he might have done yesterday. The stabbing of Robert Crawford filled him with such shame he could hardly raise his head. That shame imprisoned him here in the New World as much as if he stood in a cell in the Crumlin Road Jail in Belfast.

The sun crept over the peaks, warming his face by degrees, and his lips tingled with last night's memory of his mouth against Sofi's. Memories of his father and Jimmy kept thoughts of her away as he'd tried to sleep. Now he remembered the taste of her lips. His breathing sped up with the feel and perfume of her skin. Combined despair had pushed them into exquisite freedom in each other's arms. But it had been only momentary madness. The situation was untenable. Sofi's nearness was driving him mad, and he'd failed to get Trina to a point where a sanatorium was no longer a threat.

He should pack his few belongings. Leave today. But he couldn't turn his back on Trina just yet. He'd try one more time, though the vision of a ship and freedom by warm southern seas was fast diminishing to nothing. Instead, the picture of a dank jail cell, as if drawn by Trina's hand on paper, took greater shape and detail in his mind's eye.

~*~

Boughs of Douglas firs brushed against Sofi on her way down the hill.

Trina was fine in Matilda's care.

Neil, unable to hide the black mood that had plagued him since sunup, had trudged off somewhere on his own after breakfast.

For the first time since they'd come to the cabin, she needed to get away. Anywhere, as long as it was at a distance from Neil until she found the composure to ask him to leave.

At the base of the mountain, the hand-hewn pillars along the homestead verandah still held their form. Her grandfather had carved the shapes of grizzlies, cougars, marmots, a host of birds into the ponderosa pine. From here, the hammering on the bridge grew louder. She'd not brought Trina to the valley for her healing only, but for herself as well—to be near this bridge. But Trina was still unwell. As for herself, she'd found no peace, seeing the bridge so close, yet so far.

Kiosho rushed out the front door. Dressed as usual in worn denim trousers and faded plaid shirt, the buttons done up to his throat, he herded her into the house, throwing glances over his shoulder and down the drive to the main road.

Sofi followed him to the kitchen. "No one saw me, Kiosho. Besides, I'm beginning to think this concealment has all been for nothing."

He took a cup and saucer from the sideboard, not her grandmother's good china but his own, a wisp of cherry blossom pattern. He poured hot kettle water into a teapot. "Since this secrecy has been thrust upon me, I am diligent. But, Sofi, we believers must renounce the hidden things of dishonesty. You should come here openly to this house for me to look after you, not hide from your mama."

"Kiosho, I've explained why we can't."

Sorrow shaded his lined face. "I am praying God will bring everything out in the open, that healing may take place for all concerned." He scurried to the pantry, returning with a small box. "For the time being, take these dried blueberries for Trina. Blueberry tea clears the mind."

All she could manage was a nod. Since she was a child, Kiosho's strong but gentle hands had taken the pain out of scuffed knees or grazed elbows. If only his presence were enough now.

In the distance came the dull symphony of hammering fire-hot metal into shape. She found her ear listening more to the staccato of the riveting than to Kiosho, until he took her hand in his calloused one.

"I can see and hear what pulls on your heart, Sofi. There is an old Japanese saying—in English it is, 'Even if you hide yourself from the world, do not lose sight of your real nature.'"

She wouldn't insult him by pretending she didn't know what he was talking about. "In regards to that bridge out there, I've explained to you many times why I cannot interfere. My hands are tied."

"Perhaps your hands are tied, but the Lord's are not. While we wait on His timing, He makes us stronger through our suffering. Like steel, Sofi, we must be tempered." With the swiftness of a squirrel, Kiosho changed the subject. Thankfully, he quoted no more proverbs, but chatted with her as they used to when she was growing up.

An hour later, she left. The tops of corn were as tall as her as she waded through the field and stopped at the gorge. On the bridge above, the bolting crew had finished interlocking the triangular girders. Riveting crews worked on wooden platforms hanging over the sides of the bridge. Their small, portable forges released the odor of burning coal. She plunked down at the base of a spruce tree. Breezes snatched the sounds of industry above.

With this improvement in Trina—slight though it was—she had to press on without Neil's help. When she got back to the cabin, she'd tell him. The decision brought a sad sense of peace, and her eyelids drooped in the afternoon heat. As wind moved over the cornfield, its stalks shivered, and a screech ripped the air in two. Sofi bolted forward, her heartbeat tripping. She jumped to her feet, whirled to face the bridge, unsure of what she'd heard.

Hammering stopped. Men's shouts rebounded.

Squinting against the sunlight, it took her several seconds to see where the workers pointed.

One of the riveting platforms hung by ropes at a forty-degree angle. A man clung to the bridge deck. Another man dangled from the riveting platform, his feet swinging in nothingness.

Why were these men not wearing safety harnesses at such a height? Her father had insisted on that for all his bridges.

The man clinging to the deck hauled himself up.

Thank God, he's safe.

But the one holding on to the two-by-twelve-foot wooden platform was clearly weakening.

She wiped her sweating hands down the sides of her skirt. *Please hold on, please hold on. Oh, please, God.*

Another man crawled along the girder, reaching out, but by then the man hung suspended by one arm.

Then the air where he had hung was empty.

Sofi shook her head in an attempt to rid her mind of what had to be a bad dream—the platform swinging from the side of the bridge. Like a flapping sign over a storefront. The empty space on the bridge where that man had been.

He must have fallen on the rock-strewn bank. Her gaze followed the truss to where he'd been and estimated the height. Forty feet—what hope could he possibly have? Was the doctor on his way? This town only had one doctor, and who knew where he was.

But Neil was only minutes away.

She lifted up her skirts and ran.

~*~

The scream echoed up to the aerie where Neil overlooked the bridge. He didn't wait, but tore down the hillside and past the homestead.

Sofi turned a pale face to him where they met on the road. "A man fell. He's got to be hurt badly." She gestured down to the construction site. "Off the bridge."

He sprinted past her. It seemed to take forever to reach the site.

Sofi's footsteps fell behind.

His breath scorched his chest by the time he reached the bridge abutment.

A large group of men milled around, staring at something on the ground.

Henric arrived on horseback and swung down from his saddle. "I saw it happen on my way out of town."

All the men working on the bridge had come

down from the scaffolding, their faces blanched, talking in muted tones.

Neil pushed his way to the middle of the crowd.

A man twenty or younger lay unconscious on a gurney. He bled from abrasions to the head, face, and arms. Someone else—a first-aid man, Neil assumed—cut open the left leg of the man's bloodstained trousers to expose the femur puncturing the skin.

Neil hunched down beside the injured man. "Hold his head steady until I say otherwise."

"I know what I'm doing," the first-aid man demurred.

"I said, hold his head steady."

With a quick, appraising glance at Neil, the man did as he was told.

Neil opened the patient's mouth. No loose teeth, only superficial bleeding. Nothing to block the airway. The chest rose and fell at an equal rate, though the pulse was weak. "Is this where he fell, or did you move him?"

"This is where we found him. We only laid him on the gurney like you see."

Neil pulled back the patient's eyelids. The pupils contracted quickly and equally. He palpated his fingers along the spine and neck. No vertebrae sinking or sticking out, but it was too soon to rule out a head wound or spinal fracture. He lifted the man's shirt to check his abdomen, looking for distension or bruising. None that he could see as yet. But dropping forty feet, Neil could only hope there was no damage to the internal organs.

He sat back on his heels and looked up to the bridge, where the man must have fallen from, and studied the soft patch of sandy ground where he lay. If he'd hit the ground a few feet farther out on those boulders, he'd be dead. Amazing. Still, at such a height, why were these men not protected by safety harnesses?

Neil bit back his rising anger at the cavalier attitude of builders. At the moment, this patient's leg needed surgery, and soon. From Neil's vantage on the plateau these past weeks, he'd seen no hospital as he'd overlooked the town. Only a doctor's surgery on Main Street.

Workers stood in a circle around him and the patient.

"When's the doctor getting here?" he asked.

"Doctor's going to be a while," someone said. "Delivering a baby across the river."

Another man who appeared to have some authority pushed his way into the group and swore at Neil. "I'm chief engineer. We'll get him ready to move to the surgery, and we'll wait for the doctor."

Neil stood to face the engineer. "That bone's a mess. If it isn't set soon, he could go into shock or bleed to death."

"Don't you think we can see that?" The engineer stomped a few feet away and cursed under his breath.

Neil grabbed hold of Henric's arm. "He needs surgery. Surgery I can do."

Henric's eyes narrowed. "We've got first-aid men from logging camps and mines who've seen every kind of injury. Only a doctor would know more than they do at this point."

"I am a doctor."

Henric's blond brows lowered. "That explains a few things."

"If you don't let me work on him soon, you could

lose him. I can't rule out internal injuries."

Henric ran a hand over his jaw.

Footsteps ran up from behind. The group surrounding the injured man broke apart, and Sofi reached them, panting. "Neil, can you do anything for him?"

Henric's gaze didn't let go of Neil's for an interminable length of time. He gave one sharp nod. "Move him to Doc's surgery." He jutted his chin toward Neil. "This physician will treat Gunnar."

The chief engineer whirled back to Henric. "You're a big man in these parts, but I say we wait for the local doctor."

"Seems every time I turn around, there's a new chief on this job, and I've known Gunnar since before he could walk." Henric glared at the engineer. "I say this man will work on him until Doc Enckell gets here."

Neil didn't have time to argue.

Henric barked an order, and men carried the gurney to a Model T truck parked by the foreman's shack. Sofi and Neil slid into the truck bed. Two of the workmen jumped on the running boards.

The noon sun beat down on them, but the patient, Gunnar, felt like ice. Henric got into the driver's seat and pressed the horn, letting its baleful holler move people out of the way. He raced the vehicle at top speed into town. The short journey took only minutes, and they stopped in front of a two-story white clapboard house. A shingle with the name, PETTER ENCKELL, MD, swung from an elaborate cornice.

Neil raced inside while Henric oversaw the men carry the gurney. At the sink, Neil turned on the tap to lather his hands with a cake of lye soap. "Set him on that table. Get blankets. Hot-water bottles. Move that instrument tray close to the table. Fill basins with sterile water. Then boil more. Locate bandages, splints." He pulled a clean apron from a hook and draped it around himself. "Are you sure the local physician isn't in town?"

Henric moved closer. "He's on the other side of the river, five miles away. Apparently his wife is with him too."

Neil looked across Gunnar to Sofi.

Like him, she'd washed, put on a clean apron, and stood waiting for instructions.

He blinked in confusion. He'd never asked, yet here she was ready to help.

And Henric had followed Neil's instructions like a hospital orderly.

While the others gathered the items he specified, he took Gunnar's wrist and counted. The boy's pulse had grown rapid and thready, his pallor a dull gray. Shock was setting in. The patient moaned. Neil brushed the hair back from the young man's forehead. The patient's blue-veined eyelids flickered open.

"Gunnar, I'm here to help you. You're going to be all right, old son." He palpated Gunnar's abdomen. "Do you have any pain here? Or here?"

Gunnar moaned. "My leg..."

"Right."

Sofi stood ready with a basin of sterilized water. Neil wrapped a hot-water bottle in a blanket and tucked it next to Gunnar's side. He covered the patient with the other blanket and laid the exposed, injured leg on a clean sheet.

Neil pinned Henric with his gaze. "I need you to unlock that cabinet, for the ether."

The tall Scandinavian retrieved the key from the doctor's desk, opened the cabinet, and passed to Neil a bottle of clear liquid. Neil measured the ether on a sponge, placed the sponge into the inhaler chamber, and fitted the mask over Gunnar's mouth and nose. As soon as Gunnar slipped into unconsciousness, Henric grasped Neil's arm.

"It'll only take a moment." Henric bowed his head and began to pray.

Sofi too lowered her head and moved her lips to Henric's appeal for the Lord to guide Neil's hands, to bring Gunnar back to full health and strength.

To Neil's shock, the other rough-dressed men in the room bowed their heads in silent prayer as well. Neil rubbed his arm that stung from Henric's grip. He wanted to get started.

At last, they raised their heads, though in truth it had only been thirty seconds.

Gunnar was in a deep sleep, his breathing low and steady. Neil picked up a scalpel, cut into the leg to open it enough to get a good look at the injury. Then he bent to the tedious job of flushing out each tiny piece of debris, each clot of dried blood and bone fragment. The world narrowed to this one patient on this table. This one wound. The dormancy of his soul, his need to bring healing, stirred to life. Helping Trina with her psychological dilemma was one thing, but now his fingers tingled with the satisfaction of doing what he'd been born to do.

He had no concept of time, but gave a nod to the two workmen to come forward. They grasped Gunnar's leg as he instructed and with brute strength pulled, allowing him to line up the femur. He tied the splint firmly to the leg and became aware of a clock ticking nearby. He left the wound open to let the licensed doctor observe it, and to allow air to flow.

Pulling his shoulders back, Neil dropped the used instruments into a metal basin. If he'd been alone, he would have hummed a tune or even danced a short jig here in the doctor's office. The patient would be just fine.

Sofi took the basin, her brow quirked. She must have seen the grin on his face that he found hard to conceal, but without a word, she washed the instruments in the sink and set the two men from the bridge to cleaning the surgery.

Henric sat in the corner, his complexion waxy while Neil removed the soiled apron and leaned over the sink, splashing cold water on his face. He stopped himself from whistling.

The sound of a horse and buggy barreling down the street filtrated through the house to the surgery. A moment later, the local doctor, carrying a black medical valise, rushed in.

All desire to whistle left Neil. It was time to be accountable, and the reality of his precarious situation came grinding back. And the patient's situation gathered weight. Another life might have been lost due to sheer negligence. This Gunnar could easily have died like Da had in the shipyard. Neil squared his shoulders. "The patient doesn't appear to have any internal—"

"You're a doctor?" The local man grazed Neil with one look.

"A resident at...Belfast City Hospital for the past four years. As I was saying, the patient's bleeding is under control. The limb is warming up, and I've left the cavity open for your inspection. I find leaving it open for a while helps with infection. The pulse above and below the fracture is steady and growing stronger."

Dr. Enckell touched Gunnar's cheek, pulled back his eyelids, and inspected the leg, repeating the same steps Neil had performed at the bridge site. His frown lightened. "Looks good." He turned to Neil. "You've done an excellent job, it appears. With good post-operative care, Gunnar should be fine."

Some of the tension in Neil's shoulders melted. Maybe he could slip quietly away.

Sofi took hold of Neil's arm. "If Gunnar is safe, then we should be leaving."

Dr. Enckell raised an eyebrow, seeing her for the first time. "When did you get to town, Sofi?" Not waiting for an answer, he turned back to Neil. "But certainly, go on now. We can talk more later, but, Doctor...your name before you go?"

The truth stuck in Neil's throat. He could give him the surname *Macpherson* that he'd given Sofi all these weeks, but what if the doctor checked by sending a telegram to the hospital in Belfast? He let Sofi draw him out to the front porch before Dr. Enckell could press him further, as if she knew to distract the doctor.

Consumed with his desire to see to the patient, the local man didn't repeat his request for Neil's name.

On the front lawn about thirty men from the bridge stood. A smattering of women from the town stood around too.

He should have realized that in a small town like this, news would travel with the speed of a lit fuse. Bridge and townspeople peered at him, tamping down all the lightness he'd felt during the surgical procedure.

A gangly man from the construction site stepped

forward. "Is Gunnar going to be all right, Doctor?"

"I think so."

Kiosho rushed up. "Trina is safe at the cabin with Matilda." He cast his gaze over the large assembly. "The lid on the pot of secrecy has blown."

Neil lifted a hand in resignation and slumped down on the porch swing. Planting his elbows on his knees, he let his head droop.

Hushed voices of townspeople droned like a lazy bee in a nearby bush.

He lifted his gaze to meet Sofi's.

Her eyes sparkled with suppressed excitement, the same excitement he'd felt inside. For a second, maybe three, he savored her smile.

But Kiosho was right—the lid on the pot of secrecy had blown.

As for Trina and Sofi, the truth that they were here would leak out of this valley by the end of day. It would reach Seattle soon.

The proof that he was a doctor lay inside with Gunnar's leg that was nicely pinking up with good blood flow. He'd given the name of his hospital to Dr. Enckell. He might as well have given him his full name, and the address of the police headquarters in Belfast.

11

Sofi couldn't hold back her smile, in spite of the fact that Neil had kept such a secret from her. Her mind shied away from the reason for that secrecy. But then...she'd run away with Trina, hidden her from their mother. Whatever his reasons, Neil had to be as innocent as she was. Now all was exposed. She'd known Gunnar Bjornson most of her life, as she knew these people congregating on the lawn.

There'd be prayer meetings tonight at the two churches in town for Gunnar's recovery.

The sense of belonging to something good and old wafted over her with the scent of roses in the doctor's garden. These Swedish immigrants had brought their Christian devotion from the old country just like her own grandparents. Nothing felt right after Papa drowned, but here in this valley, she felt the rightness of belonging to these people, to her roots in Christ. And a longing to stay here. To have Neil stay here too. She tried a shy smile, but he avoided her gaze. That small shaft of hope—hope for what, she didn't know—dwindled.

He was still hiding something, but at least he'd confirmed what she'd known for weeks.

Several townsfolk yelled out hello to her in Swedish. Pastor Svendson, Mrs. Larson, and Mrs. Helsing darted up the stairs to hug and greet her. "When did you get to town? Where's your mama? So sorry to hear about your papa."

Their warmth and chatter washed over Sofi as Neil sat on the verandah, staring at his clasped hands. In the surgery when he was working on Gunnar's leg, she'd never seen him so at peace, the strong, sure way his hands went about his work, as if injected by medicine from heaven in the form of God-inspired labor. Yet now Neil acted as if he were ashamed.

Henric pushed open the screen door and drew her away from the townswomen. "Best you and Trina go to your grandparents' homestead, or come out to my place." He spoke in an undertone only she and Neil could hear. "Sofi, I've arranged for Larson to take you. I don't imagine you want to answer a load of questions at the moment...or mention how long you've been in town...or where."

Heat flashed up her face. Though they had Matilda and Trina with them at all times, the fact Neil slept only twenty feet away in the barn could stain their reputations. But in truth, her burning face had to do with the way she'd thrown herself at Neil last night. She also felt the weight of whatever shame burdened him.

Henric turned to Neil. "You're welcome at my place. In fact, I'd like nothing better...Doctor."

Neil tilted his head toward the surgery. "The patient?"

Henric sent him a wide grin. "You saved Gunnar's livelihood as well as his leg. If you feel up to it, Doc wants a chat with you."

"The doctor is pleased with the surgery?"

"Perfectly."

"Then if it's all the same to you, Henric, I'll take you up on that offer to stay at your place a few days, but I'd as soon get out of here now." Still Neil avoided her eyes.

Her gaze climbed to the hidden plateau. If she and Trina moved down to the homestead and Neil to Henric's house, the old cabin would be empty once more, and that brought its own emptiness to her heart.

Henric's brows leveled at Neil. "I guess I can understand, but Doc will want to have that chat soon. Professional courtesy and all."

Larson's greengrocer van pulled up, and Henric escorted Sofi through the crowd to the waiting vehicle. On her way to the truck, she caught sight of the chief engineer she'd seen earlier at the bridge. He stood with the workmen, keeping his distance when it would be appropriate for him to be inside talking to the doctor. During the emergency she'd not paid much attention to him. Now it struck her. This man was a stranger, not one of the engineers who had worked with Papa through the years. Nor did she know the construction foreman, one of Wetzle Steel's men.

Never mind that Trina was still ill. Never mind that Neil hid secrets. Never mind that she longed for the same joy in her life that she'd seen on Neil's face when he'd acted the doctor he really was. Her heart pounded with the thrust of a steam-driven hammer. How dare that engineer stand there so callously when one of his men lay inside the surgery after falling from the bridge?

She marched across the lawn to the man, only holding herself back from poking him in the chest. "Why were those men not using the safety measures my father recommended?"

The engineer backed up. "Your father, miss?"

"Yes, my father, Fred Andersson of Andersson and Bolton Engineering. I'm his daughter, and I'm asking why those riveters were not harnessed to the structure."

The man's Adam's apple bobbed. "Miss, it's not necessary. If you wish to discuss it, I suggest you do so with Mr. Bolton. He's due back tomorrow to prepare for the inaugural crossing of the bridge."

Her gaze searched the crowd, looking for Charles, though the engineer said he wasn't here. Granted, as consulting engineer, Charles didn't need to remain on site during the entire erection of the structure, but for the first time since Gunnar fell, she realized she'd not thought of Charles. He could very well have been here today, and she'd not once thought of the danger to Trina if he had been.

Henric led her to the grocer's van and opened the door to help her into the front seat.

Neil climbed into the back of the van.

Kiosho squeezed into the front with her, and the grocer motored away from the surgery, with Henric following on his mare.

In a daze, she glanced back at the townspeople who dispersed from the doctor's front lawn. Charles was due back in Orchard tomorrow, the engineer had said. When poor Mama heard her daughters were in the valley, would she dig her heels in and enlist Charles to bring them home to Seattle?

~*~

Roselle didn't know what day it was. If she looked out the window, she'd see Mount Rainier, but she didn't want to look. The last time she'd been to Rainier, she and Freddie had celebrated their twenty-second wedding anniversary. Memory gleamed like a sunbeam.

Freddie pulling her into his arms, saying, "Happy anniversary, *älskling*."

The memory danced away like a puff of a dandelion. She held back a cry, reaching out to keep it. At least she had made him happy. He had been pleased that she spoke English so that only a little of her Swedish showed. He had been pleased with the way she dressed and comported herself. This farmer's daughter had become a lady. But an old phrase of her mama's kept running through her mind: "A piece of bread in the pocket is better than a feather in our hat."

Her hands shook. It took all her strength to open the drawer in the small table and take out the amber vial. Shame stuck to her like molasses. If Mama were alive, she would have scolded. "Clean the chicken coop, Roselle. If you are having trouble sleeping at night, then *arbete gör sömnen söt*, work sweetens the sleep." No, Mama would never approve. Nor would Sofi approve of her reliance on this medicine. But Mama had gone to heaven long ago. And Sofi and Trina were...only God knew.

How many drops? She pressed her fingers to her brow. Three? Five? Ten? She poured the drops into her coffee. The glass bottle clinking against her china cup boomed through her head. She returned the bottle to the drawer. Only a moment and the shaking would stop.

Frida knocked on the door and came in, but had no time to speak before Charles pushed past her. He laid the back of his hand across Roselle's brow. "Dear Rosie, how ill you look. I can't bear to see you suffer like this."

"News, Charles. Do you have news?"

"Relax, dearest Rosie. Let me help you." He leaned close and took her hand.

She should order Charles from the room for such intimacy, but she had no one else to rely on. "Charles? Any news?"

"The people I've sent out have nothing to report. Now do as I say. Relax."

She tried to do as he said, but her headache had become a hammer. "My medicine."

Charles moved from the settee. The desk drawer rattled.

But hadn't she just taken some medicine? *Jah*, but...how long ago?

"Yes, dear, I have your medicine. Take a good...long sip. Lean back." His voice grated, but her limbs took on the familiar heaviness...shackles at her ankles...yet laying a blanket over her heartache. Covering it.

"Rosie..." His voice came from far way, but she felt his nearness. Why must he always sit so close? The crackling of paper pulled her back to the room, and her eyes darted open. Charles held a sheaf of papers, a pen. "A little business, Rosie."

"What is it?"

"Business papers."

"Can you not sign them?"

"These need your signature, Rosie."

The dullness of her thinking couldn't cover up the fact that Charles seemed worried. His brows rammed together as his eyes shifted from her to the patio. A sheen of perspiration dotted his upper lip. Her head felt heavy, but she forced her gaze to follow his.

Two men sat at the wrought-iron chairs. Men she did not know. One of them was the size of a mountain, a derby perched on his head. The shorter one with a brilliant green silk vest and bow tie stared through the glass at her and Charles. Their clothes were of poor taste. Not the sort of people Freddie used to associate with.

"Who are those men, Charles?"

"Only a couple of...couriers for Heinz Wetzle."

"From the steel foundry?"

"Yes, Rosie. Here is where you sign."

Her medicine was taking over. Sleep only heartbeats away. She reached for the pen, and Charles directed her hand. She made her signature as best she could.

Frida opened the door and burst into the parlor. "Madam," she shrieked, "it's the police on the telephone. They've just learned where Sofi and Trina have gone."

Roselle tried to stand. Her heart battered against her ribcage. She fell back on the settee as the color and shapes of Frida and Charles ran together as if on a rain-drizzled window. *Thank You, God, for finding them. Now...please...find me.*

12

Sunday morning, Neil savored the comfort of a real bed, but he'd never trade those weeks sleeping in Sofi's dilapidated barn for the finest room in the finest mansion. Henric's place, not as opulent as the Andersson mansion in Seattle, was a grand home of cedar beams set on a timbered slope. The house was quiet now that Henric and his housekeeper had left for church.

Down the hall, he found the bathroom, and a copper, claw-footed tub. Hot water steamed from the tap, and Neil washed up with a cake of spice-scented soap, dunking himself over and over for good measure. Wrapping a towel around his waist, he lathered the badger-hair brush in the bowl, applied the soap to his face, and shaved away his stubble with the straight razor.

Henric had left a clean shirt, charcoal-gray suit, a pair of polished shoes on a chair, no doubt hoping Neil would join him at church today. But Neil had no time for religion. Da remained faithful to his invisible God. But that wasn't for Neil. People were made of muscle and bone, blood cells. People had to save themselves by taking responsibility to make things right in this world. At least that was one thing he could agree with Jimmy on, even if the way he and his brother went about it was diametrically opposed.

He pulled on the white shirt with pale gray vertical stripes. After attaching the stiff collar and turning down the wings, he knotted the silk tie at his throat. Glad of the haircut Henric's housekeeper gave him last night, he combed his wet hair back from his forehead. With the day promising to be warm, Neil planned on carrying the gray sack coat folded across his arm. It was half a mile to the Andersson homestead.

He told himself it was for Trina that he visited today, but he wasn't fooling himself. He must be mad to torture himself like this. *Let her sister get well soon, Lord, so that I can leave this valley...and not need to see her again.* He let out a grunt of self-disgust. Him not wanting to darken the door of a church, and here he was on a Sunday muttering a prayer.

~*~

Matilda's Scottish burr jarred with Kiosho's Japanese staccato. Their mild haggling in the kitchen brought a smile to Sofi, but her smile fled at the sight of Trina sitting at the table, drawing yet again another picture of the night Papa died. Was this slight improvement enough to keep the threat of the sanatorium from her?

All night, Sofi tossed, and this morning, she wakened with the conviction—if Charles was coming to the valley, this was where she'd make her stand. This was where Trina would be healed. Sofi felt that with every fiber in her heart, though this morning showed little evidence. But that was faith, believing in what the Lord could do, when all seemed contrary.

With that thought bolstering her faith, she'd attended church this morning, the first time since Papa's memorial service.

With Matilda beside her, Trina had sat quietly enough, her foot tapping a restless rhythm, but she'd held her arms tightly throughout the entire service.

As soon as they'd made it back to the homestead, Trina rushed to the sideboard and snatched up the sketchpad. Her knuckles shone white as she gripped the pencil, almost stabbing the paper to inflict a deep scoring as the image grew.

Sofi went to pat Trina's shoulder, but Trina shot from the chair with the sketchbook clutched against her chest. She stood, her eyes wide as if imploring Sofi. Imploring her for what?

"Don't you understand, Sofi? It's my...it's my fa..."

"It's your what? Tell me."

"I can't." Sobbing, Trina ran from the kitchen out to Kiosho's garden.

Matilda watched her go. "She's only taking a day or two to get used to another change, Sofi. Wasn't she as bright as a button yesterday, for a while?"

Sofi slumped against the sideboard. "This drawing idea of Neil's has only made things worse. Last night was another bad night."

"Neil's ideas haven't hurt either. 'Tis been my experience that there are many steps to getting through grief. It takes time." Matilda patted Sofi's arm and left the kitchen to strut along the verandah in search of Trina.

Her sister drifted from pillar to pillar on the wraparound porch, a look of perplexity stamped on her face. Still holding the sketchpad close, her fingers traced the intricate animal carvings.

Kiosho dried his hands on a tea cloth. "Matilda is right."

"I don't know anymore, Kiosho. So little

improvement."

He took her elbow and shook it. "Remember what I used to tell you. The love of God, all around. Like these mountains that circle this valley. First, Trina and you must go through different canyons of sadness, but He will bring you out to open spaces."

She allowed herself one sigh and tied an apron around her waist. "I believe, Kiosho. But there are days I feel such a coward, and all I know to do is the next thing at hand." She pulled a loaf of Kiosho's freshly made bread to slice it.

He carved a cured ham. "Keep doing the work God puts in front of you. He will show you the way." His hand stilled as he reached for a jar of horseradish. "This reminds me, now everybody in town knows you are here, when will you go down to the bridge?"

She hoped if she didn't answer, he'd move to another topic, such as when Charles would most certainly arrive. No such chance, Kiosho only geared himself up to speak further. "Go down, Sofi. See if they are building your bridge the way you drew it."

The sharp tang of horseradish tickled her nose, and she used this excuse to turn away from his too-observant gaze. "My bridge?"

"You drew that bridge, and your papa made no changes to those blueprints. If you were a boy, all would be different, but your papa was a proud man. A silly man."

She didn't know what to make of Kiosho's tirade that she should take charge of the bridge. That was ridiculous. But she wasn't going to back down on the safety measures. If Charles was coming today, she'd corner him.

Kiosho's frown scored deeper. "While you are

down there, ask why money is not given to the men who have been hurt, or to Johanson's widow."

Her gaze clamped on his. "Are you saying Mrs. Johanson has not received any compensation money?"

"Yes, I am saying this. No money. Henric helps her, but now young Gunnar will need money while he is getting better. He became married last year."

Her mouth went dry. "My father had a special account for that compensation money."

"Since your papa died, things are not the same."

"Henric knows all this too and never said a word to me? Why didn't he write to Charles and get it sorted out?"

"He did write. He talk to Charles, but Charles keeps on saying he will look into it."

"I can't believe this. Charles is a meddling so-and-so, but I had no idea he was negligent. Why has no one mentioned this before?"

"How could I or Henric say this to you? You come into town so no one sees you. You hide up in the old cabin and worry over Trina. In some ways you are no better than your mama hiding in her house."

She lifted her chin. "You know I'm upset about the safety measures. I will look into that. And I promise I'll look into the compensation money. I'll take it out of my own trust fund if I have to, but what do you expect me to do about the bridge? You know how my father felt about a woman pursuing a career."

The old Japanese man threw up his hands. "Very silly. God has different work for all of us. It does not matter if you are Jew or Gentile, Swedish or Japanese, man or woman. Christ died for all, and He has special work for everyone. Your grandfather taught me this when we first met in the gold fields of Canada."

She thrust the sandwiches together, crushing the bread in the process. She'd do all she could to fulfill her family obligations about the money, but the bridge?

Kiosho's gaze lifted to the hallway through to the screen door. Someone was coming up the drive to the house. Without bothering to hide his amusement, he nodded toward the porch. "Your young man is coming to call."

She sent a swift glance to see Neil on the porch and hissed at Kiosho, "He is not my young man." But she took her time untying her apron, to let her scalding cheeks cool.

Kiosho sent her one of his inscrutable looks as Neil knocked. All last night, memories kept her as restless as Trina, memories of the gentle way Neil had spoken when he stopped her from driving away from him in Seattle. The way his hand lingered on her shoulder as he'd helped her into her coat that night by the fire. Her insides flowed with honey whenever he was near, but it was the height of foolishness to care for a man with secrets. A man with a girl back home. She remembered that name clearly written on the envelope—Alison.

A smile played about Kiosho's resolute features as he ushered Neil in. "Ah, good, I am glad you are here. Sofi has decided wisely to face Charles when he comes to the valley. So what is the plan for today, a picnic to provide calm before the storm?" He gave Sofi a long, meaningful look. "It is the Lord's Day. Tomorrow will be time enough for work."

Ignoring the glare Sofi sent him, Kiosho rushed to the back door, throwing out orders as he did. "Finish the sandwiches and cake. We will take the wagon. I do not trust that fancy horseless carriage of yours. Come,

Trina," he called outside, "we must find your grandmama's picnic basket."

Trina didn't protest as Kiosho steered her into the kitchen. His wiry frame, coursing with energy, seemed to knock her out of her private world into the present.

Even Matilda bowed to Kiosho's wishes and wrapped the cake as ordered.

Only Sofi hesitated. She gripped the kitchen sink and stared hard out the window at the mountains, warm pewter peaks above the tree line. Neil had been with them all this time, and now in her grandmother's kitchen she found it hard to turn around and say hello. She turned, a quiver running through her middle at the sight of him.

Gone was the gardener in worn work clothes. A slender man in crisp, elegant clothing, his hair trimmed and swept back, showing his distinct widow's peak, stood straight and proud. Sadness still haunted the set of his mouth. But the way he held his shoulders, the stalwart lift of his chin—here stood the man that deep down, she'd always known he was.

"How's Trina?" Neil's gaze sought hers.

Discussing her sister helped to hide how his presence shook her to the core. "Bad dreams last night. These drawings seem to increase her anguish."

"She's feeling sadder?" He ran a hand over his chin, and she longed to know what his smooth skin along that hard jaw would feel like beneath her fingertips. "Sofi, I'm convinced one day she'll awaken." He cleared his throat, his eyes straying to her hair that had fallen from its pins. "Like a sleeping beauty."

She pushed her hair from her shoulder. "I'm trusting in that confidence of yours."

"It's not so much what I'm doing, Sofi." His voice found that deep level that had become so achingly familiar. "It's you, and your steady assertions that she will get well."

His gaze clouded with confusion and she tried to understand what he refused to put into words. Perhaps if she hadn't acted the wanton floozy the other night and kissed him, they could have remained friends. He might have shared his burden with her.

Kiosho burst into the kitchen, towing Trina by the hand, and broke their gazes.

"Look, Sofi." Trina gave her a weak smile, showing off their grandmother's basket. "It's been a while since we used this."

Kiosho hauled Neil out to the barn to hitch the horses.

Half an hour later, Sofi sat beside Kiosho in the front of the wagon while Neil helped Trina and Matilda into the seat behind. Kiosho kicked the brake loose and snapped the reins. The two Clydesdales started the slow grade that wound back and forth up the side of the mountain. Cedars and pines on each side of the narrow road covered them in shade, until they reached an altitude that stunted the trees. The wagon reached the first of a series of sharp turns, and the road clung to the edge of the cliff.

Sofi never felt fear at these junctures, but looked behind to see how Trina fared.

Her little sister leaned against the armrest and peered over the valley, her fingers plucking at the pages of Sofi's sketchpad on her lap. Neil sat next to her, talking in a hushed tone. With her features crunched in thought, Trina gave him quiet responses that Sofi wished she could hear. When Trina glanced up at Neil, her absorbed expression cleared somewhat, and her smile wobbled. But it was a smile. Another honest-to-goodness smile.

Kiosho clicked his tongue, and the horses plodded on. At the summit he reined the Clydesdales in and settled them under a shady tree.

The wind, carrying a clean pine fragrance, blew unimpeded as though they'd reached the top of the world.

Trina jumped from the wagon to run along a pathway strewn on either side with blue and purple lupine, pink phlox, yellow arnica, and red Indian paintbrush.

"Trina!" Matilda yelled, huffing after her.

Only a few feet to Trina's right, the path dropped to plunge into a flower-dotted meadow. Grasses swayed in the breeze.

Her sister flew with her arms wide like she used to do.

Kiosho took charge of the basket and jockeyed with Matilda for first place, running after Trina.

Neil stayed behind with Sofi, sweeping his gaze three hundred and sixty degrees.

Above the tree line, gray peaks scraped the sky, some still capped with snow. In the distance, pale blue-and-turquoise ice from glaciers filled crevices between serrated granite heights.

Quiet awe filled his face.

She could only hope that up here, for a while he could let go of whatever pain he was hiding from the world, and from her.

They strolled side by side along the pathway, their hands brushing together once or twice. A warm wind whipped at their clothing and hair. Here and there, stunted pines flanked the path. At one spot, the trees hedged in, narrowing the path, forcing her and Neil closer. Their hands touched. She wasn't sure which one of them clasped the other's first. His cool palm lay against hers. His fingers entwined with hers. Up here, they didn't feel like a man and a woman, but two children, no different than Trina scampering along the path.

Trina stopped when she reached her favorite place, a dip in the meadow where glaciers—though miles away—seemed close enough to touch.

Sofi and Neil waited on the path.

Trina plunked into tall grasses and twirled a bloom of Indian paintbrush along her lips.

Matilda and Kiosho were busy unpacking the lunch basket.

Unless the others looked their way, she and Neil could have been alone, ensconced in the scent and shade of the firs. With their hands clasped, Sofi studied the ground at her feet. Her gaze travelled up the length of Neil as he moved to face her. Their hands tightened. Their eyes met. Warmth throbbed through her. A muscle high along his jaw pulsed. Wind blew a strand of his hair into his eyes, his look of utter hopelessness holding her mesmerized.

With a shake of his head, he released her hand. The breeze suddenly felt cold, and it felt like yesterday—yesterday when she'd felt the sooner Neil left, the better. Before she did something foolish like fall in love.

~*~

He was a doctor, for goodness sake. Neil raked his

hair back. He should be able to control these emotions. Maybe it was the thin mountain air that brought on this dizzying sensation.

Sofi turned away from him, the light going out of her eyes. She perched on her knees to set food out on the blanket.

He had to stop himself from gaping at her.

Mountaintops stretching for miles tugged him away. Up here, nothing obstructed his vision of earth and sky. Only the wind broke the intense silence. For a moment, he allowed himself to picture in his mind— standing with Sofi, looking out over this vista. Him holding her close with her back to him. Her hair softly blowing against his face.

Kiosho called to him, dissolving his musings that could never be.

Neil joined the small group, where the old man poured a cup of tea as if Neil sat at home in an Irish parlor. He nestled against a large boulder. If life had gone as he'd imagined, he wouldn't be here on an alpine meadow. He'd be home in Ireland, working at the hospital and the clinic, taking care of Mother and Jimmy, and soon Jimmy's child. But Neil's self-made plans were shattered by uncontrolled anger and the thrust of a knife.

Matilda wandered off to take in the view.

Kiosho packed the remains of the food in the hamper.

As the silence grew, Neil didn't look at Sofi. He didn't want to see her growing mistrust. Back there, they'd almost kissed again. That would have been the height of lunacy.

Trina huddled on the blanket and drew feverishly.

He touched the corner of the sketchpad. "Can I see

what you're drawing?"

"Yes," came her almost-inaudible reply.

He studied the sketch. Using the flat of her pencil, she'd drawn strong horizontal lines and left not a fraction of the page white. The top half of the sketch appeared a slightly lighter shade than the horizontal bar at the bottom. The bottom half was blocked in, black and shiny from her lead pencil. It took him a while to recognize that faint spaces here and there resembled the swells on a body of water. She'd drawn a blank sea. The *Cecelia* was nowhere to be seen. Only a surging, dark void.

He thumbed through previous sheets to find page after page of the same thing. "It's empty, Trina."

She shivered. "I know."

"Is this what frightens you?"

"I dream it every night. The water..."

Adrenaline raced through him. He could sense the same rush in Sofi beside him as she leaned closer to Trina. But he had to ignore Sofi and focus on her sister. "Tell me about the water."

"So far down. Never ending." Trina licked her lips.

"The ocean didn't use to frighten you."

Her brow lifted, and she rubbed her arms. "I used to love the feel of the spray when Papa and I sailed *Cecelia*. I'd come home soaking wet. Matilda would scold me. Papa would laugh."

"And now?"

"I hate the sea." A feral edge hardened her young face. "I hate the sea. Now...it never leaves me."

Sofi made a slight movement to reach out to Trina.

Neil shook his head. He understood her desire to comfort, but Trina had to keep remembering.

"Trina, what happened that day?" Just as he'd felt the day he put Gunnar's leg back together, joy danced a jig through his veins. His patient was close to getting well, but he must tamp down his excitement. Remain calm. For his patient's sake.

She lifted her gaze, perhaps searching for the Juan de Fuca Strait. "The noise...thunder and lighting. It came so fast." She curled her feet to sit Indian style, her arms around herself. She began to rock. "I saw Papa in the water for a while. He disappeared. I couldn't..." Her face crumpled. "It's my fault he's dead. My fault. Oh, Sofi, I'm sorry. I sent Papa to that cold, dark place."

Sofi pushed her sister's hair off her brow. "It's not your fault. Shh, *älskling.* You're not to blame for being unable to save him out on open sea. You're only human. Only one small person. A person I love so much."

Trina's shoulders heaved. "You don't understand, Sofi. I sent him there." She dropped her face into her hands. "I sent him to that dark, unknown grave, so far below. I should be there. Not him."

Sofi opened her mouth to comfort Trina, but Neil held up a hand to stop her.

"Trina, how did you do this?"

Kiosho watched Trina, his eyes dark orbs, while Matilda dropped to her knees close by.

Sofi didn't seem to be breathing.

Neil waited for Trina's sobs to ease enough for her to speak.

"Papa said that I had surpassed him at sailing. That now I was the teacher. We'd gone out that day, though he felt a change in the wind. He told me to remain close to the harbor." Her voice grew fainter.

"So we did. Stayed close to shore. But Papa was tired from his travels. He fell asleep. I was bored close to land, and the wind was barely five knots. No clouds. Azure sky. I took us out. I kept the *Cecelia* from heeling too much, to give Papa a rest." Silent tears streamed down her face. "Papa didn't wake until the squall was right behind us. Before I knew it, the wind had jumped to twenty-two or maybe twenty-five knots. I couldn't control her. She heeled over. We were in the water. She was filling up." Trina's chin quivered. "Papa was trying to make it to the boat. When she went under, she took him too."

Sofi tucked Trina close. "You've been blaming yourself all this time."

"I thought...I thought I knew best."

"You made an error of judgment, Trina. Maybe Papa went too far with his praise of your skills, building you up to take risks, but you can't blame yourself. A storm came. And you and me are only frail human beings."

Trina seemed to drink in Sofi's words.

They both turned to search Neil's eyes for confirmation.

For months now, self-preservation had stopped him from being a doctor. Now at least, with Trina able to express the horror of her guilt, she was on the way to full health. Perhaps Sofi would start to mend too. He almost felt like the man he used to be. Almost. He reached out to touch Trina's hand. "Trina, you couldn't possibly save your father." But his own words ricocheted back on him, and he held back a flinch. He'd been unable to save *his* father, and had he really saved his brother from their own personal storm?

At long last, Trina's sobs gentled.

The old Japanese man thanked him with a hand on his shoulder.

Matilda hung back until Neil nodded her over to Trina.

Sofi's smile shone through her tears. "You're going to be all right, *älskling*."

Much of Trina's trauma was still trapped in that dark place beneath the surface of the sea. But on this flower-dotted and sun-filled meadow high above the world, he'd taken her back, and she'd opened the door to her buried emotions. At the moment, the patient appeared drained.

He felt invigorated, and Neil strode fast from the picnic site, along a copse of stunted trees. He walked until he found a fallen log. He picked up a cone and threw it, startling a chipmunk. Now that Trina was speaking coherently, he was sure he could convince Dr. Enckell to be her advocate against her going to a sanatorium. There was nothing here to hold him. It was time to go, catch that ship, sail away to a new life. He could leave. Leave Sofi.

Her footsteps fell behind him.

The startled chipmunk dashed up the tree, glaring down at them from a safe height and scolding as if it considered them the most foolish animals it had ever seen.

Neil released a half-amused grunt. Only people made life more complicated than it needed to be. But what choice did he have?

"You did it, Neil. For a while I doubted, but you did it." She sat next to him, beaming.

He stared out over the mountains. "As I told you earlier, from the start it was your bravery, your faith, I admit, that helped your sister."

The warm wind whistled past them. A carpet of alpine flowers spread around them, but he hardly saw them.

Sofi barely moved.

"I'm leaving. I'm sure you'll agree that's best." Words clotted in his throat.

"How soon?" Her brow puckered.

So there would be no argument from her. Somehow, that stabbed at him. He'd thought...he'd hoped...ach, what was the sense? He turned brusque. "I'll pick up my bag from Henric's. Be on my way tomorrow. Trina will soon be who she used to be."

"And the truth. About you?" Her words leaked out on a breath.

It was easier to ignore her question. "Time heals, Sofi." But did it? When grief tore the heart out of people, did time heal? He hated giving her platitudes. And he dared not look at her, but his eyes strayed to her lap. One shining, single tear plopped and splashed on her folded hands. He could have been strong if she'd stayed away. But the perfume of her nearness, the low, melodious kindness of her voice exposed his wants, his dreams, a wife, a home. His blood ran brighter through his veins. He took her upturned face in his hands, his breath going shallow. If things were different, this girl, this woman, could be his, the only woman who'd ever penetrated his self-reliance and made him aware of his own needs. She brought wholeness to him, healing to him.

She closed the gap between them.

Wind whispered through the pines and cedars as he grazed his lips along hers. He trailed his mouth along her cheek and down the warm softness of her neck. He drew in the sweetness of her lips. But it wasn't right, and he pushed away. He may be a lot of things, but his father had taught him to be an honest man. By kissing her, he was saying he wanted to marry her. And he could never marry Sofi.

He rose to his feet and braced his shoulder against the trunk of the pine, where the bark jabbed through his shirt.

She stood behind him. The feel of her palm resting against the taut muscles of his back made him shiver.

"Neil." Her voice broke. "Please tell me the truth."

He shut his eyes. As in surgery, a deep cut brought pain, but eventually that cutting brought renewed life. The image summoned a bitter chuckle, but at least it helped him force his face into the semblance of a smile. "I've done it again—acted the cad. Sure, 'twas only a kiss to say goodbye, Sofi. Nothing more." He worked hard at keeping his face stiff to not reveal how the rejection in her eyes was shredding his resolve. Looking away from her to the mountains cresting like blue waves, he listened to the wind disturb the pines. Minutes later, he glanced over his shoulder.

Her slender form in white shirtwaist and black skirt was already a speck in the distance. Sunlight glowed like gold on her hair. A moment later, she disappeared below the crown of a hill.

"Aye, Sofi, run, for I'm no good for ye. If you knew the truth, you'd not want to be tied to the likes of me."

13

Neil cast frequent glances at the back of Sofi's taut neck. In the front seat beside Kiosho, her hands fidgeting in her lap was the only movement she made.

Trina slumped against Matilda's arm, asleep.

At the base of the mountain, Neil asked Kiosho to stop. His weak excuse that he wanted to walk into town to meet Henric would conceal the fact he couldn't bear riding with them back to the homestead a moment longer. He jumped to the ground and couldn't stop his gaze from seeking Sofi's, but she refused to meet his glance.

Kiosho flicked the reins, and the wagon moved off.

Trina awakened and over the back of the seat sent Neil a ghost of a smile.

Matilda did too.

The wagon trundled down the road, taking them to the Andersson homestead.

Neil's vision blurred. So that was that. How long would it take to forget Sofi? Ach, he was a blighted fool. Blood pounded in his temples. His muscles coiled. A foot away stood a tree, and he struck his fist into it, stopping only short of breaking a bone, though blood trickled down his fingers. His lack of control over his emotions sickened him. Sure, it was a similar, shameful display the night Da died that had set it all up. Dominoes toppling, setting in motion events that sent him running to the ends of the earth.

He could still feel his hands gripping Robert

Crawford's suit lapels that night after his father had been brought to the hospital. When there was nothing more he could do, he'd turned from Da's lifeless body and run out to search Belfast for Crawford. He found him outside the fancy hotel he lived in. He'd hauled Crawford close, only inches away from the whites of the shipbuilder's startled eyes. He could still smell brandy on the man's breath. Hear his own voice barking into Crawford's face, "Because of your filthy greed, my father's dead. I'd like nothing better than to put my hands around your neck and squeeze the life out of ye."

He'd thrust Crawford from him so that the man had fallen. It was then Neil had become aware of the crowd standing around them. At the periphery of his vision...his young brother making his way through the bystanders. Jimmy had watched his every move. Heard his every word.

Now Neil braced himself with his arm outstretched to the tree. Waited for his breath to slow. If only he'd kept his emotions in check. Been a better example to Jimmy. Because of his loss of control that night and that stupid threat he'd uttered, he'd lost everything.

The road into town with an assortment of clapboard houses beckoned. A white corniced steeple shaded the roadway, where purple clematis trailed along a split-rail fence. At the side of the church, Neil found an out-of-the-way spot beneath a massive cedar. He sat at the base of the trunk. His head slumped to his chest. A whiff of biscuits baking brought memories of home. He tried to picture what Jimmy was doing at this moment, but couldn't. Maybe that was just as well. Thinking of Jimmy only tightened that feel of a noose around his neck.

Memories of his father's face slid past, too fleeting to grasp. The picture of Sofi's taut neck was clear enough, though. The sun inched lower, and the quietness of the Sabbath took some of the sting out of the day. He must have sat there a good hour, until footsteps trod the gravel path.

Henric stood a few feet away. "I figured you'd be at the homestead with Sofi and Trina."

Neil shaded his eyes against the sun behind Henric's head.

The big timber man measured him with a look. "Come on in. I was about to set out the songbooks."

Inside the building, the familiar smell of wood and the musky scent of hymnals met Neil. He hadn't given God much heed these last few years, but the simple task of setting books into the pockets at the back of each pew brought a strange rest to his tumbled thoughts.

With the last pew filled, Henric handed him the local newspaper. "I didn't notice until I got home from church today."

Under yesterday's date the headline blazed, "New Doctor in Town Saves Life of Local Man." Neil's mouth went dry. Under the headline sat a fuzzy photograph of Sofi and him on the doctor's front porch. It was only a local paper, but he couldn't take the chance on word getting back to Ireland. Robert Crawford was an Englishman. His death was not something the British would forget.

Henric's eyes searched his. "It appears this acclaim doesn't please you."

"It's gratifying, to be sure." Neil's attempt at nonchalance didn't work.

The tall Scandinavian ran his knuckles along his chin. "Neil, if I hadn't got the impression from the first moment I met you—that you're an honorable man—I would not have let those women stay on the plateau with you for one single minute. Sofi and Trina mean the world to me." Henric's voice became grainy. "And Rosie...But you're a complication in this business I can't figure out." A shadow darkened Henric's face. "Sofi tells me you lost your father recently. I know something about grief, watching my dear wife suffer till the cancer took her. At times I swear I felt God crying with me."

Something invisible struck Neil in the chest. The last thing he wanted was some platitude. Nothing good had come out of the grief he, Jimmy, and Mother shared.

Henric sat in the pew. "What I'm trying to say, Neil, is that I trusted you with the safety and reputations of those girls. I'm asking you to trust me."

"I only came by to tell you I'll be heading out tonight."

Sunlight shone through stained-glass windows casting tints of red, blue, and yellow on the far wall. The reverend entered from the door to the garden and smiled at them as he walked up the aisle to sort his notes at the pulpit.

Henric's shrewd gaze didn't waver from Neil. "Sorry to hear that. You fit into this community just fine, and there's more than one who would be your friend."

The church doors opened and the first of the evening worshippers came in, along with the organist. Moments later, the notes of the hymn "Immortal, Invisible" belted out, and the church began to fill.

Henric gripped Neil's hand in farewell and left him to take a pew up front.

Neil readied himself to leave, when Sofi's voice carried to him on a warm current of air.

At the back of the church, she spoke to several women while searching for a place to sit. Her hesitant smile dissolved when she saw him.

He'd hurt her enough already, but couldn't summon the will to walk past her and out the door. Instead, he sank into the pew.

At the pulpit, Henric led the hymn sing.

Neil stood when everyone else did and let the music whirl around him.

But the Bible story was too simple—King David running from Saul, who'd accused him of treachery. David couldn't go home. The pastor read from a psalm, "When my spirit was overwhelmed within me...refuge failed me...I cried unto thee, O Lord: I said, Thou art my refuge."

Neil sank his chin on his clenched fist. In the biblical story, the dominoes of King David's life had also toppled because of the treachery of another. It was true his own threat on Robert Crawford's life had set it all up. The threat he'd made under the madness of grief would poison his soul until the day he died. But as with King David, it was the treachery of another that forced him to run. It was his foolish, brash, bullheaded younger brother who'd put into action what Neil had only uttered.

It was Jimmy who'd plunged the knife into Robert Crawford.

The congregation stood for the benediction.

Neil tried to catch a glimpse of Sofi. He started to make his way toward her, but the congregation filled the aisle. A small child stood in the crush, and he lifted her up and set her on a pew. The child's mother smiled and reached for Neil's hand. A chorus of voices rang, all congratulating him, hoping he'd stay in town. Neil caught the eye of Dr. Enckell, who sent him a smile of approval. Neil waded through the press as Sofi reached the door. In a minute, she'd be gone. The clamor of the small mob following Neil rose in crescendo when he got to the back of the church.

Sofi waited on the boardwalk. Her eyes glistened, but he wasn't sure if she was holding back tears or anger.

The sun hung suspended on the horizon between mountains when it seemed the entire town burst from the church with him. A flash of sunlight glinted off a metal sign from across the street.

With the sun's aura blinding him, Neil made out the silhouette of a man clutching a bag. He felt a premonition before his sight cleared. The coppery tones of the setting sun lit the man's face where he stood on the wooden boardwalk under the sign to Elfreda's Hotel.

A young man, slender-boned like himself, not overly tall, pushed his dark hair back from his forehead to show a widow's peak.

It was like looking into a youthful mirror. It always had been.

14

All through service, Sofi barred tears from falling. She could trust Neil with a thousand things, but not with her heart. She'd been nothing more than a stolen kiss.

As he'd plowed his way through the congregation, his eyes had been fixed on her. Now Neil's gaze shifted to something across the street. Instantly, his stance became watchful.

She followed his line of sight.

A young man, a younger copy of Neil, crossed the road.

Neil met him in the middle.

The congregation eddied past the two of them like a stream around a stone.

"Jimmy." Neil's face twisted with conflicting emotions.

The younger man wrapped his arms around Neil so that they swayed together.

She put a hand to her mouth. *His brother.*

"You look terrible," Jimmy said to Neil.

Neil gave him a wan smile. "Aye, and I suppose I missed you too." He set Jimmy at arm's length. "What are you doing here?"

Jimmy puffed out his chest. "Sure, there's nothing wrong with me wanting to see my brother. And like you, I want to make me fortune."

"Make your fortune? What about Alison? The child's not due for another few weeks." Neil dropped his hands from Jimmy's shoulders. "Surely you didn't leave her alone with a babe coming?"

Breath caught at the back of Sofi's throat.

Neil's hands fisted at his sides. He'd freely volunteered that he had a brother. If Alison was a sister, why had he not mentioned her? Alison must be the reason for the lines of despair on Neil's face.

Sulkiness overtook Jimmy's grin. "Alison's fine at home with Ma. Stop your nagging. I'm hoping to get work and send money home to them."

"If you'd wanted to leave Ireland…and come here all along…why? Why did you let me take the—" Neil glanced over his shoulder at Sofi.

Her heart lurched at what she thought was longing, but Neil pulled Jimmy away from her hearing, and she stood frozen outside the church. The way Neil ushered his brother away from her made it clear. He might steal a kiss from her, but he'd never share his life.

~*~

Neil firmed his jaw at the sound of Sofi snapping the reins and the buggy driving off. He and Jimmy walked along the boardwalk, and he watched as Sofi's buggy disappeared at the crossroads. Sitting on the bench outside the closed drugstore, he sank his head into his hands. He heard only half of Jimmy's voyage across the Atlantic and his long train trip from New York to Washington State.

Neil shook his head to clear it. When would he get control of *his* life? Every time he thought he'd taken the reins, something would come along, and his life charged off like a spooked horse. As Jimmy talked, the fact broke through that his young brother experienced a much more enjoyable voyage than Neil had. But then Jimmy had not had to run to this land like a hunted animal.

Neil cut in. "Why'd you come?"

Jimmy's expression shifted to a childish glower. "It shouldn't always be you who gets the good things in life."

"The good things in life?" Neil sputtered. "There's nothing good about having to leave my home, my life, everything I'd worked for, and run with the police on my tail. That coming from you, Jimmy, is..." He stepped away to settle his breathing.

The moonlight showed a feverish brilliance in Jimmy's eyes. "You've started a new life here. That's all I want. You had it all back home, the big man with the education, becoming a doctor and all. When we got your letter, I thought this was my chance."

"Jimmy, I did what I did so you could marry Alison, be a decent father to that baby of yours, and take care of Mother. You did marry Alison, didn't you?"

"Aye, I married her."

"I would have taken care of all of you the rest of my days, but my hands are tied. You, Jimmy, above all people know how tied they are."

"Ach, you're building that up too much. Sure, you're safe here. And you never had it as hard as me. After you became a doctor, you didn't have to breathe in steel dust every day like Da and I did. If I'd stayed in Ireland, there would be nothing for me but the shipyard."

Neil drew back. "In time I could have saved enough to send you and Alison to the States, if that's what you wanted. But Robert Crawford dying stripped me of all ability to do anything."

"Well, Crawford deserved to die, didn't he." Jimmy's voice turned husky. "And will ye not be bringing that up. Your letter said you were in a place that was building a bridge. Sure, you told me about the steel work, so I packed me bag that night."

Neil rubbed the throbbing pain at his temple. That one stupid letter he'd sent.

The police may not have gotten hold of it, but this was almost as bad.

"When'd you arrive?"

"A few days ago." Jimmy's good humor returned in an instant. "I got off the train in Seattle, caught another to some place called Skykomish. A farmer gave me a ride to this place."

Neil formed a fist and strode down the street. His brother sprinted to catch up. Neil grasped him by the shoulders. "Did anyone follow you? Any policemen?"

Jimmy ran his tongue over his lips. "No. I'm sure of it."

A dead weight settled in Neil's stomach. "What happened after I left home?"

"The police were always coming around. They wanted to know all about us."

"What else?"

"They asked about...your scalpels."

Neil stalked away until the boardwalk ended and the worn path took him to the outskirts of town. Wind moaned through the gorge, through the steel skeleton of the bridge.

His brother uttered a thin mumble. "You're worrying too much. The English coppers won't come all the way over the Atlantic."

"You know very well Robert Crawford had friends in high places."

"Aye, friends like him who care only about making money off the backs of others." Jimmy's voice rose. "Da tried to tell Crawford we needed safety measures in the yard. It's because of him rushing the job that Da's dead."

"Negligent as he was, he didn't deserve to die the way he did."

Jimmy stood in front of Neil and stabbed his fingers into his own chest. "Well, I know inside here that he did deserve that. An eye for an eye."

Coyotes yipped and howled in the distance. Whatever prey they hunted, Neil felt its fear.

He lifted his head, taking in the stubborn set to his brother's mouth. His gaze dropped to Jimmy's hand that had used a knife to rob a man of his life. Dear God, had he done the right thing by protecting his brother? All he'd wanted was to stop the pain his family were feeling over Da's passing. Give Jimmy a chance to live a decent life to make up for the one he'd taken.

He laid an unsteady hand on Jimmy's shoulder. "It's not safe for me to stay here. Scotland Yard can't ignore the murder of an Englishman in Ireland. And the United States has extradition laws with Great Britain."

"I just got here, and you tell me you're leaving." The whine returned to Jimmy's voice.

"You took a chance coming here, because I never intended staying here at all. I should have been on a ship months ago."

"If that's the case, why are you still here?" Jimmy's brow wrinkled. "Is it something to do with that girl, the one standing outside the church waiting for ye?"

"Never you mind about her. I'll see you settled, and in a few days be off. A few days won't hurt me."

"So, do you have a place here in this town? Ach, you've done well for yourself, haven't ye, Neil, old son." Jimmy picked up his bag and followed him with the eagerness of a child.

But Jimmy wasn't a child. All Neil's life, he'd looked after him, and now he wished his brother was anywhere in the world but following one step behind him.

"I have no place of my own," he said. "Only a safe place we can use for a day or two. Then I'm gone. Do ye hear me, Jimmy? You'll have to be a man and look after yourself."

15

The sun had set by the time Sofi pulled up to the homestead. Her intention had been to put the horses away for the night. That was, until she reached the drive leading to the house.

Charles's dark green limousine was parked outside.

Kiosho rushed out of the barn as if he'd been waiting for her. "You want me to get Henric?"

She gave a quick shake of her head and climbed down from the buggy.

On the darkened porch Charles's cigar flared.

If he expected her to act like a truant child, he had another thing coming. She strode past him into the house.

He followed into the front room.

Her gaze flitted about the room, to her grandmother's red-flocked wallpaper, the crystal droplets fringing the lampshades. Here too, Charles had made himself at home, his satchel open, papers strewn over her grandmother's lace-clad table. He narrowed his eyes through a haze of smoke. "Well, I've made eight or nine visits to the bridge this summer, and here you were under my nose the whole time. You certainly caused your mother and me no end of worry." His stiff attempt at a smile failed. "Come now, Sofi, I don't expect a fulsome welcome, but some civility is in order."

The strength of her voice surprised her. "You'll

receive civility if you promise to be civil in return."

"That's a bit uncalled for."

"Not when the last time I saw you, you were convincing my mother that Trina needed a sanatorium. As it is, Trina is fine. Made an amazing recovery in fact."

"Is that so? Your sister is upstairs with Matilda. Apparently old Matilda feels it necessary to barricade Trina from me."

"Can you blame them?"

"Enough, Sofi. I only want to arrange for your safe travel home. The sooner you and Trina go back to Seattle, the better."

Home? It would be good to get home and see their mother, especially if her concerns for Mama were real. But could she trust Charles to give her no more trouble over Trina?

Her gaze fell to the papers on the table. With a pang, she recognized the blueprints for the bridge. She tenderly touched the drawings as if they would bring her father back for a moment. The times she would work out the mathematics and bring it to him to see his face flood with pride.

Charles's voice broke in. "With the inaugural crossing of the bridge only two days off, I have back-to-back meetings in town, a dinner tomorrow night with the state representative, as well as representatives of the railroad, so I'll have my chauffeur take you to Skykomish where you can catch the train to Seattle."

"Trina is fine where she is, Charles. There's no need to discuss this further. Especially since we have something else to discuss."

"And what would that be, Sofi dear?"

She held on to her anger. "A man fell from a

riveting platform yesterday. He could have been killed. Why are you not implementing the safety measures Papa insisted on?"

Charles waved a hand as if dismissing an annoying fly. "Not necessary. Nor is it law. Besides, the men work much faster without harnessing—"

"I also found out yesterday none of the compensation money for our injured workers has been released, nor has that for the Johanson widow. What's holding up this money?"

"In all fairness, Sofi, as the design company we're not obligated to pay any compensation. That's Wetzle's responsibility as the builder, and so are the safety measures. This was something your father and I often disagreed on."

She couldn't help the rise in her voice. "Papa also never wanted to do business with Wetzle Steel."

Charles leveled his gaze at her under lowering brows. "I'll tell you the same thing I told your father time and again. There's more money to be made in the building of structures than in the design, but all he ever cared about was the artistry. He had no need to make money. Your grandfather left him plenty."

She thumped the arm of her chair. "Exactly. And the money for the trust fund was my father's. Andersson money. Not Andersson and Bolton's. Ethically, Charles, we must provide for the people hurt while building our structures. Better still, keep them safe."

He slashed a hand through the air. "Sofi, when your father died...there were financial difficulties. Certain liabilities. I had no choice but to use a great deal of the company's capital. To keep us out of the red."

"What do you mean? Papa told me a year ago of the company's financial stability." Heat pulsed through her. "I want to see the books."

"See the books?" Charles blinked slowly.

"Mama inherited my father's half of the business, but she was in no fit state when Trina and I left in June. I think it only fair I step in and help her with her responsibilities until...she's well."

His gaze shifted imperceptibly to his left. "Your mother is perfectly capable of taking care of her own affairs. Why, I have dinner with her every evening."

"If that's the case, why didn't she come with you?" Even with grief drowning their mother, surely she would want to see for herself that Trina was well.

Charles's chuckle held no amusement. "Sofi, you are not a partner in the firm."

Her gaze dropped to the blueprints again, to the computations down the side of the drawing. Her eye snagged on the corner of the page, drifting to the mathematics again. That equation...

Charles sat opposite her. "It's as if you don't trust me. But I'll show you the accounts when we get back to Seattle, if you wish. I want nothing more than your peace of mind, dear."

If he said *dear* one more time, she'd scream. To calm herself, she shuffled the blueprints with one finger. "I'll consider going back to Seattle, Charles. I'll leave early in the morning if you instruct the office staff to show me those books tomorrow. Then I'm coming back here to the valley."

Charles followed her gaze to the blueprints. His nostrils flared as his mouth became a solid white line. He leaned across the space between them and stuffed the blueprints into the satchel, taking little care whether they tore in the process. "Fine, Sofi, fine. I'll see those accident victims receive the full due your father specified. Once this bridge is finished and we're paid, well, then we'll have the funds." He snapped his satchel shut. "Will that make you happy?"

"I insist on proper safety measures. And I want to see the ledgers."

"Sofi, please go home and take care of your mother and sister. It would do her a world of good to see Trina doing so well, as you say she is." He hurried to the door with his satchel under his arm.

"How strange, Charles, that you should say that when only a few months ago, you told me I was not of an age to make decisions for them. What has changed, I wonder?" She waited as he hesitated at the threshold to the porch. "Aside from that, the ledgers, Charles. I want to see the ledgers."

A flush mottled his neck. "Sofi, stop worrying over things your father never meant for you to be concerned about. Quite frankly, it's none of your business." Charles dashed down the steps, got into his car, and motored along the driveway.

The brass lamps on his car shone in the dark as she watched it turn toward town. What had changed? In Seattle, he wanted to control her. Here in the valley, he wanted her to remain in Seattle. A small sigh came from behind her, and she whirled.

Trina was sitting at the bottom of the staircase, and she held herself the way she had been doing since Papa died.

Sofi's heart moved to her throat. It appeared Trina had relapsed. *Oh, please, God.* The day weighed down on Sofi's shoulders. With her altercation with Charles, and now if Trina was slipping away from her again, she wanted to close the door and never open it again.

But Trina stood and slipped her arm through Sofi's, watching Charles's car drive out of sight. Her chin lifted, but her voice matched Sofi's weariness. "Don't let him scare you, Sofi. The enemy's all talk. Just talk."

16

With her back against a carved post on the verandah, Sofi twisted her hair at the back of her head and secured it with a comb. All morning, a weak sun labored to burn off the fog. Though her sister was much better today, bad dreams had plagued her last night. The swirling mists of Sofi's own mind hadn't allowed her to rest either. Things Charles said...and hadn't said...the blueprints...something missing...but as morning crept toward afternoon, the haze lifted. The bridge became visible.

Trina came out, holding a plate of just-out-of-the-oven oatmeal cookies, and they sat together on the top step.

"I can't believe it, Trina. You're your old self again. I missed you."

That vacant look Sofi had become familiar with these past few months clouded Trina's gaze for a moment, though it was soon replaced by the lucid pain of sorrow. "I am here with you, but I'll never be the same. Papa's dying changed me."

"It changed us all."

Trina dipped her head. Her unbound hair fell, covering her face and exposing the vulnerable nape of her neck. "I'm not sick, Sofi. Nor am I a kid, even though you protect me like I am."

"You're no kid. Not with the bravery you showed the night Papa died."

"But I used to be a brat up to then. Charging in

where angels would shudder. Didn't I?"

There was no sense denying it. "Papa was a bit too lenient with you at times."

"And Mama?"

Sofi pulled Trina close. "Papa made things too easy for all of us. Grandmama said all the starch got washed out of Mama when she left the valley. Hardships make us strong, I guess."

"I don't feel stronger, just sad." Trina lifted a languid hand and let it drop to her lap. The house sheltered them from the humid wind, creating a pocket of air that captured the scent of honeysuckle. "There's something wrong with Mama too, isn't there, Sofi?"

"I want to go to Seattle, bring her here, but..."

Clouds hid the sun, and the humid wind divided the corn into green swathes. Something cloyed at the back of Sofi's mind, sticking to her thoughts like this moist heat stuck to her skin. Whatever it was, it eluded her. But her mind stumbled on something yesterday evening, sitting with Charles. The arc of the bridge drew her eye again.

"I'm not the only one who's clammed up, Sofi."

Tears pricked at the back of Sofi's eyes. "I wish I had some of your courage, like you, charge in where angels would shudder."

Trina's gaze tracked to where Sofi's rested. "It's your bridge, Sofi. The sailing skills Papa gave me were just for fun. I could be as daring as I wanted. But he never let you do anything real with all the learning he gave you."

Sofi held back a grunt of amusement. "You call it my bridge."

"It should be you down there in charge, not Charles."

"I used to worry that I was too bossy. Mama used to scold me for always trying to solve everybody's problems, especially when you got into trouble."

"I think it's time you stopped taking care of me and Mama. I'm thinking Papa was as wrong about you as he was about me."

Her little sister had grown up. But if she stopped taking care of Trina, how was she to fill her days? What was she to do with her energy, the desire to do something with her life?

"Sofi, you're smart. That's something I don't have. Oh, I used to be able to race a yacht, but there's not much call for that. There is a need to build bridges. Just because you're a woman shouldn't stop you." Trina's dimples emerged with her smile. "Come on, I dare you." Though she spoke lightly, her smile melted. Her newfound strength was fading fast.

Sofi's chest tightened. "You may not need me anymore, but there's still Mama."

"Leave Mama to me. It's time I took care of someone, and you do what you need to do."

Sofi turned to look at the huge steel structure. Her bridge beckoned.

Kiosho had also urged her to go down there.

What was it about those drawings in Charles's satchel that bothered her? Something...down in the right-hand corner...something missing. The truth blazed and she held her breath. The blueprints didn't bear her father's approving initial. None of the drawings she'd seen last night had. Her designs for the bridge had been altered. The math changed. She'd gotten a glimpse, but in talking about the compensation money, she'd failed to look closer. Why had she not gone down to the bridge before this? She half rose.

Last night, Charles said he'd be busy with meetings in town all day. A dinner tonight. He'd not be in the company Pullman today at all. She could drive over there. With any luck slip into the office and look at the working blueprints. There was no time to lose. The inaugural crossing was scheduled for tomorrow.

"Sofi, what is it?" Trina pulled at her sleeve.

"I'm not sure, but I've got to go down to the bridge."

"I'll come with you."

She hugged Trina to her. "You may think you're a hundred percent, but you're not ready to charge down any hills yet."

Trina slanted a look at Sofi, with a light in her eyes Sofi hadn't seen for a while, that mixture of mischief and mystery, and courage. "All right. But promise me, Sofi." Her tired smile stretched. "Promise me you'll do something that I *would* do."

17

Metallic dust clung to the hem of Sofi's skirt at the bridge site. The reek of burning coal in the riveters' forges covered up the fresh scent of the valley. Hammering punctured the air as the riveting gang worked feverishly to finish the structure.

She didn't like the answers Charles had given her last night, or the lack of them. Charles told them little of his past, but he'd never hidden the fact he liked fine things. When her father bought the blue Cadillac, Charles bought the same in green. This past year, Charles seemed to have increased his personal wealth. Or was the money he used to build his new home in Seattle's hills out of company funds?

That wasn't the urgency now, though. She had to see for herself if Charles had replaced her designs for the bridge with his own. Had he left enough of a safety factor?

Near the abutment, the Pullman car sat on a spur track running parallel to the main line. The chief engineer was far enough away, directing a team of riveters. She was about to step up to the Pullman but stopped. A man on the bridge looked down at her.

Neil's brother. He flicked a pocketknife open and shut. The blade was not a blade, but a sort of tool. A spike, six inches long and curved. A marlinspike. Jimmy didn't brace himself against a girder, apparently confident on a slender riveting platform. He tilted his head, seemingly as puzzled about her as she was about him.

If he held answers to her questions about Neil, she didn't dare ask. There was always this Alison. An intense spat of hammering pounded the truth into her heart. Whether Neil stayed or went, it made no difference to her life.

A workman called out to Jimmy, then measured the depth of the hole in the eyebeam. With a hand signal, he sent the message to the heater standing by the small, portable forge. They needed rivets six inches long. Jimmy hailed the man with a raised hand and bent to pick up a set of tongs.

She wanted to stop the work right then and there until she could arrange for harnesses for them. But she had to find the proof first, proof to stop the work completely. And the chief could come back any minute to the Pullman car.

She gripped the iron railing, stepped on the foot rail, and pulled herself up to the vestibule. Inside the Pullman, it was as if Papa would walk through the maple-paneled corridor at any moment. In the patina of the mahogany table, she saw her own reflection and that of the white quilted silk on the ceiling. And there on the table, the working blueprints. Her eye travelled to the bottom corner. Just as she thought, her father's initial wasn't there. She checked the date. These were not the drawings she had finished.

Through the window, she could see the chief engineer make a beeline for the Pullman. There was no time to study these blueprints. She rolled up the drawings, stuffed them into the bag she'd brought, and hurried off the vestibule. On her way off site, she stopped at one of the barrels holding scrap metal and retrieved a sample.

"Sofi?" Neil's voice startled her in the midst of hissing sparks and pounding steel. The area around his mouth was white from the hard compression of his jaw.

"I thought you were leaving." Holding nothing back of the rawness she felt, she slipped the steel sample into her bag.

"I'm only here to help my brother get a job." Neil glanced at the bridge as if to confirm he had a valid reason for being here.

"I saw him just now. Though we've never met properly, it's obvious he's your flesh and blood. It appears he's staying, at least for a while, but what about you?" At the hurt on his face she regretted the harshness of her tone.

"I'm only staying a day or two, until Jimmy gets settled, then I'll be on—"

"Yes, on your way, Neil. You'll see your brother settled here, yet you're planning on going to who knows where. All those weeks up on the plateau—I thought at least we were friends."

His Irish accent took on a husky lilt. "Sofi, you're a beautiful, strong, intelligent woman. You don't need the likes of me around."

"Why, Neil? What are the likes of you?" She put into words the thoughts she'd tried to smother for weeks. "You had to leave Ireland, didn't you?"

He sucked in a breath. "Aye."

His simple admission left her stunned. "What did you do that was so terrible?" A horrible truth glimmered. "Something went wrong. Someone died. One of your patients."

"No patient of mine died because of any error on

my part. At least I don't carry that burden."

"It's something to do with your brother."

"I've told you all I can, Sofi." Neil took her elbow and walked her to the buggy.

"You never did tell me how your father died. Or speak of anyone else...in your family." She couldn't bring herself to say the name *Alison*.

He looked back at the bridge. "My father was a riveter, like Jimmy. He fell from the scaffolding on a ship to the ground fifty feet below."

"When?" She touched his arm, wanting his arms around her like they had been yesterday. Even now, when he seemed to have more secrets than she'd known.

"My da died this past spring. There was a man who could have done more for the safety of men like my father, but didn't bother because it would only cost money."

"Will you stay at Henric's until you leave?"

His gaze dropped to the ground. "That's the other thing, Sofi. We stayed at the cabin last night, but now Jimmy's been hired, he'll live in the quarters for the riveting gang. Do you mind if I stay there another night?"

"Then you'll be on your way?"

He gave a short nod.

Some horrible offense hung over his head. She didn't trust herself to share her own fears with him over the bridge. Right now, she couldn't bear his nearness. Nor could she ask him outright who Alison was. "Stay at the cabin as long as you want, Neil. I have no use for it any longer."

~*~

Neil let Sofi go. He turned back to the bridge to assure himself that Jimmy no longer needed him, but he couldn't fool himself. It was only to give him a minute to try and shut out the hunger that Sofi's presence stirred within him. Though watching the riveter's ballet of throwing white-hot steel always made his stomach harden to a lump, at least it distracted him.

He picked out his brother from among the men and expelled a long sigh. On the bridge deck, or on one of those meager platforms hanging over the side, one slip, one fumble...from that height...and a man could die.

On the deck, Jimmy rapped his elongated tongs against the cone-shaped catcher can, waiting for the man known as the heater. The heater sent Jimmy a nod and thrust the peg of steel into the portable cast-iron forge. When the peg of metal glowed to a molten white, he pitched it forward. Jimmy caught it in the catcher can and inserted the glowing rivet into a hole in the girder. With the same concentration Neil would use with a scalpel, Jimmy waited for the bucker to place his buckling tool against the head of the rivet and for the riveter to hammer it home.

Their father had been equally expert as a riveter on the ships in Belfast.

A whistle blared for the end of the day, and Neil met Jimmy as he came off the abutment. Together they went down to the riverbank strewn with rocks and boulders, close to the soft patch of ground where Gunnar had fallen. If Gunnar had fallen a few feet in any direction...

Neil shook his head.

But Gunnar lived. As if a giant hand guided him to fall in a safe place. But that was nonsense. He believed in science, not in God.

The work crew moved in clusters toward the water.

Sunlight usually made the stones shimmer under the green ribbon of river, but not today. Clouds rolled in.

Neil hunkered beside Jimmy at the base of a jack pine. "Now you're here in Washington, it's probably good that you are. As soon as you can, though, promise me you'll bring Mother and Alison and your wee one over."

"Will ye stop harping like an old woman. I'll bring them over when I have the money."

Neil ran a hand around the back of his neck. "Look, we both have a chance for a fresh start. I have to start over somewhere else, where the police and newspapers can't catch up to me, but you can make a good life for yourself here. Promise me you'll live by Da's example."

"I've already said I will." In a nervous gesture, Jimmy pulled a pocketknife from his trousers and flicked it open, exposing a blade.

Neil couldn't take his eyes off the pocketknife. It was the one Jimmy'd won in a bet a short while before Da died. Jimmy flicked the knife open. Open and shut, open and shut, unaware of Neil's mesmerized stare. Jimmy gouged at the wooden stump he sat on. A sick feeling invaded Neil's gut at the sight of that slender, flat blade.

Jimmy saw his disgust and turned red to his ears, snapping the knife shut and stuffing it in his pocket.

Neil stomped a few feet away until his breathing

settled. He'd never asked. Never wanted to know. But of course, that had to be the knife that killed Robert Crawford.

18

Kiosho followed Sofi into her grandfather's study.

Sofi placed a set of scales on the desk. She dabbed a handkerchief to her moist neck. "How's Trina?"

"She's gone off somewhere with Henric. Just up and left, the two of them, half an hour ago."

With her sister out of the way, Sofi could concentrate on the task at hand. She removed the steel sample from her bag. Her father had held a longstanding dislike of Wetzle's foundry. Their company's relationship with Wetzle had been Charles's domain, which Papa had argued with him over. If she suspected Charles of changing her designs and mismanaging the accounts, was it possible he'd gone a step further? Cut costs on materials?

Kiosho adjusted the scales to weigh the steel rod as if it was fifty years ago when he and her grandfather panned for gold on the Fraser River.

She swept her hair off her shoulder. A proper analysis was needed to determine if this steel had been blasted long enough in the furnace. Only half aware of Kiosho leaving, she weighted the blueprints down and sharpened a pencil. She pulled a slide rule and sheet of paper toward her and bent over the blueprints. Three-hundred-foot span...thicker steel in this section required to carry the tension...her pencil scratched as algorithms and formulas blossomed on the page.

Matilda's and Kiosho's voices rippled from the kitchen as they canned peaches. The afternoon waned, but Sofi bent over the blueprints again and redid the computations. A third time. A sixth. Each time, her calculations gave her the same answer. She slumped back in the chair. Her creation that she'd dreamed of for years needed thicker steel in various places. Charles had indeed changed her designs.

Sofi crossed her arms and strolled out of the house, down to the cornfield. Half a mile away, the bold and ethereal strokes of her pencil stood tangible against Washington's twilight sky. A thing of beauty, but it had no strength. It would fall. Maybe not right away, but one day in a few months, a year, or ten. The inaugural crossing was scheduled for tomorrow. Railroad men and politicians were gathering in town, but none of them would believe that her father had taught her at home what others took years to learn in a college.

She rubbed her hand down the side of her skirt. If she could find the original drawings with her father's initials, she could show them to the head of the Great Northern Railroad, or the state representative. Maybe Charles kept a copy of them in the safe in the Pullman car. If he was attending the dinner this evening, she could go there now.

Grabbing her bag containing the stress computations and steel sample, she raced out of the study to the barn. Ignoring the buggy, she headed for Papa's limousine. From the corner of her eye, a long-legged, black-and-white shape loped along the porch.

Odin jumped into the car and gave her one glance before staring through the windshield.

Laughter erupted from Sofi in a gulp, and she leaned her head against the dog before starting the car.

Matilda darted out of the house.

Sofi called out as she drove away, "There's something I've got to find in the Pullman car."

~*~

The cabin echoed with memories. Neil swung the axe, let it plunge into a log.

If Sofi ever came up here, she'd find this wood stacked and ready for her.

With the heel of his hand, he wiped the sweat from his eyes. He'd wash, eat some of the food Kiosho had brought, and wait for sleep. If sleep would come. Earlier, he'd dissuaded Jimmy from coming by. The thought of Jimmy and that pocketknife—opening and closing, opening and closing—came between them, gouging from his heart the last sliver of innocent brotherly affection.

Night edged in. From the bluff, he watched lights twinkle in the Andersson homestead. He wanted to go down there, but he couldn't bear to see that growing mistrust in Sofi's eyes. He lifted his cup of tea and lowered it again as beams coming from an automobile's headlamps lit the road.

The vehicle neared the crossroads and, at a fair clip, turned in the direction of the old wooden bridge.

Throwing the tin cup aside, he started down the hill. The Andersson barn was empty except for the wagon and buggy. Nothing in the stalls but the horses. The limousine was gone.

He ran up the porch steps and banged on the door. He waited. Why was it taking so long?

Finally, Matilda held the door open.

"Is Sofi here?" He had no time for niceties.

"She left the house not fifteen minutes ago."

"Where's she going at this time of night?"

Matilda's mouth tightened. "She said she was going over to the railcar at the bridge. I'll have you know, I don't care for her running off in the dark like that."

"What would she be going there for?"

Kiosho raced down the front hall from the kitchen to join them. "All we know is she is worried about her bridge. Something about blueprints."

"What do you mean hers?" His voice came out rough.

Kiosho pointed at the bridge now shrouded in darkness. "Sofi designed that. It's hers."

Neil stuck his hands into his back pockets and pushed out a hard breath. He knew she liked to design bridges. He'd encouraged her to go to school and learn. But that bridge, so complicated and beautiful, was hers? How true her talent really was. Why had he not seen it before? Her sketchpad was filled with the minutiae of detail.

By now, she'd almost be at the Pullman car.

He turned and took the road at a run. If he crossed the new bridge, he could meet up with her on the other side.

19

Light from the shed in the new railway switching yard spilled out, along with the smell of baked beans and coffee.

Sofi stopped the car beside the Pullman.

The hum of a mouth organ floated on the humid wind. Men's voices droned around cooking fires and covered the crunch of her footsteps on the gravel siding.

She pulled up to the vestibule and used Papa's spare ring of keys that he'd kept at the homestead. After struggling with several, one of them unlocked the door.

In the main bedroom, she found Charles's silver-backed brush and comb on the dresser. His clothes hung in the closet, but his satchel was not to be found. She hunched down beside the bed and prayed he hadn't changed the combination. With a click, the safe opened. Invoices, letters to the railroad, stacks of cash bills, bags of coin, but no blueprints. A clock chimed eight.

Her small flame of hope snuffed out. There was no time to drive to Seattle with the hope that the original drawings might still be in her father's office on Pioneer Square.

Outside, the bridge drew her. Darkness cloaked her presence as she picked her way over railway ties to the abutment and out to the middle of the deck.

Clouds shifted. Only a sliver of moon and stars

gave a trace of light to see where ties ended and empty spaces began. Sixty feet below, the tributary rushed.

Was she deluding herself, searching for her original blueprints? For so long her need to craft and shape refused to die, so that tonight she couldn't ignore Kiosho's or her headstrong sister's urging to lay claim to her work, even if it meant failure. It wasn't cold, but she shivered. Standing on this high bridge, she had nothing to hold on to but steel ribbon of triangulated trusses. A gentle voice seemed to speak in her spirit. *Your duty includes the dreams I give you.*

Were her aspirations God's business? A quiet joy started in the center of her being. This *was* her bridge.

A noise startled her. Footsteps on the deck came toward her. In the inky night, whoever it was didn't speak. But ten feet from her, she recognized a white shirtfront, a white scarf looped around someone's neck.

A man in evening clothes. It had to be Charles walking across the bridge. The dinner must have finished early. It was only Charles, yet her pulse skipped. Why didn't he speak? If he had nothing to be ashamed of, he'd call out. People only hid who they were when they'd done something wrong. Like Neil.

She turned to go back, to get off the bridge before he reached her. Her intent had been to avoid him, but now the best she could do was get to the abutment and talk her way out of why she was here at such an odd hour.

Heartbeats later, Charles stood at her side and took hold of her elbow. Too many quiet seconds slipped by as the river churned below. "What are you doing here, Sofi?" He didn't seem to care that she had no answer. A tinge of bitterness tainted his tone. "A little congenial company would be nice. I've had quite a night, I don't mind telling you. For months, Great Northern wouldn't release a penny until the bridge was opened. Now that event is at hand, the bridge committee is dragging their feet in making their payment. The town wants this. The state wants that. Perhaps now you can appreciate the bind I'm in."

"You talked with the man in charge of the railroad tonight?" She took a few steps.

"He's gone back to Skykomish with his secretary. He'll be coming up by train for the inaugural crossing." He tilted a look at her, his voice too soft. "Why do you ask?"

The abutment was still several feet away. "No reason."

He stopped them both. "You were seen in the Pullman car today. Why, Sofi?"

The end of the bridge felt too far away. Nothing but air beneath the gaps in the ties. Nothing to guard her from the emptiness over the river. But why should she fear him? It was only Charles. Only Charles, who had allowed men to drop, perhaps to their deaths. Charles, who'd altered her bridge so that it was unsafe. Charles, who refused to let her look at the books. And he knew she knew. But he wasn't a criminal. He was her parents' colleague. All the same, she tried to pull her arm from his hold.

"What are you up to, my girl?"

"This is a ridiculous place for a conversation." She forced a light tone.

"Also a ridiculous place for a young lady to come at night."

In the dark, she couldn't make out his expression. His fingers constricted above her elbow. Her pulse hammered in her ears.

Odin's bark shattered the air.

Charles jolted, but kept his hold on her.

The dog stood at the edge of the decking. His gangly shape, hardly visible in the dark, pawed the ground before the first gap in the ties.

Men around the campfires came running, their voices stabbing the night air.

Charles laughed, but she heard the nervousness beneath it. "Your dog frightened me out of my skin, Sofi. We could have fallen." He called out that all was well and walked her to the abutment. Flickering light from cooking fires lit the hard line of his mouth.

Her pulse started to slow, but Odin crouched, baring his teeth at Charles.

"Call your dog off. The stupid animal thinks I mean you harm."

She grasped Odin by the collar, but after snuffling his nose into her skirt, he growled again at Charles. With her feet on solid ground and men not far away, she wrenched her arm from Charles's grip. "I want the inaugural run cancelled. The structure isn't strong enough. A few more months—"

"My dear girl, the bridge is complete. If you want your precious accident compensations paid, then the opening must occur. We all need this."

"We do not need a bridge that isn't safe. This steel is not the thickness I—and my father—specified when we designed it. This bridge needs to be strengthened, and I'm going to see that gets done."

"My dear Sofi, you're acting like a spoiled child." Charles's normally jovial tone returned.

She doubted he'd meant her any harm on the bridge. She'd been a fool to imagine that. She swung to face him. "This bridge is my design."

"Oh, come now. You're letting your father's overindulgence make you think more of your artistic aptitudes than you ought."

They walked past the workers' sleeping cars and stood in the light from the switching yard.

Odin's hackles were still raised.

She grabbed hold of Charles's sleeve. "Think what you like, Charles. I'm going to stop you."

His wide-eyed glare reflected his cowardice. He was all bluff and bluster like Trina had said. No true power. "What's making you do such outrageous things, Sofi? First, you run away, taking your sister with you instead of leaving her to medical professionals. Now you're telling me how to run the business. Is the grief over losing your father driving you to do the unthinkable?"

What a strange thing to say. He may be a meddling fool, but fools could be dangerous. "Is that the case with you, Charles? What anxiety in your life made you act the traitor to my father? You are not the man you used to be." She shook, but not from fear as she walked the dog to the car.

If the man in charge of the railroad had gone to Skykomish, then she'd drive there tonight. He was one of the men who'd built Washington into the state it was today. He had the power to make men listen, and she had to make him listen to her, original blueprints or not.

20

Sofi's limousine turned on the road in the opposite direction of town when Neil reached the switching yard. He slapped his hand against his thigh. He'd missed her by minutes. But it was her at the wheel going with the velocity of a slingshot. And if he saw correctly, she had the dog with her. There was nothing for him to do but go back to Orchard and wait for her return. He'd just begun to make his way across the bridge again when another car pulled into the yard and drove up to the Pullman.

By the light in the switching shack, two men got out of one of those fancy new speedsters. One of the men loomed over the other, his derby set at a jaunty angle. He and his companion sauntered up to the railcar as Charles stepped out of the shadows. "Well, well, Mr. Bolton, I imagine you didn't expect my company this evening."

Neil backed up. The whole scene had a clandestine quality. He slid below the bridge decking, close to the spot he'd hidden their first night in the valley.

Charles's voice held no welcome. "You didn't have to follow me from Seattle, Forbes. I'll get the money."

The man called Forbes thumbed his derby back from his forehead. "Mr. Wetzle gave me two options. One—get a satisfactory answer from you regarding payment. Or two. Well, Charles, I'd rather not go into option two at the moment."

Neil had a perfect view where he crouched within the lower cords of the bridge.

The larger man stood behind Charles and pulled Charles's arms back as he shunted him to the brink overlooking the gorge.

Neil darted deeper into the shadows.

Only a few feet away, the three men stared down at the river.

Forbes spoke over the sound of frothing water. "Quite a ways down, isn't it."

With a nod from Forbes, the other man pulled Charles back from the brink and straightened Charles's tie and lapels. Forbes reached into Charles's pocket and pulled out a cigar case, lighting up three as if they were out for a friendly chat.

The glow of Charles's cigar wavered, matching the shake in his voice. "Mr. Wetzle will have his money. Roselle Andersson signed her husband's accounts over to me."

"That will pay off merely half what you owe. There's interest on that loan."

"What more does Wetzle want? It's only a matter of a few days. And there was talk of me going into partnership with him."

Forbes steered Charles toward the Pullman car. "Though Mr. Wetzle is highly interested in your firm, you've failed to pay your debt by the date promised."

Charles sputtered. "As soon as the bridge opens and the bridge committee pays me, I can take care of what I owe."

Forbes waved his cigar, casting ribbons of red light in the dark as the three men climbed the vestibule. "So you've said. That's exactly why Mr. Wetzle wants us to stay right here. To make sure this bridge opens."

Neil didn't move until the door to the Pullman closed. He didn't know what to make of it, only that Sofi was worried about this bridge and these thugs were now a part of the equation—because thugs they were. He braced his hands on an eye bar to hoist himself up, and his fingers brushed a rough patch of steel, the same way as his first night in the valley. He rubbed the crumbling metal between his fingers. This was what worried Sofi. This was not simply a random rough patch. There was no sense waiting here, though.

Jimmy was only fifty yards away in the iron crew's lodgings.

Neil wasn't sure if he was exasperated or relieved when he found Jimmy happily crouched around the campfire listening to a lurid tale told by one of the crew.

He looked up when Neil came upon them and brought his cup along to follow Neil into the trees. As soon as Jimmy opened his mouth, whiskey-soaked breath sullied the space between them. "And here I was thinking my big brother'd had enough of me and was sailing off into the wide world without a word of goodbye."

"I need your help and can only hope you're sober enough for the job."

"You're beginning to sound like Da."

"Well, I'm beginning to think Da's stand on taking the pledge of sobriety was a wise one, especially when I see what the drink does to you."

Neil couldn't see Jimmy's face in the dark, only the outline of his bent head illuminated by the fire beyond him.

"All right, Neil."

The broken tone in his brother's voice acted like a

poultice and drew the anger out of Neil. He was no longer sure running from Ireland had been the right thing. But looking at his brother's bent head only affirmed that he could never have let his brother be hanged. "Jimmy, do you remember the girl, Sofi?"

"Aye." A smile entered Jimmy's voice. "You're sweet on her, aren't ye?"

"There's something going on with this bridge opening. I don't know what, only there are some unsavory characters hanging about with the boss man in that railway car. Sofi may come back, and I want you to keep watch. If she does, send word to me at the cabin. I'll come down straightaway."

Jimmy's head jerked up. His hand went to his pocket, to that ruddy knife no doubt. "Unsavory characters, you say?"

"Aye, Jimmy. I'm only asking you to watch. Nothing more."

21

A water tower, depot, railroad shacks flanked the tracks running through the center of Skykomish. It was almost two in the morning when Sofi arrived at the white clapboard hotel. Like all railroad towns, Skykomish never slept. Men hailed each other in the dark as they shunted a train off to a siding. It had to be too late to see the man in charge of the railroad. He must have already retired hours ago if he was to attend the crossing of the Orchard Bridge tomorrow.

The gentleman had sat at her father's table once or twice. An Irish immigrant, he had risen in Washington's hierarchy and had strong sentiments on what was best for the state. If anyone could stop the opening of the bridge, it was him.

She secured Odin in the back of the car and strode into the hotel foyer. The clatter of dishes from the restaurant met her, and the hum of voices from railway men playing poker. At the front desk, she registered, but before retiring asked that a message be given to the railroad man. She hoped she could speak with him the next morning.

The hotel clerk peered at her over a pair of bifocals. "The gentleman has already left the hotel, miss. On his way to Seattle."

She was so sure he'd be at the inaugural run. Disappointment welled. Her head ached. Her knee was stiff from driving. She'd driven all this way in the dark, creeping along winding roads around mountains just to see this man. No one else had the kind of clout he did. She felt the questions in the clerk's eyes as she backed up. When her knees reached the edge of a chair, she dropped into it and sank her head in her hand. What now?

Voices from the card room leaked out. A voice she recognized?

She rose, stiff with weariness, and peeked through the door. Blue cigarette and cigar smoke smothered the room, but one man wearing a dark broadcloth suit stood out in a room filled with roughly dressed railroad laborers. The railroad gentleman's assistant, Jonathan Simmons, sat at a table, a scowl on his features at the hand of cards he'd been dealt.

It was a long shot. Jonathan Simmons may be second in command, but he'd have to do. *Dear God, make this man listen.* She placed her palm against the door and crossed the room to greet Mr. Simmons. Her outward stillness didn't match her skittering insides as she offered her hand. "Mr. Simmons, I am representing my late father in regards to Andersson and Bolton's latest undertaking, the Orchard Valley Bridge."

He threw a jack of spades on the table, his mouth thinning at having his game disturbed, but he stood and took her hand. "*You* are representing Andersson and Bolton?"

She would not appear cowed in any way. "Fred Andersson's daughter, Sofi Andersson."

"What can I do for you...miss?"

"Can we speak somewhere private?"

Jonathan Simmons gave his hand of cards a look of regret and indicated she proceed him to a corner table.

Hiding her trembling hands below the table, she met his eyes head-on. "There are difficulties I wish to make you aware of with my father's last project."

"The new link? But it's completed."

She squared her shoulders. "I've dreamed of that bridge opening up the northern Cascade Range, but only when it is safe to do so." She kept her voice steady. "Tomorrow's inaugural must not take place. It grieves me greatly, but the current administration of my father's firm has mishandled this project. With my calculations, I am convinced that bridge will weaken."

"Miss Andersson, calm yourself. Such wild allegations on the eve of the opening."

Her fist landed on the table with a thump. "Mr. Simmons—"

"Miss Andersson!" He raised his palm to her. "We have track laid on the other side of Orchard connecting to the main line. I personally will be on that train scheduled to cross the bridge and proceed into Orchard at precisely one PM." His brows rose higher when she tried to speak. "We cannot cancel these arrangements on the whim of a delicate young lady."

She locked her gaze with his. "Mr. Simmons, that bridge is my design. I know every ounce of steel and thickness it requires. I'm convinced the combination of weak steel, changes to the original design—that with friction from a locomotive, and if a violent stream of air slams against the solid surface of a train—my bridge will not hold."

His face turned a burnished red. "You've read too many train-disaster stories."

"You must listen to me. Greater tenacity is required in the steel."

"Now, now, Miss Andersson. Leave men's work to men. I'm sure that's what your father would have wanted. I'm afraid I must bid you good night." He strode to the door.

"My calculations say we need—"

"Good evening to you, Miss Andersson."

She stood at the table, numb. Would no one listen to her? No, of course not. She could speak with a hundred men in power, and each one would see a debutante in front of them, never an engineer.

~*~

Dawn struggled to take over the night. From the plateau, Neil watched the bridge and the crossroads. Wind had risen, pushing humid air into hot gusts. At last, at five in the morning a black Tin Lizzy created a small cloud of dust as it sped at nearly twenty miles an hour up to the Andersson house. Henric's car had also left sometime yesterday, as well as Sofi's, and Neil took off, half running down the hillside to meet the Model T on its way up.

Henric leaned out the car window. "Thank God. I was coming for you."

Neil jumped in. "What's happened? If someone's sick, you'd best get Dr. Enckell."

Henric spun the car back the way he'd come. "It's you I want. I hate to say it, Neil, but it's your ability to keep a secret I need. She needs this to be kept quiet."

"She?" Neil's insides twisted. "Sofi?"

"No. Rosie. Her mother. I just left her at the homestead with Trina."

Neil breathed in the small comfort that it wasn't Sofi who needed his skills as a physician.

"Trina and I drove to Seattle yesterday," Henric continued. "It was time Rosie came back to the valley."

Neil was pleased for Sofi's sake that her mother

was here, but his concerns for her outweighed everything else. "I was looking out for you too. Sofi went off somewhere last night after talking to Charles. And there are some men with Charles that I don't like the looks of."

Henric threw him a wide look. "But you saw Sofi drive off on her own?" He clenched the steering wheel. "Let's trust the Lord all's well with her, because right now, her mother is far from fine. It's the laudanum. It's taken hold. You do what you can for Rosie, and I'll ask around and see if anyone's heard from Sofi. I'll drop by and talk to Charles too."

They reached the homestead and ran into the house to find Sofi's mother in the large front bedroom. She paced from the window to each wall of the room and back to the window.

Matilda hovered near, her arms outstretched as if to catch a child learning to walk.

Trina sat on the bed, holding out a glass of water to her mother.

Henric took Roselle's hand.

In a nervous spasm she thrust his hand off, yet was cognitive enough to give him an apologetic look. "Henric...sor—sorry." Her glassy-eyed gaze shifted away.

Neil stayed in the doorway, observing her.

She veered from the window to cross the room and threw a glance at him, but otherwise ignored his presence. "Trina." She swallowed convulsively and spoke to Henric. "Trina...should not see me this way..." At least she was perceptive enough to understand and protect her daughter.

"Mama, I want to help you." Trina tried to take her mother in her arms.

Roselle shrank from her.

Henric addressed Kiosho and the girl. "Take Trina to my place. Trina, do as your mama says. It'll help settle her." After Kiosho had taken Trina, Henric sent Neil a pleading look. "Can you do anything for Rosie?"

"When was her last dose of laudanum?"

"She thinks she took some yesterday morning, but she's not sure of the passage of time. It may have been earlier. Or later." Henric drew a hand down his face. "I drove all night, thinking it best to get her here. Trina thought so too. When we started out, she wasn't too bad."

Neil counted back. By her symptoms, Mrs. Andersson had probably calculated correctly. It would be best to assume she'd had none of the opium tincture for at least a day and a night and was in the middle of shaking loose from the drug's grip.

Roselle rubbed her arms and shivered. A moment later, she sat on the edge of a chair and ran a hand across her sweating brow. She stood and paced again. Her hair fell about her shoulders.

Neil took a step closer. "When did these symptoms begin?"

Henric scratched his head. "At first she slept restlessly, but kept crying out in dreams. She became more and more anxious, and nauseated a few times on the last leg of the trip."

"Mrs. Andersson," Neil said. "Will you be seated on the bed and let me examine you."

She drew her fist under her nose. "Where...do I know you? Yes...I remember. Policemen in Seattle. Came to the house." Her gaze clouded. "They...were looking for you. Showed me your picture."

The hairs at the back of Neil's neck stood. Were

the police on their way? Were they American? Scotland Yard? He pushed down his fears. "Mrs. Andersson, I'm Dr. Neil Galloway. I've been treating your daughter." At least it felt good to use his real name. He paid no heed to the shock on Henric's face.

Her teeth chattered. "I need my medicine."

She didn't resist when Neil helped her sit on the bed and took her wrist.

Her pulse ran like a steam engine, as did her breathing. Her pupils dilated, but at least they were equal in dilation, and her body trembled like quicksilver. This exhausted woman was only in the middle of the battle. If her withdrawal symptoms escalated to severe in the next few hours, she ran the risk of seizure, and she'd need a hospital or at least Dr. Enckell's surgery in town.

Matilda looked at him expectantly.

Neil rolled up his sleeves. "Matilda, prepare a clear broth. Bring a pitcher of water for now. Henric, my instruments are in my bag up in the cabin. Will you get them?" He leveled a look at the older man. "I'm afraid my secrets may have caught up to me. I'm asking that you trust me no matter what you hear. And...I'll be leaving as soon as I know Sofi is safe."

Henric's pause lasted several heartbeats, but he nodded.

Neil stood. "After you bring my bag, go to the pharmacist for a bottle of belladonna. I hope he'll give it to you without question, as I can't give you a prescription."

From the threshold, Henric spoke across the room to Sofi's mother. "I'll be back soon, Rosie."

Roselle's gaze flew to his.

Neil chafed her hands. "It's all right, Mrs.

Andersson. Sure, you'll be feeling better in no time at all."

22

In her room on the top floor, Sofi had only a snatch of sleep. This morning, all she could do was return to town and talk to the state representative who would be arriving for the ribbon cutting. She hurried through her grooming at the washstand, pulled her clothes on, and buttoned up the side of her boots. It would take several hours to drive to Orchard. She'd best have something in her stomach.

The same drone of voices filled the restaurant. Most of the tables were already taken by railroad men who cast glances her way.

A tall blond man in a well-tailored gray suit entered behind her, removing a black Stetson from his head.

She weaved through the tables to one by the window. She didn't notice the tall man at the table next to hers until with a quick smile he held a chair for her. As soon as she was seated, he sat at his table and proceeded to read a newspaper.

She ordered coffee and flapjacks and stared out the window.

Cloud lay like a blanket over the mountains and pass, but a hot wind moved, bringing a trace of cold, a forerunner of something coming off the Pacific.

Conversation flowed around her. She had no other option but show the state representative and the town authorities the blueprints she'd drawn in her sketchpad. Prove to them with her own calculations the difference between what Charles was building and what she had drawn. But there was so little time. She couldn't take the chance they'd listen to her. There was only one thing to do. Go back to Orchard and stop the train before it crossed the bridge.

Facing the authorities was the daring thing Trina urged her to do. Strangely, this moment didn't feel reckless. A calculated risk, yes. One that required courage and wisdom, and she felt God's smile. He had narrowed and funneled her circumstances to bring her to this decision. This must be faith.

The low tones of two men talking at the table nearby penetrated her thoughts. She hadn't noticed the tall man in gray had been joined by another. Her heart skipped a beat. She sat still. And heard again what yanked her from her reverie.

The man in gray pushed the newspaper across the table and tapped it. "What the Anderssons' maid told us is confirmed. Macpherson's the name he's going by, but Neil Galloway was definitely in Orchard as of Saturday."

The hairs on her arms rose. Neil Macpherson...Neil Galloway? Her Neil...? They spoke of the Andersson maid.

The shorter man who'd joined him whipped the paper off the table. "At last, some progress." His crisp English accent quivered with excitement.

She pretended she studied the view through the window beyond them. The tailored suit of the younger man sported a gold watch chain looped in front of his waistcoat. His hat sat on the table. The Englishman in brown tweed kept his bowler on his knee, which jerked with nervous energy.

A quiet burst of laughter erupted from the

Englishman. "I've spoken to a conductor who saw a man fitting Jimmy Galloway's description getting off a train here on Saturday. The man's sure Jimmy hitched a ride to Orchard. I've the younger brother to thank for leading us to this valley, and those daughters of Mrs. Andersson's. A coincidence? Certainly not. Good police work. I'll soon have Neil Galloway clapped in irons."

Her insides turned over.

The younger man spoke in a dry tone. "Yes, with Dr. Galloway clapped in irons, that promotion you mentioned, Webley, will soon be yours."

"About time too, Joel. I've worked too hard to be passed over again. Perhaps with the promotion I can get transferred out of Ireland and back to civilized England."

The man called Joel looked over a sheaf of papers. "I'm puzzled by your Scotland Yard autopsy report, though. There's nothing to suggest what type of weapon the decedent was stabbed with."

The Englishman clipped out, "Had to be a scalpel, didn't it? Who better to take a life than a doctor?"

"A scalpel? I don't think—"

"Of course it was a scalpel." The Englishman, Webley, grew red in the face. "Besides, only days earlier, Neil threatened to kill Crawford. He was seen standing over the body. That's the thing you've got to understand about the Irish—they're always fighting. This Neil Galloway, putting on airs, getting himself an education, thinking highly of himself, will always, only ever be...good-for-nothing Irish."

Shaking began in her inner core. Neil...accused of murder. Stabbing. She carefully set her cup on the saucer and stared blindly out at the mountains that under the heavy cloud cover appeared a dull jade. From the corner of her eye she caught the man called Webley craning his neck as he looked over the restaurant.

"It'll be a few hours before that train for Orchard arrives. It's a sore trial waiting in this blighted place, the back of beyond."

The younger man's words slid out in a low tone. "I'm sorry you find our Washington State such a trial. Most Continental visitors compare its pristine beauty to Switzerland."

Webley sat back. "Have I trod on a nerve, Detective Harrison? Well, once you've escorted me and my quarry back to New York to catch our ship, our paths will part, and I'll be leaving this charming frontier patch. As it is, I must send a telegram to my superiors in Ireland with my progress." With that, Webley marched out of the restaurant.

Sofi rose stiffly as though she'd aged a hundred years. The waiter came with her order balanced on a tray, but she swept past him. Thankful she'd already paid her hotel bill, she ran out of the foyer and down the steps to her car. She'd been so angry with Neil for his secrets. But Neil had given Trina nothing but compassion. He'd put himself at risk to save Gunnar's life. The contradictions in him persisted. But murder? The man she'd kissed, who'd held her in his arms, a murderer? What little faith she had in Neil slammed up against the Englishman's accusations. Think, Sofi, think. Don't feel. Put him out of your mind. There was the bridge to think of. Yes, her bridge.

The train was supposed to slow before reaching the bridge. It would come to a stop to allow Charles to board before it steamed into Orchard. The only safe place to stop the train was the switching yard. The limousine's top speed was only thirty miles an hour. On rough road, much slower.

She'd have to hurry to beat the train that would leave Skykomish in a few hours. Minutes later, she banged on the front window of the mining store. The owner snapped his suspenders into place and opened the door to her with a mild grumble. Rummaging through the tools, she found what she was looking for, a large sledgehammer, a variety of wrenches, a hacksaw, most importantly, a set of bolt cutters.

She paid and ran to the car under a sky bruised with cloud. Her only clear thought—and may the Lord forgive her—she must break the law. Stop that train. And when she saw Neil, do what? Warn him? Or tell the sheriff?

23

Neil sank into a chair and checked his pocket watch. Almost noon, yet outside it looked as if night was about to fall. Wind shook the house, tinkling through the lamp's crystal beads. Rain beat the windows. At last, though, Roselle's pulse steadied, she dropped into a natural sleep, his fears of a seizure dissipated. As long as Roselle never touched laudanum again, she'd be fine.

The hard line of Matilda's mouth assured him not a drop of the stuff would ever pass Roselle's lips as long as the Scottish Virago lived.

He opened the bedroom door to find Henric sitting in a chair on the landing. Neil touched him on the shoulder. "She'll be all right in a day or so."

Henric released a deep sigh.

"Any news of Sofi yet?" Neil asked as they both started down the stairs.

"The sheriff sent out wires, but we've heard nothing. She's probably hightailed it to Seattle to talk to someone about the bridge, from what I've pieced together from Kiosho and Matilda."

"And Charles?"

"He seemed his usual pompous self, getting ready for the day's festivities, and I couldn't see anything to indicate there was something to worry about. Those two men are still with Charles. So Sofi—wherever she's gone—should be fine. In fact, I should be getting into town myself." Henric stopped at the door to the kitchen and gripped Neil by the elbow. "You're sure Rosie is all right?"

"I wouldn't leave her unless she was stable. Keep her on the belladonna and plenty of fluids until the sickness passes."

Neil stopped to listen to the wind. "Can the bridge be opened with this storm?"

"Even a gale like this can't stop that train coming into town. But you, my friend, need some coffee." Henric filled a cup for him. "Now will you tell me why you went as white as a ghost when Rosie mentioned policemen last night? Neil, as your friend, I'd like some sort of explanation."

Neil held the cup in his hands. Henric was probably right. Sofi was most likely in Seattle, safe and sound from this storm, going about the things that mattered to her. Those two thugs seemed more interested in Charles anyway. In fact, with the light of day—or lack of it with this storm—this was the perfect time to slip away. Jimmy was settled. The police on their way, and his last reason to stay was gone. Before he went, though, Henric deserved as much truth as he could give him. "Aye, you'll find out soon enough, I suppose. The English police want me for the stabbing death of a man called Robert Crawford."

Henric sat across from him, his expression immobile.

"Crawford worked for an important man, Sir William Armitage—not that that should matter in life and death. Crawford came from England to oversee the building of a new line of Armitage's ships in the Belfast shipyard." Neil played with the handle of his cup. "During the building of one of those ships, my father died. He slipped from scaffolding fifty feet to the ground. That night while our family grieved, I went looking for Crawford. He cared not one whit that a man died building the ship. Walked past me as if I were pestering him for a coin. I lost my temper...took him by the throat and threatened him. A few days later...after my father's funeral...Crawford was killed."

"Who killed this man?"

He met Henric's gaze. "I was found over the body. My scalpels, smeared with Crawford's blood, lay beside his body. The police were coming. Someone shouted that I'd done it. I ran. I ran to the morgue at the city hospital and stole a dead man's papers. For a while I became Neil Macpherson."

Henric leaned forward. "You've hidden who you are, but I don't believe you're a liar. And I don't believe for one minute you stabbed this man. You're a doctor. You were there to help. Even if you did threaten him a few days before. So why run?"

"It doesn't matter, Henric. It's me they're looking for."

Henric's mouth firmed. "They'd send a policeman all the way here to look for you?"

"It's because of Crawford's connection to that English peer."

Matilda came into the kitchen. "Mrs. Andersson has woke. I'll be making her a cup of tea." She shuffled toward the stove.

Henric pushed back from the table. "Why don't you go on up and attend to her, Matilda, and I'll bring up the tea."

Matilda shuffled back up the stairs. Henric's brow creased to a sharp V as he busied himself arranging a tray. He opened the door, and wind lifted the lace curtains. He returned with a tendril of honeysuckle and placed the damp blossom on a white cloth next to a teapot and china cup and saucer. Lifting the tray, he said to Neil, "I'll be back in a few minutes. When I do, I want the truth. You're still hiding something." He left the kitchen and went up the stairs.

Neil drained the remainder of his cup. He filled his bag with foodstuffs from the larder. After grabbing his coat, he was out the door. The cornfield would hide him from Henric's view if the big Scandinavian looked out. Neil burrowed into his wool coat. If it weren't for this gale, he could walk over the new bridge and be across the gorge in no time. Instead, he started down the incline toward the riverbed and the small wooden bridge that was more sheltered from the wind. Rain soaked his face, and he pushed the ever-present thoughts of Sofi away.

Henric would look after her.

In fact, if Neil's suspicions were correct, Henric would like nothing better than to look after Roselle Andersson and her daughters.

Neil hunched his shoulders against the slicing rain. If he kept off the roads and worked his way to the other side of the gorge, he could stop by the ironworkers' camp. If he couldn't say goodbye to Sofi, at least he could bid farewell to his brother. The wind shrilled as keenly as a whistle behind him as he started toward the gorge.

24

A gust of wind pummeled the car. On the drive from Skykomish Sofi had stopped the limousine several times to clear the road of rocks and branches. The storm wasn't what chilled her to the bone, though. If these winds built in force and funneled through these canyons...if her bridge was as weak as she felt it was...

She clung to the steering wheel with frozen fingers as the car bumped into the switching yard. Her bridge lay a hundred yards off. She glanced at the watch pinned to her shirtwaist. She'd gotten here in time. *Dear God, keep Neil out of sight.* On the way here, she'd made her mind up. She loved him. Dear Father in heaven, she loved him. And loving him the way she did, she could not be the one to inform the authorities where he was. No matter what he'd done.

No one stirred in the ironworkers' camp. They must all be down at the new station in town to watch the initial run across the bridge. The gale would hurt no one in the station. Only the bridge and those crossing it by train were at risk.

On this side of the river, smoke spiraled out of the stovepipe chimney on the roof of the shack. There was no guarantee the switchman would listen to her either, and no time to waste in trying.

Howling wind thrust her against the car as she got out. Rain trickled down the back of her collar as she grabbed the bolt cutters, and Odin slunk low beside her as they fought the wind over to the switching stand. The acrid smell of creosote from the rail ties added to the nauseous squall in her stomach. But no movement from the shack yet. A high-pitched screech echoed faintly. *Please, God, let it be the wind and not the whistle of the train.*

At the switching stand, the padlock secured the rails in place. She opened the jaws of the cutters, her hands straining as she squeezed, struggling to cut through the chain. She didn't have enough strength to sever it. Her hands throbbed. The links held strong. Tears sprang to her eyes. *Please, God...*

She felt the cutters roughly pulled from her as she was pushed aside. Her heart dropped. Wet wind blew her hair into her face. She'd been stopped so quickly. Failed so easily. She dragged the hair out of her eyes to face the switchman.

But it was Neil's brother, Jimmy.

She tried to yank the cutters back from him, for all the good it did.

He held them in an unyielding grip. "I'm trying to help ye, ye fool of a woman. I can see plain as day what you're trying to do."

"I've got to stop this train," was all she could get out.

Jimmy pulled the chain from the padlock and let it clank to the ground. "Aye, so I see." He nodded toward the Pullman. "I know a thing or two about steel, and that bridge has too much pig iron. Sure, they've painted over the holes in places you can hardly see. High uppity-ups, making money out of the lives of innocent people by cutting corners." He lifted up the weight lever on the switching stand, shifting the track points so that the signal swiveled from green to red.

"Lock it down," she said, her thoughts consumed by the coming train.

He fastened the switch. "Now the lock's broken, we've no way of securing it." He bent over the ground, inspecting the gravel.

"I was going to put my car over the track."

"Your car will only stop them for a few minutes." He picked up a piece of wire buried in the gravel and wedged the wire deep into the keyhole, jamming the lock. "That'll stop them for a while longer."

He followed her as she raced to the limousine.

She shooed Odin away, jumped into the driver's seat, and drove the car toward the track.

Jimmy pushed, and the car bumped over one rail, jolting her.

She bit down and tasted blood. Shouts came from two directions, and the blood in her veins crackled like ice.

The switchman, brandishing a shovel, ran from the shack. From the Pullman railcar, Charles and two men raced toward them too. One fired off a gunshot.

Jimmy hauled Sofi from the car.

Her knees buckled, and he pulled her with him to the siding close to the trees.

Charles bolted toward the switch stand. The switchman did the same. The other two men ran to her car. Jimmy shoved her out of the way behind a large boulder, and she landed with a thud. "I daren't let anything happen to ye, miss. Neil's forgiven me a lot, but he'd never forgive me that." Rain plastered his hair to his head. He crouched, ready to spring at Charles coming toward them.

Clutching her stomach and trying to breathe, she stared as he pulled from his coat a pocketknife and flicked it open.

~*~

The airstream shrieked over, under, and through the bridge's steel trusses.

Neil was only twenty yards from the workers' lodgings. Was that the wind or a train whistle echoing along the canyon floor? Branches and leaves littered the wet ground. Rain slashed. It felt more like November than August. And the river had swollen.

He stepped through the trees.

Charles's limousine sat next to the Pullman car. So too did the speedster he'd seen last night, but there was no sign outside of the men who owned it.

Neil's footsteps crunched on ballast stones when a loud crack reverberated to the treetops. A flock of crows scattered on the wind. It took a moment to make sense of the noise.

A gunshot surely.

Neil ran past the Pullman to where the shot had come from, dropped his duffle bag. He tried to make sense of the chaotic scene.

Several men, Charles included, darted from all directions toward the juncture where the main track shunted off to the siding. A railway man and Charles both hauled on the switching stand, banging at the lock.

A flash of blue caught Neil's vision.

Sofi's car. On the track! But it was blessedly empty.

Two men were attempting to push her car off the rails.

His stomach turned to lead, his gaze ricocheting

from man to man. It was a gunshot he'd heard. He was sure of it. Who held the gun? What or who had he shot at? And where in blue blazes had Sofi gotten to? The bigger of the men lifted the car's fender off the track while the shorter one shoved from the back.

Without warning, a streak of black and white bounded toward the bigger of the thugs, a whirl of legs and fur. Odin. He growled and leapt, knocking the man to the ground. If her dog was here, where...?

Neil's knees turned to water.

His brother was crouching in the center of the yard, ready to spring, knife in his hand.

"Jimmy! No!" Neil shouted.

But Jimmy leapt at Charles.

Neil ran toward them.

Jimmy had Charles in a grip.

The switchman strove to pry them apart.

Neil had almost reached them when the shorter of the thugs turned from the car. Slowly, the gangster lifted a gun, aiming at the constantly shifting men. A second shot splintered the air.

Neil's vision went red. The world all but stopped. He couldn't move his limbs as Jimmy and Charles scuffled on the ground. And then a third shot. A guttural cry cut the air. Neil's limbs began to move of their own accord as the thought filtered through his mind—that cry had come from him. He lunged.

Somehow in the stew of wrestling arms and fists, the gun dropped to the ground.

Before Neil could reach for it, the larger man, bleeding from gashes from the dog's teeth, tossed Neil aside like a child's toy. Neil landed hard, his head hitting the railings. His eyes blurred and his thoughts swirled into an unintelligible mass. Stunned, he leaned on an elbow in the gravel, trying in vain to focus.

The two gangsters half carried Charles, who limped and clutched at his thigh, to the parked speedster. The car chugged to a start and drove off in a spurt of wet gravel.

Realization gradually returned as the car roared away. His pulse drummed. Rain drizzled down his face. No hope remained in the growing stillness.

Odin whined, and Sofi knelt at Neil's side and helped him stand. Sofi!

It must have been only minutes since he'd first entered the switch yard. Where had she been? Nor could he see the switchman. Only Sofi stood, pale and grubby with mud and leaves, but whole, while Jimmy...

Sofi looked off to her right, her face contorting. On the other side of the track, his brother sprawled face down in the dirt. With that same sense that the world had slowed, it now wound down to a stop.

Neil stumbled over to Jimmy.

Blood seeped over the back of his brother's shirt. Dropping to his knees, he reached his fingers to Jimmy's neck, knowing the truth before he touched the carotid artery. An image of Jimmy as a little boy flashed into his head—an impish grin when Jimmy was still an innocent lad. That remembered face didn't match the one before him with its vacant eyes and unearthly stillness. That silenced voice.

The gale howled through the canyon, beating the trees.

Sofi's hand moved across his back to cup his shoulder. "Neil." She gripped his arm. Her voice brought him out of a tunnel of darkness. "Neil, Jimmy tried to help me. He protected me." Her grip tightened.

Snatches of what she said flitted around him. "Train is coming. Questions asked...go to the cabin..." What was she saying?

A train whistle penetrated the chasm of his thoughts.

"I understand why you needed to hide." Her voice became grainy. "There are police detectives on that train, looking for you."

"How do you know?" He looked again at Jimmy lying irrefutably lifeless before him. It wasn't possible.

As if her words were reaching from across the canyon, she said, "This is what you couldn't tell me. Accused of murder. I understand."

Something collapsed inside him. "You say that as if you understood I'd broken a favorite plate. I'm accused of murdering a man. Taking a man's life."

Her face grew pinched as she held back tears. "Whatever you did, you must have had good reason. You're not...you're not a cold-blooded murd—" Her voice broke and she linked her fingers with his. "There's no time. Go to the cabin. I'll make sure Jimmy is cared for."

He raised his gaze to the leaden clouds. "It doesn't matter anymore."

A train whistle sliced the air.

Blood drained from her face. "It does matter. Go! Take the back roads." She pushed at him, crying openly. "There's money in my car." She thumped him in the chest so that he stumbled backward. "Go, Neil. What are you waiting for?"

He started toward the Pullman where his bag lay, but turned back, opening his hands and letting them fall. The forest would swallow him quickly enough. But just a few minutes.

"There's no time." She rushed at him. "If it eases your heart, I believe in you. I know you, Neil."

"How can you know me?"

"Because in spite of it all, who you really are shone through."

"I want to tell you, Sofi." He shook his head. "I didn't kill anyone. I can't go with you thinking that. All this time, I've been protecting Jimmy."

With her hand on her heart, she choked as if coming up from water. "You're innocent. I've known it all along. Jimmy could tell...Jimmy..." Her eyelids fluttered as the truth settled. Jimmy could no longer say anything in Neil's defense.

"There has to be something to prove your innocence," she whispered.

"It's my word against theirs now. Jimmy's taken the truth with him."

A plume of smoke billowed a half a mile down the track. "Go," she cried.

A moan came from nearby.

Neil lifted his head, searching for where that all-too-human noise had come from.

25

They found the switchman lying behind the stack of ties, clutching his leg, a bloody contusion at the side of his head. Neil wadded a neckerchief to press against the injury. In this rain he couldn't see how badly the man had been hurt. He might only be suffering from concussion, but it was the leg wound that worried Neil. He blinked at the welcoming forest, curling his fists.

Sofi gripped his arm. "I'll see he gets to town. It's only a leg wound. Go."

The man groaned.

Sofi was right. He should run now. But Neil couldn't. He couldn't make sense of anything. Half his family gone in a violent manner. The law chasing him. Jimmy dead from a murderer's bullet. But his hands knew what to do. He pulled back the injured man's eyelids. The pupils dilated equally. He ripped open the blood-soaked trouser leg, wiping at seepage. It was as he feared, a bullet wound, but he couldn't see much else. Rain fell in rivulets down their three faces. He had to get the man inside that shack to examine him.

Sofi pushed Neil away. "I'll see to him."

"My bag, it's over there. Bring it, Sofi."

The broken look she sent him sheared a piece off his heart, but she ran for his bag as he carried the patient to the shack. The dog bounded beside him.

"Clear the table," he ordered when they were inside.

She helped him lay the man on the table covered by oilskin cloth and raised glistening eyes to Neil. From the last curve in the track, the chug of the train's pistons began to slow. Brakes squealed.

Neil examined the wound and released a sigh of relief that jarred with frustration. The bullet had missed the femoral artery and passed through the leg. The patient would be fine. Though the man gritted his teeth in pain, his pulse remained steady. He did not need immediate surgery. Neil could have left him in Sofi's hands as she'd begged and been deep in the forest by now.

Outside, the locomotive slid past. Red-white-and-blue bunting beribboned the front of the cowcatcher. Steam rose under flanged wheels as the engine hissed to a stop.

Neil laid his hand on the patient's shoulder. "You'll be fine as soon as we get you to town."

The patient gave him a grateful smile as passengers disembarked the train. Clamoring voices increased to a din.

Neil caught Sofi's gaze as the door swung open.

A man in a top hat and morning suit marched inside. A ribbon rosette on his lapel marked him as a railroad dignitary.

Sofi seemed to know him and moved toward him in a listless fashion.

Several automobiles rumbled to a stop outside.

From where he stood, Neil could see through the windows that one of them was Henric's Tin Lizzy and the other, the police van from Orchard.

The crowd converged around his brother's body still out beside the tracks where he'd been forced to leave him. The local constable, Sheriff Dahl, pushed through the crowd and entered the shack with several men behind him as well as Henric. The local sheriff hitched his stocky frame to appear taller. "We got word there was trouble this side of the bridge." He raised bushy brows at Sofi.

The railroad dignitary glanced in alarm at the switchman on the table. "Miss Andersson. What is going on here?"

"Your questions can wait." Neil tore a clean cloth into a narrow strip. "What's urgent is that you do not allow that train to cross this bridge. Because if Miss Andersson stopped that train, there's a reason. And this man needs to be taken to surgery." He wrapped the strip of cloth around the injured leg and checked the pulse above the knee and below the wound. "Someone find a blanket for this man," he ordered, ignoring the railroad dignitary's grunt of displeasure.

"Are you out of your mind? I'm Jonathan Simmons, assistant to the man in charge and as soon as that track is cleared, my train will proceed into Orchard."

Sofi searched the shack, returned with a rough comforter, and tucked it around the patient. "I'll be happy to explain why I stopped the train." She raised her voice so the growing crowd could hear. "If you care about the safety of your passengers, Mr. Simmons, you will not let them cross."

Mr. Simmons purpled, but he had no chance to speak as Sheriff Dahl indicated the patient. "Is he going to make it, Doc?"

Neil rolled his stethoscope into his bag. "He needs to be transported to town immediately."

The pain-thinned voice of the switchman rose up from the table. "She stopped the train...Charles

Bolton...went off with two men..."

The sheriff patted him on the shoulder. "Who shot you and the dead man outside?"

Neil cut across the questions. "One of Charles Bolton's companions shot him and Jimmy." The image of his brother lying on the ground burned behind Neil's eyes.

Sheriff Dahl arched his brows. "I'll talk to him when he's sewn up and rested. But you, Doc, tell me about this man who's been killed."

"My brother. Jimmy Galloway."

"Well then, I have an unexplained death out there. As for the train going on into town, that's railroad business."

Mr. Simmons elbowed his way next to Sheriff Dahl. "The inaugural run will continue."

One of the passengers stepped forward, a tall man with a raincoat to his knees and a black hat shading his features. "Mr. Simmons, I'm Joel Harrison, a representative of Pinkerton's Detective Agency. In view of this rather significant allegation, I strongly suggest you do not take this train over that bridge until you verify these allegations are unfounded."

Sheriff Dahl stuck his thumbs under the lapels of his jacket. "I'd listen to him, Simmons. I've worked with Joel here before, and as I recall, he's saved the railroad's bacon more than once. Last thing we need is another train disaster in these parts."

At the mention of recent train disasters, Mr. Simmons smoothed his mustache with the back of one knuckle. "Very well, but I want an inquiry set up in Orchard this afternoon."

Neil locked his gaze with Sofi's, but directed his words to Henric. "Make them listen to her, Henric. We both know who designed this bridge, and it's about time everyone else did too."

Henric's mouth firmed as he nodded.

The shack erupted with voices talking at once.

The local police started shouting instructions along with Jonathan Simmons.

Neil didn't notice one of the passengers moving to stand beside him until the man spoke in an English accent. This older man in a brown tweed suit and bowler hat almost whispered in his ear, and Neil got the sickening feeling the man was immensely amused. "Well, well, Dr. Galloway. At long last I may introduce myself—Inspector Webley of Scotland Yard, at your service."

The tall man in the long raincoat and black hat moved to the other side of Neil, barring him from escape, as if he could now with the shack crammed with people.

Inspector Webley's whisper grew to a proclamation that silenced the commotion. "Dr. Neil Galloway, I'm here to arrest you in connection with the murder of Robert Crawford."

Neil met the satisfied gleam in the inspector's eyes. Surprisingly, he felt nothing. For months, he'd thought he'd feel the terror of an animal with the breath of hunters scorching his neck at this moment. But the truth that he'd never see his brother again, and in a few minutes never see Sofi again, erased that fear. It was over and done. Neil sent a smile to ease the stricken look on her face.

Joel Harrison, the Pinkerton man, took Neil by the shoulders. With surprising gentleness he turned him around. "This way, sir." Rain pummeled the trees but the wind had calmed as the Pinkerton man pulled

Neil's hands together behind his back.

Neil flinched as the lock on the handcuffs clicked.

26

In the pandemonium, Sofi hadn't noticed the English inspector or the Pinkerton detective. Yet, with all the noise inside and out, she heard the cold click of those handcuffs. That small sound cut off her ability to speak, threatened to cut off her ability to breathe.

Henric rushed to the inspector. "You're not taking this man anywhere."

"Indeed I am, sir. I have the writ of extradition." Inspector Webley peered at Henric.

Sofi reached Henric with a gaze, and he called out to the sheriff. "Check to see if this inspector's got the right papers."

Sheriff Dahl strolled over to the English policeman. "If you're going to arrest this man on American soil, then he'll be taken to my jail first. If my questions regarding the shooting are answered to my satisfaction, and if—and I mean if—your paperwork is in order, only then will I release him into your custody."

"The documents *are* in order, and I will take my prisoner with me this evening." Inspector Webley scowled.

"We'll see." The shorter local man eyed the inspector.

Sofi's eyes sought Neil's but he turned away, and she was forced to watch as if in a dream as passengers, dignitaries, railroad men, and lawmen overran the switching yard.

Men in formal broadcloth suits held top hats to their heads and plowed along the track to view her bridge.

Women with skirts flapping in the wind used black silk umbrellas as shields and stepped onto the abutment.

The switchman was carried out to the police van. That vehicle drove off on its way to town.

Soon after, Jimmy's body was carried to a truck and also driven to town.

Neil's only motion was the rhythmic spasm of a nerve high on his jaw.

She wanted to move closer. Comfort him somehow. The moment was snatched as the two visiting detectives led him out to a car. Neil too was driven away, and a band tightened around her chest. She closed her eyes. Odin nuzzled against her hip, and she pulled softly at his ears.

"Sofi." Henric drew her close. "The sheriff's got some details from the switchman. He's going to talk to Neil in town, and he wants to talk to you. Sofi?"

She'd saved her bridge for the moment, but images of Jimmy scuffling with Charles looped through her mind at an ever-increasing pace. "Take me to the jailhouse. I've got to tell them Neil is innocent."

"No, Sofi, Neil's right. You've got your own explanations to make."

As if on cue, Mr. Simmons clamped a hand on her shoulder. "Miss Andersson, you've placed me in the humiliating position of having to send this train back to the main line."

Henric pulled back his shoulders, ready to defend her.

She captured his hand in hers. "I tried to tell you

last night, Mr. Simmons. I hope you'll credit me with at least stopping the train safely."

The railway man's eyes narrowed to slits. "Credit you? I'm going to press charges."

Her clothes imprisoned her, heavy and damp. Let him have her arrested. Maybe she had done something illegal, but probably worse in his eyes was that she'd delayed the sacrosanct Great Northern train schedule.

Mr. Simmons's brows beetled. "We don't take tampering with the railroad lightly, Miss Andersson. You will face prosecution."

~*~

The storm had blown itself out by the time the sheriff marched Neil up the steps of the Orchard jailhouse. Before passing through the door, Neil glanced down Main Street. The white clapboard church drew his eyes until his gaze dropped from the steeple to meet the steady scrutiny of Joel Harrison.

Once inside the jailhouse, the local lawman and his deputy walked Neil to a back hallway containing three empty cells. The deputy released him from the handcuffs, and Neil shook his wrists to stimulate circulation.

With only his deputy in attendance, Sheriff Dahl sat on a wooden chair and proceeded to question Neil.

The Pinkerton detective and the English inspector had no choice but to cool their heels in the outer office.

Twenty minutes later, the sheriff stood. "I'll check your statement with the switchman, and with Sofi. If all three statements agree and I'm satisfied you weren't involved in the shooting, well then, Neil, I'll have to give that Englishman access to you."

As the steel-barred door clanked shut, a cold sense of aloneness brushed Neil. Though the jail smelled of carbolic soap and metal—clean—it still brought back the waking nightmare he'd imagined prison would be. Dank, dripping walls, the smell of frightened men. The only fear he smelled was his own. But Jimmy was gone. He couldn't hurt his brother by telling the truth now. *Dear God, was there a chance?*

27

Inspector Webley sauntered down the hall to stand outside Neil's cell.

Joel Harrison followed.

Neil took the bars in his hands. "I've got something to say. I was too late to save Robert Crawford's life, but I did not kill him."

Webley swept Neil with a sour look, disbelief grinding through his voice. "Innocent men don't run."

"They do if they're protecting someone."

"And who would that be?"

Neil looked at the floor and at Webley again. "My brother."

"How convenient now he's dead."

Hearing the finality of those words *he's dead*, Neil sucked back air as billows of loss rolled over him.

Kneading the brim of his hat, Joel Harrison's grave eyes scrutinized Neil the way they had since the moment they'd met at the rail yard. "Start at the beginning, Dr. Galloway. Where were you the night Crawford died?"

"I was working. In a free clinic that I helped out at when I wasn't at the hospital. We'd just buried our father that day. I needed to get away from the house full of grieving family and friends. So I went to the clinic. About seven in the evening, Jimmy came running in. He said...he said he'd stabbed Robert Crawford."

"Did you see a weapon on him?" Joel asked.

It was hard to get the words past the lump in his throat. "Jimmy had recently won a pocketknife. And there was blood..."

Webley cut in, "Your brother isn't alive to say what he did or didn't do."

"Jimmy came to me at the clinic in a panic at seven in the evening." Neil gripped the bars tighter. He was repeating himself. He had to slow down and tell it right. "Jimmy told me where he'd left Crawford. In a back alley not far from the shipyard. He was in such a state he didn't want to come with me to see if Crawford was alive or dead." His throat tightened.

Jimmy, so full of energy and foolishness, was truly gone.

"Did anyone see your brother at the clinic then?" Joel interjected.

"No one. The other duty doctor was in the back having his tea. The nurse was there as well, sterilizing instruments in the autoclave. I packed my valise. Shouted out that I was leaving to see a patient." He cast a glance in Webley's direction. "I told my brother to go home. Told him...if anyone asked, to have our mother say he'd been with her the whole time." He ran his hand around the back of his neck. "It was wrong, but it was only until I had a chance to think. I left the clinic. Found Robert Crawford where Jimmy'd said." His breath became shallow. "Crawford wasn't dead when I got to him, but the wound was deep. He was slipping away fast."

Joel's voice broke through. "You're sure this pocketknife of Jimmy's—or any weapon for that matter—wasn't lying in the vicinity?"

"I can't remember. Maybe. No. Jimmy must have taken it with him. It was then I knocked my bag over, as I reached for gauze. My scalpels fell out. I heard people shouting. Then Crawford's pulse stopped. He was gone. And I knew if Jimmy was brought in for questioning, he'd surely be hanged." His hands flexed on the bars. "People were coming. I decided to protect my brother." His voice dropped to a rasp. "I've always protected..."

Webley smiled a slow smile that didn't match the coldness in his eyes. "I'd have been surprised if you hadn't bleated out your innocence." He leaned close to the bars. "I talked to your mother that night. As well as your brother's fiancée. Both women categorically said your brother Jimmy was with them the whole evening."

"As I'd asked them to."

"Well, in hindsight, of course you'd say that."

Neil's voice rose. "And you never cared which brother you brought back, as long as an Irishman was hanged."

"You Irish are all the same." Webley twisted his mouth to one side. "No number of fancy letters behind your name can rid you of the stain. A more hot-tempered, bar-brawling, vicious race the world has never seen. At least your brother had the sense to stay in his place and work as a laborer in the shipyard."

Joel cleared his throat. "Dr. Galloway, tell us about the weapon your brother owned?"

Neil threw a glance at Joel. The question of Jimmy's knife again. How could that help him now?

Webley threw up a hand and stalked down the hall. "Your job, Joel Harrison, is to escort my prisoner and me to the ship in New York. Galloway's medical bag was full of scalpels with different types of blades. He could have done it with any one of them." At the threshold of the office he stopped. "Prepare yourself, Neil Galloway. You're going to start the long journey back to Ireland tonight." He slammed the door behind him.

Joel remained outside the cell. "Do you need anything?"

Neil leaned his head against the cold bars. With Webley's attitude, his slim hope was petering out fast. And he *had* run. An unfamiliar shaking began in his hands, and he became aware of his thirst. "Some water, please."

Joel brought him a large metal cup and sat on the chair outside Neil's cell.

Neil finished the water in a few gulps.

"I'm sorry about your brother." When Neil didn't respond, Joel continued. "I've read the details of this case. Apparently the British government is anxious to see it resolved quickly." Joel stared at the tip of his boot. "Perhaps they're acting a little too quickly, forcing Scotland Yard to extradite you on—as I see it— inconclusive evidence. Your brother had a hot temper, did he not? You don't strike me that way at all, Dr. Galloway."

"I did threaten Crawford. The night my father died."

"There's a big difference between threatening someone and actually committing murder."

Neil sat on the edge of the cot. Until today, protecting Jimmy had been his own choice, but now that Jimmy was gone, taking with him the only proof of Neil's innocence, these prison walls and a noose around his neck became far too real.

Joel stood and repositioned the chair against the wall. "There are things in this case that whet my curiosity. The autopsy report is unclear what type of blade was used in the stabbing. Is there anything you can tell me?"

Neil sank his head in his hands. "Nothing."

"Keep thinking." Joel softened his voice. "By the way, I'll see what I can do to help out your lady friend. She doesn't strike me as the type to cause havoc without good reason."

Neil swung his head up. "If Sofi says that bridge is unsafe, then it is."

"I've been assigned to quite a number of cases on this line the past few years. I'll do what I can. Is there anything I can get you for now?"

Neil shook his head. "Wait. Yes." He ran trembling fingers over his jaw. "I'd like to wash. Shave, if I may."

"I'll bring you a razor and soap."

Neil's words came out halting. "I'd like a Bible too, please."

The grave eyes of the Pinkerton man shone. "I'll get that for you as well, Doctor."

~*~

Neil lay on the cot after his brief wash. He felt somewhat cleaner at least. Rolling on his back, he rested an arm over his eyes. If only he'd taken that ship in June, he could have been in Indochina by now. Maybe Jimmy would still be alive, and he'd be free. But Jimmy was dead. And what little time he had left on this earth, he couldn't imagine not seeing Sofi. Touch her hair, the color of August wheat. Hair that never would stay pinned up. He pressed the heels of his hands into his eye sockets. There was no sense thinking of what could have been. He'd sacrificed everything for his brother, everything, and what good had it done either of them?

Da's face came to him. Back when he and Jimmy were only lads, the two of them hanging on to their father's hand as they walked to church on a Sunday morn. Bells chimed all over Belfast. Inside the gray stone building, Neil had listened to the minister preach of what Christ had done on the cross for all mankind, taking the punishment that people like him deserved.

Neil sat up and leaned his elbows on his knees. His hands dangled between them like heavy weights. As a boy, he'd believed in what Jesus had done. But as an adult, he'd demeaned that sacrifice. Instead, he'd tried to be Jimmy's savior. How could he save anyone, him, a fallible human being? *Lord, I've been a fool.* He dropped his face into his hands. The die had been cast, though. In only a matter of months, maybe weeks, he'd be facing his Maker.

He picked up the Bible Joel had brought him and opened to the psalm the preacher had spoken on last Sunday. "When my spirit was overwhelmed within me, then thou knewest my path...refuge failed me...I cried unto thee, O Lord: I said, Thou art my refuge."

He wiped moisture from his eyes with an impatient hand. He couldn't save himself, but needed to accept the salvation so freely offered. The church bells of home rang in his memories. And was there a hope, hope that his foolish young brother in the last few days or minutes remembered what Da had taught them? In his heart, he felt no such peace for Jimmy. But he remembered what Henric had said. It was as though he felt God beside him, crying with him, sharing in his grief for Jimmy.

28

Sun melted the mists that snagged on the mountainsides.

Sofi watched this from inside the yellow clapboard town hall as she told her story to the sheriff. Images somersaulted in her mind as she talked. She'd been cutting the padlock on the switching stand. Then Charles and two men. The shooting. Her voice was a dry wisp by the time she finished.

"That's enough for now, Sofi. I've sent out wires that I'm looking for Charles and those two men." The sheriff gave her a wry smile. "I'll leave you now to that inquisition waiting for you down the hall."

She gripped his wrist. "Neil—you're not going to let Neil go with that inspector."

"There's no way I can disregard a writ of extradition."

Squeezing her eyes shut, she listened to Sheriff Dahl close the door behind him. *Dear God...dear God...dear Father in heaven...*

"Sofi." Mayor Frank touched her on the shoulder. "We ought to join that meeting."

Biting her lower lip, she let the mayor take her arm and walk her down the hall to swing open double oak doors to the main chamber. With a sad smile, he held out a chair at the head of the large oval table. Sunlight poured through multi-paned windows, making the room unbearably stuffy.

Around the table, the state representative, several men from Orchard, Mervin Jensen—the head of the bridge committee, city councilmen, and railway men gaped at her as if trying to make out if she was some sort of animal species new to the area. The mayor of Orchard began to speak, but Mr. Simmons interrupted him. "First thing I want to know, Miss Andersson, is what you intend to do about the muddle you created today."

Mayor Frank forestalled him in a softer tone. "Sofi, please tell us your side of things."

She preferred to start by answering Mr. Simmons's rudely phrased question anyway. "I will pay for all expenses incurred, Mr. Simmons. Stopping that train was part and parcel of providing this area with the bridge they are paying for—a safe bridge that will last for generations. The bridge, as it now stands, does not meet the contract Andersson and Bolton signed with you."

"A slip of a girl like you can determine that?" Mr. Simmons sneered.

She lifted her fingers to secure a hairpin but stopped. "I make that determination with all confidence, gentlemen, because I designed that bridge."

Men's voices began speaking over each other.

Mayor Frank pounded his gavel, and order was restored. "You designed this bridge, Sofi?"

Mr. Simmons laughed out loud. "I must—"

"Quiet!" the mayor said. "I want to hear what she has to say."

At last, someone opened the windows. With a fresh breeze cooling her face, she carried on. "Yes, I designed this bridge. However, to our shame my father's partner failed in his duty by changing the specifications required and by using inferior metal." Sofi swept her gaze around the table.

These men, even those from the railroad, didn't know the first thing about the mathematics of creating a bridge.

"Perhaps it would be easier for me to show you. If I could have something on which to draw."

Someone was sent across the street to the schoolhouse to bring back a blackboard easel.

Sofi sipped from a glass of water to quench her parched throat as she waited and ignored the low drone of conversation around the table. Neil's face swam before her eyes. The ticking of a clock seemed to go on forever. The memory of Jimmy earlier today came over her, the way he crouched and sprang at Charles with that pocketknife. She flinched.

At last, the blackboard arrived.

A councilman set up the easel, and Mayor Frank smiled as he passed her a piece of chalk.

Taking a deep breath, she swept her arm and drew a strong, fluid arc across the board. Quickly sketching in the steep cliff sides, she added the triangular shapes of trusses, and her bridge came to life. With short jabs of chalk, she marked crisscrosses at various sections. "Here, gentlemen, is where the steel is too thin. This will escalate stress in these thinner sections." She wrote a series of formulas on the side of the board and underscored them.

"It's not just the dead load of its own weight that the bridge must sustain, but the tonnage of locomotives. Plus, the wind-shear factor in these canyons will slam against the flat sides of railcars, acting in a similar manner as wind filling canvas sails on the surface of water—"

"How strong were the winds today?" one of the railroad dignitaries asked.

"Forty miles per hour," another man volunteered.

"Which means the wind-shear factor is..." Sofi scratched the chalk on the board and ran the calculation. "Which means on days like today." She quieted her voice. "My bridge, as it now stands, will collapse. Maybe not today, but one day. Lives could be lost."

For a moment silence reigned, then the room burst with another barrage of questions.

She answered them one after another. Through the windows she watched late-afternoon sun angle over the mountains as she reiterated her claims and went through the math for the umpteenth time. Her throat grew hoarse from talking.

Mervin, from the bridge committee, wanted her to go over what percentage of pig iron was safe for a bridge this size. What was her opinion of Wetzle Steel?

She rubbed her aching brow, drank another glass of water. She'd been in this room for more than three hours.

Mr. Simmons stood, the disgruntled look still pinching his face, when the state representative also got to his feet and waved Mr. Simmons down. "Seems to me we should call it a day. The people of Orchard obviously vouch for the character of Miss Sofi Andersson." He broke off when Joel Harrison entered the room, strode to the mayor's chair, and passed him a slip of paper. Just as quietly, he left.

Mayor Frank read the note, passed it to the state representative to read, who then addressed the meeting. "I have here a telegram from the gentleman in charge of the railroad. Great Northern Railroad will not press charges until it is confirmed that Miss Sofi Andersson has acted irresponsibly. Until then, taking into consideration these allegations she has made, there will be no loads added to the bridge until due consideration of the facts is made."

The state representative raised a brow at Mr. Simmons. "So it seems your employer feels there is nothing to be gained by pressing charges prematurely." He turned to the rest of the table. "Because, gentlemen, if Miss Sofi Andersson is proven correct, we may very well find ourselves in the position of thanking her. However, Miss Andersson..." The representative's gaze pierced Sofi. "It is my sincerest hope your mathematics will withstand the scrutiny to come."

With a firm jut of her chin, she returned his steady gaze. After thanking him, she started to leave the room, but Mr. Simmons stepped in her path, wrinkling his nose as if he smelled something slightly off. "I have never met a young woman brought up to your position to push herself forward in such an unbecoming manner."

"I'm sorry you find my manner unbecoming." Her voice faded but she pulled herself up to her full height. "I have no desire to push myself forward. Quite the contrary, sir. However, my mathematics will stand. Now if you'll excuse me, please."

After closing the door to the council chamber, she leaned her back against it and released a ragged breath. From here, she could look down Main Street and see a portion of her bridge. It had taken her a while to learn that the labor of her heart was God's inspiration. It was only right that she act in confidence to protect that labor. But weariness weighted her feet as she walked across the street to the jailhouse.

29

Sheriff Dahl sat at his desk when Sofi entered the jail. Behind him was the closed door to the cells. He rubbed his chin. "I'm sorry, Sofi. Henric brought in a lawyer, but he's only confirmed that I've got no grounds to keep Neil. What's more, no word on Charles or those two men. I've been a lawman a long time, and I'm starting to get that prickle at the back of my neck."

Some of what he said seeped past her fear for Neil. "You think Charles is in danger? But he seemed to be in cahoots with those men when they tried to stop Jimmy and me."

"In cahoots with some nasty men is what he is. Joel's been sending out wires all afternoon, and we got one from the Seattle police a while ago. The descriptions you and Neil gave fit two men who work for Heinz Wetzle. Seems in addition to shady goings-on in his business, Wetzle is a major loan shark on the coast."

She should feel some concern for Charles, but because of him, their company and their lives had been tainted by corruption. All concern for him disappeared with the threat hanging over Neil's head. "Let me talk to Neil."

The sheriff unlocked the door leading to a narrow hallway. Daylight filtered in from a barred window at the far end.

Neil, the only prisoner, rose to his feet.

Her eyes went everywhere but to him. Bars, brick walls, thin cots. She didn't know what to do with her hands and ran her palms along the side of her skirt.

Sheriff Dahl set a chair in front of Neil's cell.

"I want to go inside," she said.

The older man twisted his mouth to one side.

She mustered strength into her voice. "You know as well as I do what kind of man he is."

"All right, Sofi. Only for you."

Neil waited as she entered the space that seemed too small for a human being. The pillow carried the indentation of his head. He'd recently shaved. A small nick at his neck had a dry spot of blood. Someone had brought him a fresh shirt. But he'd been running his hands through his hair, and a dark lock fell over his forehead. Her fingers yearned to brush it back.

"Did everything go all right?" he asked. "Your bridge and all?"

"My bridge will be fine. It's you I'm worried about." She kept her own voice barely above a whisper.

He turned his back to her, took the bars in his hands.

She wanted to take those few steps closer, but didn't. The way he kept his back to her didn't invite touch. "Neil, I'm sorry about your brother."

His shoulders slumped. "It was hard telling them the truth, even though he's gone."

She managed to speak through a painful throat. "The truth can't hurt Jimmy now."

"Well, it appears I did too good a job covering up the truth. Now there's not a shred of evidence in my favor. Only my word, and for the first time in my life my word isn't good enough."

"Henric told me what you told him, how this Robert Crawford hurt your family. There must be something to free you. Then we could..."

He turned, a slow smile taking possession of his mouth and eyes. "We could what, Sofi?"

A tingling travelled along her arms. "If this weren't hanging over your head, there'd be nothing...nothing to stop us from..."

Moisture swam in his eyes. "Aye, Sofi, at last, I can give ye the full truth. If this weren't hanging over me, we'd be setting the date for our weddin'. But it won't do, Sofi love. It won't do."

She trailed her fingers along her cheek to wipe away the wetness. "Because of Alison?"

"Alison?" His voice broke. "My wee sister-in-law? She's the other reason I ran, because she's expecting Jimmy's child. I wanted to give them a chance as a family, is all."

In spite of the gravity of his situation, her cheeks grew warm. Alison had not been the love of his life.

Neil's smile glimmered at her blush. "There's no one in the world for me, but you. If I were free, I'd share everything I have with you, my heart and soul." His voice grew husky. "All of me." His brief smile vanished as he hunkered down on the floor, his back to the bars. "But it still won't do, Sofi, because I'm not free." His voice grew stronger. "Strange, isn't it, both our families devastated by grief. Both our fathers, my brother. I may have been angry with Robert Crawford's greed and callousness, but I never truly wished him dead."

"Why did you run, Neil, as if you had killed him? Why did you cover up the truth for Jimmy?"

"He was my brother. Sofi, you, of all people,

should understand. My weak spot has always been rescuing those I love. So I ran. Made my way here, of all places. And met you."

Her gaze went from his eyes to his mouth to his arms that refused to hold her. Maybe it was better that way. To hold each other for five exquisite minutes, knowing they could soon be parted forever, would only crush what was left of her heart. Her breath caught. *No. No. No. This was wrong. Wrong!* Hadn't God taught her to act with courage and confidence? How dare the two of them act in such a defeatist manner? There was still time. Still something to be done.

She moved to stand beside him, hating the question on her tongue that would only bring him fresh pain. "The pocketknife that Jimmy used today, was that how he killed Robert Crawford?"

He lowered his head. "Aye, but there's nothing uncommon about a man owning a pocketknife. Most men carry one."

"You're a doctor. You must know. Wouldn't there be something about Crawford's wound to show it was made by a pocketknife and not a scalpel?"

"Even under a microscope, the difference between any of my blades and a common pocketknife cannot be told apart." His brow lined as thoughts raced behind his eyes. "It's no use, love."

"Was there anything about the wound? Something uncommon—"

"Stop, Sofi." He ran his hands down her arms. "I don't want you thinking of that. I've had to carry that awful image in my head for months. I want you to remember good things. Sweet things. Like the image of you that will always remain with me." He touched a finger to her lips. Her mouth trembled with his touch.

"I also want you to know...that if...well, if I'm not able to come back to you, I know where I'm going when the end comes."

Her heart beat a solemn dirge as coldness filled her.

When she tried to speak, he moved the pad of his thumb across her lips. "I tell you that only to give you comfort if things don't go...if things don't go as we hope. But, please, let me have these last moments with you to cherish."

He couldn't be saying these things to her.

She shook her head. "You give up so soon, Neil. You tell me to stand up for my work, flaunt convention, yet you refuse to act for yourself. Oh, you'll act bravely for others, but not for you." Her voice rang down the hall of empty cells. "Well, I won't stand for that. God gave you your life. Don't let it be stolen from you!"

His face drained of color.

For a good minute, they stood in silence.

Her voice fell to a breath. "If you love me, Neil, fight for your freedom."

"All right, Sofi." His fingers wandered from her chin to follow her cheekbone, to tangle in her hair. The breath from his whisper brushed her face. "I promise I'll fight to the end. But there's honestly nothing I can think of to do."

"No!" She threw her arms around his neck. "That's not good enough. Promise me you'll get your freedom. You will!"

"Sofi, love, don't cry." He rested his forehead against hers. "All right then, I promise. I will become a free man, and we'll marry." His matter-of-fact tone held no conviction, though. He laid his cheek against hers and ran his hand up and down her back until her sobs turned quiet.

Outside, the wind murmured.

Her palm slid from his shoulder to rest against his chest, to feel the beating of his heart. Perhaps they would never grow old together, but she'd give him what comfort and joy she could for what may be the only moments God allowed them. Her own heart raced. Lifting her face to his, she trailed her mouth over his cheek.

On a sharp breath he pulled her hard against him, locked his arms around her. Her hand, captured by the press of their bodies, felt his heart gallop. Their lips met. Tremors rippled along her nerve endings. She wound her arms tighter around his neck as his lips sought her mouth, her cheek, her neck, again and again.

A lifetime passed in his arms, and their kisses grew deeper. Tender. Slower. How long had her hands caressed the strength of his shoulders, his back? How long had her lips traced the line of his smoothly shaven jaw? Minutes? An hour? A new sob clogged her throat. No, only minutes.

His hands shook as he unlocked her arms from around his neck. His voice cracked as he held her from him. "I'll be leaving shortly. I don't want you here for that."

She reached for him but he backed away.

"But the lawyers. I can get more lawyers."

"Henric did all he could. The sheriff is driving me and the two detectives to Skykomish tonight to catch the New York train in the morning."

She tried to speak. He stopped her with his lips on hers as light as a rose petal falling. "Go, Sofi, please. If you love me, go now. I'll do everything in my power to come back to you." A nerve in his cheek went into spasm, and he turned to face the wall. "Or wait for you in heaven."

30

Sofi fled along the hallway and tore through the office, unable to look at the hard features of the English policeman. She would hire the best lawyers. There had to be a way to keep him here. But what could be done here, thousands of miles from where the crime took place? Was it as Neil said, Jimmy had taken all evidence to his grave?

She raked her fingers through her hair. Stop crying. Think. Think.

Numbness took over her limbs as she walked unsteadily past Vern and Elfreda's hotel, past Mr. Helsing's mercantile store. The aroma of cooking suppers wafted out of houses. Summer had returned after the storm, but in a few weeks autumn would come. Leaves would curl on the ground. By then Neil would be in an Irish jail. Facing a British court. Come winter, these mountains would be covered by a cold white shroud.

The boardwalk ended and she stumbled past houses, the doctor's surgery, and the meadow outside town.

At the crossroads on the edge of her grandparents' cornfield, she blindly turned to sit on a boulder. Corn stalks whispered in the breeze. She wrapped her arms around herself, tears dry now.

Neil would soon be driven past this spot.

After a while, on the fragrance of ripening pears and apples in her grandmother's orchard came the quiet voice of God and jumbled sections of the psalm she'd heard last Sunday. "When my spirit was overwhelmed...thou knewest my path...I looked on my right hand, and beheld...I cried unto thee, O Lord...Bring my soul out of prison..." Like Neil, she was giving up too soon.

The clip-clop of a horse and Trina calling reached her over the rustle of the corn.

Henric rode his mare down the road with Trina seated behind him. A few feet from Sofi, Trina dropped from the horse and ran to her.

She took Trina in her arms, feeling the tremors in the young shoulders.

Trina was working hard to be her old self, but her bravado was paper-thin.

An automobile engine rumbled and sputtered. It wasn't the car leaving town with Neil. The sound was coming from below, on the road coming up from the gorge.

Sofi's eyes stung as she set Trina from her.

Henric too couldn't find words to speak.

The noise of the vehicle engine below grew softer as it met a curve and went behind a portion of the hill. The sound all but disappeared.

Henric brushed a finger down her cheek. "We'll see that Neil gets the best legal help."

A moment later, that engine she'd been listening to roared at full throttle. The police van sped through the crossroads into town. It was the volunteers sent out to search for Charles and the two men. The vehicle squealed to a stop outside the surgery. Volunteers pulled a stretcher out of the van, bearing the form of a body covered by a blanket.

*I looked on my right hand...and beheld...*A broken

phrase of the psalm repeated in her brain with the clang of a bell. Her gaze returned to the body being taken inside the doctor's surgery. *Look...behold...at your right hand...bring his soul out of prison.* The sight of that body drew her like a magnet.

It was Charles. Of course it was him.

Her mind clicked. Charles, fighting with Jimmy? Charles, clutching his leg as he'd lurched to the car with the other two men. Jimmy had stabbed Charles. Just as he'd stabbed Robert Crawford in Ireland. She'd seen the weapon in Jimmy's hand. Sofi choked on a breath and gathered the weight of her skirts to run.

"Sofi," Trina called out.

Sofi's boots pounded on the road. She stumbled. Just as she reached the steps of the doctor's house, Willem, one of the deputies, raced out of the surgery and past her up Main Street to the jailhouse.

Dr. Enckell was already at his surgery table. He pulled the blanket down to uncover the face of the man beneath it.

She looked down at Charles's face and shuddered. She had every reason to despise him. His meddling in their family had brought them hardship. The criminal way he'd played with their business had placed innocent lives at risk. She tried to summon pity, for what Charles used to mean to their family, but her fear for Neil pushed that pity away.

Dr. Enckell covered Charles's face again.

Henric entered the surgery.

"What killed him?" She groped for her voice.

The doctor spoke to Henric. "Take her into the hall. Wait for me there, Sofi."

Henric led her to the foyer where Trina sat. Through the oval glass, Sofi could see the street.

According to the clock on the wall, Neil would be driven past soon. She'd miss seeing him, but she still sank to the settle.

Trina looped an arm around Sofi's neck. "It's going to be all right, *älskling*."

Sofi and Henric stood when Dr. Enckell came out of the surgery. "I've done a cursory examination," he said. "Looks like someone shoved Charles off Dry Gulley and he died of head injuries from the fall."

So Charles had not died from Jimmy's hand like Robert Crawford. How could she have hoped for something so horrible when she first saw that Charles was dead? But she had wanted something about Charles's death to reflect on Crawford's murder and somehow save Neil. She smoothed her aching throat. What good would that have done? As Neil said, the flat blade of a pocketknife wouldn't make much of a different wound than that of a scalpel. But Jimmy's pocketknife was no ordinary pocketknife.

She rubbed her forehead. "What is the wound in Charles's thigh like?"

Henric's face became a mask of astonishment.

"Was it done with a blade," she added, "or something else?"

The doctor angled her a look. "It was a nasty-looking gouge, not a clean cut. If it's important, I'll examine it further."

"Quickly. It is important."

"Will this help Neil?" Henric asked.

"I can only pray it does."

Henric kept his thoughts to himself and paced.

Trina didn't speak.

Five minutes later, Dr. Enckell returned. "That wound is a strange one, a downward incision into the thigh from something rounded—"

She gripped the doctor's arm. "From a short, curved spike, the width of my little finger, six inches long."

He arched one brow. "Something like that."

"There'd be no mistaking a wound like that with a flat blade. Like a wound from a scalpel?"

"Looks that way to me."

"Was a pocketknife found on Jimmy's body?"

"No, Sofi, only his clothes."

In the space of a heartbeat, she ran from the surgery. She sprinted down the boardwalk.

Sheriff Dahl and the two detectives came out of the jailhouse. They stood outside on the steps, talking with the deputy.

Neil stood between them, his hands bound in front of him.

"Was a pocketknife..." She gripped the hitching post as Henric and Trina arrived. "Was a pocketknife found at the switching yard?"

Joel's gaze darkened with questions. "No weapon was found there of any kind."

She turned to Webley. "An autopsy must have been performed on Robert Crawford in Ireland."

"Of course." He sent her a look of disdain.

Sofi took a step forward. "Today I witnessed the fight between Jimmy and Charles. I saw the knife he used to stab Charles."

Sheriff Dahl narrowed his eyes. "Willem's just told us about Charles. What's this knife you're talking about?"

"Send your men back to the yard by the bridge. Tell them to search until they find a pocketknife close to the switching stand. A special kind of pocketknife."

Webley's expression shut down.

Neil's eyes brimmed with a look that said he feared to hope. "The wound in Robert Crawford's abdomen...I didn't get a good enough look at it that night. I couldn't tell what made it."

Joel took her arm. "What kind of pocketknife, Miss Andersson? Be specific."

Her pulse tripped. "A regular blade at one end. The opposite end swings out to a spike, curved inward at approximately twenty degrees." She whipped around to Inspector Webley. "In the name of justice, compare Doc Enckell's findings with your autopsy results on Robert Craw—"

"There's nothing further to discuss." Webley's features hardened. "In my latest telegram from Belfast, I am to bring Neil Galloway back to Ireland. Send whatever new evidence you find and let His Majesty's courts decide. I refuse to spend another moment on this blighted case."

Henric and Trina uttered cries of dismay.

She managed to speak through her constricting throat. "Dr. Enckell says—"

"I will waste no further time on whims, Miss Andersson, especially with what I've seen today in regards to your activities." He barged past her, towing Neil by the arm.

Light dazzled. Her surroundings went gray.

Standing at the waiting car, Neil locked eyes with her. The area around his mouth turned white as he pressed his lips together.

At the edge of her sight, the Pinkerton man removed his hat. "Inspector Webley, would it not be prudent to look into this? We might discover sufficient evidence to eliminate Dr. Galloway from your inquiries. With a few telegrams to Great Britain, you could save your government the cost of unnecessarily returning this man to Ireland, and perhaps some embarrassment to yourself."

"We have a train to catch in the morning," Webley spat out.

"Sofi." Neil's husky voice cut through her reeling thoughts. Lifting his cuffed hands was difficult, but he managed to touch her cheek. "I won't give up." He tore his gaze from her and didn't look back as he got into the car.

Sofi watched as Webley got in next to him, Joel on the other side.

From under lowered brows, Sheriff Dahl sent a measured look to Deputy Willem. "Check that switching yard. They'll be catching the eastbound transcontinental tomorrow morning from Skykomish." He bent to turn the crank of his Model T, and the engine coughed to a start. The car pulled away.

Sofi followed a few steps, waiting for Neil to turn around. She lifted her hand, but it dropped to her side as the car drove past the crossroads and out of her sight.

He'd never looked back.

31

"Let me take you home, Sofi," the deputy's voice broke through.

She rolled her shoulders back. "No. I'm coming with you to look for that knife."

Pale and shivering, Trina stood beside Sofi, but the old spark shone from her eyes. "So am I."

Henric put his arms around her and Trina. Willem had the good sense not to argue. He settled them into the police van while Henric swung into his saddle to ride down to the gorge and across the old bridge to the other side.

In the west, the sun dipped below the peaks. So little light left.

Each minute took Neil farther and farther from her. Tree branches and leaves littered the small switching yard. A lifetime had passed since she and Neil stood in the rain, looking down at Jimmy's body.

Willem pulled a rake and shovel from the van.

Sofi took the rake and strode to the section of track where Jimmy and Charles had fought.

Willem scored lines in the gravel from the tracks to mark off sections.

Trina and Henric picked up fallen branches. They'd just started to search the ballast of stones when voices reached them.

A group of the bridge crew hurried over. It wasn't angry faces, but curious ones.

Sofi returned her attention to raking stones.

Willem questioned the men about Jimmy's pocketknife.

Comprehension lit their faces. "Jimmy had a pocketknife," one man said. "*Jah*, had it with him this morning. We vill help the young Irish doctor." Several of the crew ran back to the camp while others scored off sections of ballast.

Sofi dug through the rocks and swallowed back tears at their willingness to help.

A larger group of workmen rushed into the rail yard with rakes and tools.

Oh, please, dear God, it has to be here.

Light dimmed, and someone brought out lanterns. The whole yard was covered by the bridge crew, but Sofi remained at the place she'd seen Jimmy and Charles scuffling. An hour passed. Two. She would stay here for days if she had to. Just as she was ready to weep, a man shouted, not three feet from her.

"I found it!"

She remembered Neil's voice. Months ago, he'd taught her to focus on her breathing, in and out. *Thank You, Lord.*

The man who found the knife held it up for all to see.

Through a blur, she recognized it.

Deputy Willem was at her side in seconds and took the pocketknife. "You men vouch this knife belonged to Jimmy Galloway?"

Several of the crew chimed in to confirm.

Willem turned to her. "Is this the knife you saw Jimmy attack Charles Bolton with?"

"That's it," she croaked, swaying. Was it enough to free Neil? Was there enough time to stop that English inspector from taking him away from

American soil?

~*~

Sofi insisted on going with Willem to make sure he sent that telegram to Skykomish. It was late when he dropped her and Trina at the homestead.

Henric wasn't far behind.

Light spilled from the open door as Sofi trudged up the porch steps.

Matilda and Kiosho rushed out, their voices blending into a raucous chorus that normally would have made her smile.

Then Mama came, leaning hard on the arm of Mayor Frank.

Sofi breathed in her mother's lavender scent. Mama had gone so thin. Blue smudges bruised the area beneath her eyes, and she trembled. Yet she wore a trace of a smile. "There are people waiting to see you, Sofi."

Henric sprinted up the steps. "Rosie, what are you doing out of bed?"

Her mother gripped Henric's arm as if it were a lifebuoy. "I needed to come down for Sofi's sake."

Sofi's heart filled at the sight of her mother, who, like Trina, was trying hard to be strong. In time, they'd win. But right now, it was Sofi's time to break, and there was no privacy to unleash the torrent building inside her. Where was he now? Were they nearing Skykomish?

Trina kept an arm around her as they joined Mervin Jensen, head of the bridge committee, and Jonathan Simmons in her grandmother's parlor. While everyone took seats, Mr. Simmons stood suddenly, avoiding eye contact with Sofi.

Mayor Frank set his hat on his knee. "We can speak privately, Sofi, if you wish."

She waved a shaking hand. "I have nothing to hide."

The mayor beamed. "Fine. Fine. Well, this afternoon after you left, there was a heap of talk. With the various groups represented, the state, railroad, and bridge committee, all decided that with this alleged misappropriation of funds and neglect, we do not want Andersson and Bolton to modify the structure. Our decision is moot, though, after hearing the news that Charles has died."

It was hard to feel anything, but still disappointment stabbed. Even if Charles had lived, her father's company would not have been allowed to correct their mistakes.

Mervin leaned forward. "What the mayor is saying, Sofi, is though we don't want Andersson and Bolton to finish the project—you being the designer— we want you as a consulting engineer. Of course, we will be bringing in a new chief engineer. If that's all right with you, Sofi?"

A series of gasps issued.

Trina clapped her hands, and Mama's eyes warmed with a tired smile. Henric pressed his hand to Mama's shoulder while Kiosho and Matilda exclaimed in a combined muddle of praise and indignation as if there had ever been any question that Sofi would fix the bridge.

Sofi risked a glance at Jonathan Simmons.

He looked as if he wished he was anywhere but here.

"Well, Sofi," Mayor Frank said.

She glanced at the clock. In the morning, Neil would embark on a journey back to Ireland. She had to decide—take charge of her bridge, or go to the man she loved in his hour of need? God had made her strong for a purpose. Perhaps at another time, saying no to her talent would have been too steep a price to pay. Not now. She felt the Lord stir her heart.

No matter God's tasks, His people always come first.

She stood and forced her voice level. "Gentlemen, I'm honored, but I cannot accept. I'm relieved you're bringing in a new engineer to make this bridge safe. Perhaps that's all I was meant to do. Make it possible for someone else to...complete my vision. For personal reasons, I'll be out of the country. For an unforeseeable length of time. Now if you'll excuse me."

As she ran from the room, the rustle of standing, the murmur of voices went up.

Much later, her mother slowly came up the stairs and entered her room. Mama sat on her bed, and though her mother was frail, she held Sofi as if she were a child. Gulping tears overtook, and Sofi slid to her knees, laying her head on her mother's lap. Mama's hands stroked Sofi's hair. "Rest, *älskling*, then in the morning go find your love."

32

Her grandparents' homestead lay around Sofi like a favored quilt while the household slept. Morning would break in less than an hour. She washed, pulled a blue serge skirt over her petticoat, and did up the buttons on a white lawn blouse. She brushed her hair, but let it fall down her back, and threw a shawl over her shoulders. Her traveling valise sat at the bottom of the stairs. She'd come back for that later. Confliction pressed on her heart before she started the journey to Ireland.

Would visiting Neil in an Irish prison bring him comfort or despair?

But she couldn't let him face this alone.

After latching the back door, she walked through a row of raspberry canes. Mist touched her face with cold droplets. There was no need to hurry. She'd not be able to catch the train that Neil would be on, but she'd leave today and meet up with him and the inspector in New York. No one could stop her from boarding the same ship.

Odin padded at her side, and together they walked the road that switched back and forth up the side of the mountain to the plateau.

"You'll miss him, won't you?"

His tail gave a gentle wag in answer.

The road all but disappeared until she came to the drape of low-hanging evergreens. A maple was turning red, one or two larches yellow. She stepped into the clearing. A stream of first light hit the pine logs of the cabin, and Odin bounded off after a dragonfly.

The barn sat off to the side. Neil's barn. She climbed to the loft where he'd slept. The stirred fragrance of cedar filled her with emptiness. Above the loft, a spider had spun a web that caught the gradually growing light from outside.

She drifted to the cabin and stared at the cold ashes in the fireplace, at the table where he'd pieced together not only Trina's tea set, but also the very essence that was Trina. From Matilda's jumbled explanation earlier, he had also brought healing to her mother. On the porch she ran her fingers along the cords of wood he'd cut and stacked.

The bluff overlooking the valley drew her. The bridge stood stark against the cold pewter sky. As with her bridge, her soul couldn't grow strong without the fiery forge of pain. But how much more could God expect her to bear?

Odin sat on his haunches at her side. Together they watched a nimbus of sunlight top the mountains and throw blue shadows into the valley. The dew-soaked surfaces of her bridge turned into graceful lines of molten gold. Her face warmed with the rising sun.

But it had been night when Neil kissed her here at the edge of this bluff. Her lips tingled with the memory, the feel of his heart thudding under her palm. Her insides shuddered with the loss of what had hardly begun between them.

Holding out her open hand, she prayed without words for the fortitude to keep on going afterward if...if...

She must accept that Neil would find his joy in eternity with Christ, if not in a life here with her.

Odin's damp nose thrust into her hand. She pulled at the silkiness of his ear, clinging to this small comfort. But he turned to gambol across to the opening in the trees. Her gaze followed. A band of ochre light hit the clearing, turning the pine logs of the cabin to a warm golden radiance. Her eyes sought the dog, to where he bounded...where he now jumped and yelped in greeting.

Neil waited at the entrance to the clearing, holding back a branch.

Her heart stopped and started again.

He took a step forward, and the branch fell behind him. He was alone. And he smiled.

It couldn't be. How could he be here? Where were the handcuffs?

He began to walk toward her. "Sofi."

She shook her head.

"It's all right, Sofi love."

She stared at the opening in the trees from where he'd just come. "They're waiting for you, aren't they?" She heard the rawness in her voice. "They're going to take you from me."

He rested his hands on her shoulders. "They let me go, Sofi. Because of you, they let me go. I heard from the deputy you almost dug a hole to China looking for that knife." His smile took her back to the first few weeks here on this plateau, to the days they had to themselves before the world broke in on them.

She whirled to face the valley, feeling only the thumping of her heart against her ribs.

He ran his hands down her arms. "You're cold, love."

She shook her head, feeling the warmth of his body behind her. Could she believe that God had answered her prayers? Or would she wake to find her hopes dashed? But Neil's breath against her nape was real.

He pulled her back against him and wrapped his arms around her middle. He spoke through a soft chuckle. "Inspector Webley and Joel Harrison took me as far as Skykomish last night. Your telegram was waiting for us when we arrived. Joel convinced Webley to wire Scotland Yard and to come back here to wait on the return wire."

"You were in town last night?"

"Aye. Only a mile from you the whole time. The wire from Ireland came an hour ago. The Irish magistrate wants me to stay here until they evaluate this evidence you found. Apparently the police at home were never as convinced as Inspector Webley that I had anything to do with it."

Her mind spun.

"They let me go, love. Well, into the custody of your local law enforcement. Sheriff Dahl and Joel are down at the house having a cup of coffee with Kiosho. Webley's as mad-hot as a kettle, sitting in the hotel in town." His voice caught. "My brother had been under suspicion from the start. It was only my running that clouded the issue."

Smiling through tears, she added her arms to his in front of her, to strengthen their embrace. "And my bad advice would have kept you running when it wasn't necessary. Is it over?" she whispered.

"If all goes as Joel hopes, the magistrate at home may only want a signed deposition from me, and that English copper will be off my tail."

His lips touched her hair. "I'm praying like I've never prayed before, Sofi. I want to live my life with you. There's nowhere in the entire world I'd rather be than wherever you are."

She caressed his hands, barely able to speak. Relief fell like droplets of mist. He was here. He was real, and free.

A heavy sigh escaped from him. "We've lost loved ones. A lot of sadness."

She turned to him and cradled his face. "We'll bring your mother over as soon as possible."

"And Jimmy's bride and babe."

She searched his eyes, dark with heartache that would take time to heal. But she'd seen the healing in her mother and sister, herself as well. Healing that only came from trusting that God did bring them across deep waters and through dark canyons, and made them stronger for it. But always with His loving comfort surrounding them.

Some of the pain lessened in Neil's gaze. The hard line of his mouth softened into a half smile. "Sofi, my Sofi." He pulled her into his arms and rested his face in the crook of her neck. "I never want to be parted from you again."

Her hands moved up his back and held him close. "You never will."

"I want to build a life for you and me in this country. You'll build your bridges. Kiosho told me before I came up here that the committee wants you to finish the bridge. I'll set up a practice wherever you are."

"Why not here?"

His smile started in his eyes and molded his mouth into a grin. "Sounds a grand proposal, sure it does." He wound his hands through her hair. "I've only one more favor to ask—would you mind if we spent our honeymoon here in this fine establishment behind us?"

Laughter burst from her as she leaned her head on his shoulder. "I can't think of anywhere I'd rather go."

His voice thickened. "The morning after we're married, I want to wake up in that loft, holding you."

He crushed her to him as his mouth took hers. Her arms wound up over his shoulders to return his kiss with the same hunger. Sunlight filled the clearing when they parted. He kissed her lips once more, gently, as a promise of many more to come. With his arm around her, they strolled down the hillside to the homestead. At the start of the raspberry rows, he pulled out his father's pocket watch.

"Sofi, my love, I see you might just have time for a cup of coffee before you—as consulting engineer—get to that bridge of yours. Work begins at seven AM, precisely. Or so I've been told."

Thank you

We appreciate you reading this White Rose Publishing title. For other inspirational stories, please visit our on-line bookstore at www.pelicanbookgroup.com.

For questions or more information, contact us at customer@pelicanbookgroup.com.

White Rose Publishing
Where Faith is the Cornerstone of Love™
an imprint of Pelican Ventures Book Group
www.PelicanBookGroup.com

Connect with Us
www.facebook.com/Pelicanbookgroup
www.twitter.com/pelicanbookgrp

To receive news and specials, subscribe to our bulletin
http://pelink.us/bulletin

May God's glory shine through
this inspirational work of fiction.

AMDG

Free Book Offer

We're looking for booklovers like you to partner with us! Join our team of influencers today and receive at least one free eBook per month. Maybe more!

For more information
Visit http://pelicanbookgroup.com/booklovers
or e-mail
booklovers@pelicanbookgroup.com